# Heartbreaker

# Heartbreaker

## De'nesha Diamond

## Erick S. Gray

## Nichelle Walker

KENSINGTON PUBLISHING CORP.

www.kensingtonbooks.com

DAFINA BOOKS are published by

Kensington Publishing Corp.
119 West 40th Street
New York, NY 10018

All Kensington titles, imprints, and distributed lines are available at special quantity discounts for bulk purchases for sales promotion, premiums, fund-raising, educational, or institutional use.

Special book excerpts or customized printings can also be created to fit specific needs. For details, write or phone the office of the Kensington Special Sales Manager: Kensington Publishing Corp., 119 West 40th Street, New York, NY 10018. Attn. Special Sales Department. Phone: 1-800-221-2647.

ISBN-13: 978-0-7582-4663-9
ISBN-10: 0-7582-4663-3

First Kensington Trade Paperback Printing: February 2010
10  9  8  7  6  5  4  3  2  1

Printed in the United States of America

# CONTENTS

# Slippin'

## DE'NESHA DIAMOND

*To Selena James and Marc Gerald:*
*Thanks for believin' in me!*

# Prologue

The summer heat ain't nothing to fuck with in Atlanta. All the hustlin' niggas on the street corners looked like tall sticks of meltin' chocolate, but we're all dedicated to the grind. Shit. We had bills, badass kids, and whining baby mamas ready to stick our asses in jail if we missed one damn child support check. Bitches don't be playin' about their fuckin' checks nowadays.

When I was fourteen, I fucked around and got my play cousin, Trina, knocked up. Now I had a beautiful eight-year-old daughter I hardly ever saw. Ain't my fault. Trina's parents shipped her ass out to her grandma's in Alabama pretty much after the baby was born. Some of my niggas said I got lucky not having her ass all in my face all the time. I just know it didn't stop her from being able to reach into a nigga's pocket. So my paranoid ass was out there hustlin' too. Shit. In this muthafuckin' economy a nigga ain't got no choice. Way things be lookin', Obama was the only nigga with a good job.

One thing about walking up and down Metropolitan Parkway in my fresh tee and black AKOO jeans was that I got to hear and watch how all the shawties be bangin' it. Every one of us niggas out there couldn't walk straight because our dicks were so hard, peepin' at big-ass titties and red-beans-and-rice booties squeezed into shorts that could double for panties. There was nothing but titties and asses shakin' as far as the eye could see.

I grew up in this godforsaken neighborhood back when the street was named Stewart Avenue and its reputation for drugs, prostitution, and murder were known statewide. The tall brick buildings were crack houses, and dodging bullets was how niggas got their daily exercise. Though I wasn't so lucky one time. Caught a bullet when I was fifteen, walking out of a Freddie's Hot Wings joint. It was bullshit because it was all over shit that didn't have nothing to do with me. Some miscellaneous nigga got hot over some other nigga for scuffing up his white Air Jordans. That non-aiming muthafucka just started shooting. The bullet that nailed my left shoulder felt like straight fire. I remember hitting the sidewalk—hot sauce flying everywhere and my ass thinkin' I'ma 'bout to die.

My boy, Alonzo, claimed I was screaming like a bitch and to this day his ass hadn't let me live that shit down. That's alright, though. What goes around comes around—and as big as my dawg's mouth is, it's just a matter of time before some nigga blaze his ass up. Now I wasn't wishin' that shit on him. I'm just sayin'. Muthafucka thinks he knows every fuckin' thang.

Alonzo and I were cool and everythang, but I'd be lyin' if I didn't say that every once in a while we got a friendly competition between the two of us goin'. Nuthin' serious or anything. Though I might have crossed the line when I hooked with one of his baby mamas before I got locked down. But shit, what the nigga don't know won't hurt him. Besides, if he was so crazy about her, he would've given her his last name.

I survived that night outside Freddie's. 'Round here what doesn't kill ya makes ya stronger.

The crack houses were gone, but the buildings still felt like brick bars for people who were still strugglin' to make it out. That included my ass. Gettin' out wasn't as easy as it sounds. The street game ain't no joke. Most niggas I knew jumped into this shit 'cuz money didn't come no easier. The one true thing about drugs was that the product sold itself. But easy money knew how to hypnotize muthafuckas too. It convinced our weak asses that ballin' out of control was gonna last forever.

It never does.

And if you didn't wind up facedown on some hard concrete, then you're certainly gonna feel the cold pinch of the po-po's handcuffs when you least expected the shit.

"Delvon, yo ass ain't worth shit!" Tiffani, a dime piece I'd spent the last two nights fuckin', shouted from across the way.

I rolled my eyes at the sound of that bullhorn she called a voice. I kept it movin' though, hopin' I could outwalk her.

"I know you hear me, Delvon," she shouted, practically blowing my damn eardrums out when she rolled up on me.

I finally stopped. She mushed me on the back of my head. "I shoulda known that your ass hadn't changed a damn bit."

I laughed at her stupid ass. The only reason I was putting up with her shit was because she was ghetto fine and had pussy that tasted like candy. "Hey baby." I attempted to pull her into my arms, but she pulled back.

"Don't *baby* me, Delvon. You said you were gonna give me twenty dollars so I can get some damn diapers for Kanye." She ran her hands through her tight weave and then crossed her arms, waiting for the next lie I was 'bout to tell.

"Look, I'm gonna get you your twenty."

"And what—my baby is supposed to just chill in pissy diapers 'til you feel like showing back up?"

"What the fuck? It ain't like that l'il nigga has my DNA."

Tiffani's face twisted so hard, it looked like it was about to pop off. Still, twenty dollars for two nights' worth of pussy was a bargain no matter how you sliced that shit up. "Look. I said I'ma gone get you your twenty. I just haven't swung by the ATM yet." I reached for her again, and *again* she stepped out of reach.

"Nigga, does it look like I have Boo Boo The Fool stamped on my muthafuckin' forehead? Yo ass ain't never *dreamed* of having no damn bank account."

I laughed because she was straight up tellin' the truth.

"The shit ain't funny, *Delvon*." She held out one hand while cradling a fist in the center of her hip. "Give me my shit."

I thought about fuckin' with her for a bit longer, but judging by her mean mug shot, she seriously wasn't in the mood for it. Fuck it. I was tired of dealing with her trifflin' ass anyway. "Here. Take your muthafuckin' twenty." I pulled out a fat roll from my mornin' hustle and peeled off a bill, and to show just how generous my ass was, I peeled off an extra one. "Here. Consider it a tip."

Tiffani snatched the two bills out of my hand, but then eyed the roll I was stuffin' into my pocket like a Doberman drooling over a ham bone. Flippin' the script, her voice suddenly dripped with honey. "You comin' back over tonight?" She eased up on me, rubbin' her titties on my arms. But I ain't going out like that. I've gotten my nut. Now it was time for me to find a better grade of pussy to get me through this hot-ass summer. It wouldn't be hard. A pretty nigga like me ain't never had no trouble slidin' into home base.

"Nah. Nah. I'm cool. Thanks for the pussy, though. I'll recommend ya to a coupla my partnas." I stepped back and spotted a new dime piece sportin' some short shorts that had the bottom of her ass cheeks peekin' out and winkin' at me. "Goddamn!"

Li'l shawty hit me back with a wide smile. I bet I could bust that shit wide open behind one of these buildings. I reached down and readjusted my hard dick while lickin' my lips—a sign to let li'l shawty know I was down for whatever.

"Oh, hell naw." Tiffani jumped into my line of vision and got her cobra neck workin'. "How the fuck you gonna play me like that?"

"What?" I asked, blinking and playin' dumb.

"Fuck you, muthafucka. Yo ass will never change." Tiffani's nose twitched like I was somethin' nasty stuck to the bottom of her Payless shoes.

"Why? Because I keep shit real? Girl, you better go on with that." I laughed. "You know what I was about when you hooked up with my ass." From the corner of my eyes, I see Alonzo strollin' down the block, bouncin' a basketball and chattin' with that Crazy Larry. "A-yo! Alonzo! Wait up!"

"What the fuck? We're talkin'," Tiffani whined.

"Correction: you're talkin'. I'm walkin'. Later."

"Nigga, hold up," she shouted after me.

I tossed her a couple of deuces and kept it movin'.

"Alright," she yelled. "You're gone get yours one of these days. Watch!"

Alonzo and Larry seen me comin' and held up. As I rushed across the way I saw a couple of other niggas that had been hangin' on the block since my ass was in diapers. The original gangstas they called themselves—or O.G.'s. They used to be hard; now they look as if they were allergic to cocoa butter or Vaseline. Ashy from head to toe and lookin' as if they hit the glass dick on the regular.

Their surprise at seein' me back on the block was clearly etched into their faces. Truth be told, nobody was more surprised than my ass when my sentence was reduced because the state couldn't afford to hold so many niggas on bullshit charges.

Hell. What amount of weed they busted me for couldn't have gotten a cockroach high.

"Yo, nigga." Alonzo laughed, swappin' dabs. "I thought you'd still be gettin' your dick wet or I would've hit you up sooner."

We did a one-arm hug and then pulled back like the shit never happened. "Just takin' a little break." A coupla more honeys squeezed past us standing on the sidewalk. I turned, my dick following the one with the jiggling booty like a homing device. "What—y'all can't say excuse me?" I asked with my slick, on-the-prowl smile already in place.

The one chick that was so high yella she practically belonged in a Crayola box smiled. As her hazel green eyes performed a slow drag down my six foot two, muscular frame, I knew my pretty caramel complexion and my honey-colored eyes was making her think how pretty a baby between us would be.

Alonzo stepped out front. "What's your name, li'l mama?"

I bit back my annoyance at the nigga interruptin' my flow.

"Jelissa," she purred.

"Jelissa, nice." Alonzo reached up and lightly brushed a curl away from her cheek, making sure to caress the side of her face. When she smiled, it was over his shoulder at me and I knew my ass was in. For the first time, I noticed the orange Creamsicle in her hand. She put it up to her mouth and unfurled this incredibly long pink tongue and started lapping up the melting icicle like a porn star practicing for her close-up. My shit was hard as fuck.

"You got a man, Jelissa?" Alonzo asked.

"Yeah," she admitted to my surprise. "But he ain't here

right now." She cut a look toward me. The kind of look that promised nothing but freaky, butt-nasty sex, and you know a nigga was always down for that shit.

Impatient, Crazy Larry started bouncing his basketball. "We playing or what?"

"Y'all go on ahead. I'ma holla at Jelissa for a minute," I said, easing in between my man and what I hoped to be some sweet pussy.

Alonzo looked pissed, but I've always scored more bitches than he did. You'd think by now he would accept the shit.

"Sheeeit," Crazy Lazy grumbled.

I looked over in time to see Crazy Larry rollin' his eyes. Then Larry just put it to me straight. "Look, nigga, we ain't got all day to wait for you to play with some more busted-ass ghetto pussy."

Jelissa snapped out of her sex trance. "Hey!"

He ignored her. "When you get through busting a nut with her, why don't you just meet up with us tonight up at The White Room?"

"The White Room? Where the fuck is that?" I asked.

Alonzo smirked. "Aww man, it's this sweet spot out in Alpharetta."

I laughed. "Y'all niggas hangin' out in suburbs now?"

Crazy Larry wrapped one of his big, meaty arms around my neck and damn near put my ass in a headlock. "Yo ass gonna be hangin' out there too once you see the bitches that joint rakes in. Bitches with money." His eyes shifted back over to Jelissa. "Not these used-up hos we got still hangin' out here. You'll probably need a shot or something after fuckin' with this one. Didn't I hear yo ass got chlamydia or something?" he asked Jelissa.

My dick just shriveled up.

"You know what—FUCK YOU, muthafucka." Jelissa's sex kitten act was long gone and she was clearly in full bitch mode. "I ain't gotta take this shit."

"Then take yo skank ass on then." Larry laughed as if he got a high from pissing her off. "Ain't nobody stoppin' your ho patrol out here. But I bet Lamon ain't gonna like hearing you giving his shit away to every Tom, Dick, and Delvon."

Jelissa's yella ass turned white.

I couldn't help but laugh.

"Yeah, that's right," Crazy Larry kept on, smirking. "I know your boy. Nigga locked down and *this* is how you roll?"

Jelissa's friend, a thick big girl in clothes two sizes too small, moved back into the scene and tugged on her girl's arm. "C'mon, Jelissa. These niggas are whack."

"Y'all bitches are whack," Crazy Larry corrected, cupping his dick as he looked Jelissa's friend up and down. "Why don't you go home and dust that dandruff off in that whack-ass weave. Maybe then I'll let you ride some of this good dick. I love big girls."

"Kiss my ass," the girl shouted, smacking her round romp.

"Wash it and maybe I will." He flicked his tongue out as if to show her what she was missing.

I was cracking up. If these bitches didn't know that this crazy nigga would say just anything by now then their asses deserved exactly what the fuck he was shovelin' out.

Jelissa gave me a nasty look and I couldn't do anything but shrug my shoulders. Hell, I didn't do nothing to their stupid asses.

"What the fuck ever." She cut her eyes and I was left to watch her strut away.

Crazy Larry's heavy hand slammed across my back. "I ain't never seen a nigga get more strung out over pussy in my life."

I rolled my eyes. "And I ain't never seen a nigga do so much cock blockin' in all my life. What's up with you, nigga?"

"Shit. I just did your ass a favor and this is how you act?" He tossed up his hands as if saying I was on my own.

"Alright, y'all. Squash that bullshit," Alonzo said, sounding as if he was tired of the fake drama. "D, why don't you just come out to The White Room, check it out, and see if you like the vibe? Hell, it ain't like you got shit to do anyway. I'm sure by now you done pissed off whatever bitch you've been fuckin' with anyways."

"You know me so well." I laughed.

"Then it's settled," Crazy Larry declared. "You're hangin' with your boys tonight. Now let's go play some damn ball before I fuck around and lose my muthafuckin' high."

I gave in. Why not? Maybe it was time for me to leave these ghetto hood rats alone and find myself a real classy woman with *no drama*.

"9-1-1, what's your emergency?"

"Hello? We need help! There's been an explosion. Please send the fire department!"

"What's the address?"

"2355 Abbott's Way. It's the Walkers' estate. Please hurry. There were people inside!"

"We're on our way. Do you know what caused the explosion?"

Silence.

"Sir?"

"Yes. I did it."

# Chapter 1

*C*lick.

I know that sound better than anything in the whole world. It's the sound of handcuffs, lockin' a nigga down. In this case: it's me, Delvon Jackson. Fuckup extraordinaire. Shit. I can't believe I'm back in this position. The Atlanta cop behind me jerks my wrists up, and as a reflex I clamp my back teeth together to bite down on the pain. But this muthafucka don't give a fuck. He's too busy reading me my so-called rights. That's cool because I don't really hear him. I'm too fuckin' mad at myself at how this whole shitty situation went down.

"Watch your head," the cop says, but he still rams my shit into the frame of the back door. "Sorry about that."

Dazed, I don't even say anything to the ignorant muthafucka. All I can think about is her. My eyes burn, but I hold back these damn tears 'cuz no matter what, I ain't no bitch and I ain't gonna go out like that. But . . . goddamn! Sabrina was my world.

*To the left of this parked police car, the Walker Estate is engulfed in flames. Not until Officer Asshole slams the door do I get a break from the intense heat rollin' from the burning mansion.*

*My bottom lip trembles as I close my eyes for a brief moment. I quickly realize my mistake when Sabrina's beautiful smile flashes behind my eyes.*

*"Delvon." The memory of her sexy, husky voice whispering my name echoes in my head. I loved the way Sabrina used to moan and gasp my name in a whisper wheneva we were funkin' up those expensive-ass silk sheets she loved so much. Not to sound like no punk or nothing but I swear to God my heart hurts so bad I want to rip it out of my chest. Damn. I loved that woman. I peel open my eyes and glance out of the police car's window and watch a mixture of firemen and random volunteers battle the tall flames.*

*I really fucked up this time. And I don't mean kinda fucked up. I mean my ass is going straight to jail. Do not pass Go and I can forget about collectin' a muthafuckin' thing.*

*Officer Asshole slips in behind the wheel and I can feel his heavy gaze tryna blaze a hole in the center of my forehead. After a long silence his hard, gravelly voice asks, "Why did you do it?"*

*I swear to God a knot about the size of a fuckin' baseball lodges in my throat. I lick my thick lips and try to breathe.*

*"You might as well gone and confess. People already comin' out the woodwork droppin' dime about how you been stalkin' the place."*

*I glance around and see snitchin' niggas gathering around the burnin' house like it was a goddamn communion bonfire. I finally cut my gaze away to meet Asshole's black gaze through the rearview mirror. "People don't know what the fuck they're talking about."*

*One of the cop's thick, bushy, black eyebrows jumps up to the center of his forehead. "No?"*

*I don't answer because I know he knows I'm lying.*

*I look away.*

*"Okay." The black officer shifts in his seat. "Then maybe you have an answer to why you're even here since they filed a restraining order on your ass."*

*"She didn't file that shit. Her husband put her up to it."*

*Asshole's gaze hardens. "Guess you showed him, huh?"*

*My gaze refocuses on the burning house. It looks like the fire department has given up on saving it. Those goddamn tears come back in full force. If I was any kind of man, my ass would have been inside that damn house instead of Sabrina.*

*"Maybe you'll have some answers down at the station," Asshole says after it's clear that I dismissed his ass a few minutes ago.*

*I sit there and watch the fire for what seems like forever. Finally Asshole's partner, a short, plump, black woman with thick black hair slicked back by at least a tub of hair gel, jumps inside the car.*

*"Did he say anything?" she asks her partner.*

*"Naw. I'm sure he's too busy tryna think up a lie," Asshole tells her, and then starts up the car.*

*"The shit better be good," she passively warns. "'Cuz you're certainly lookin' at the needle for all this shit."*

*My heart drops as we pull away. The tall, roaring flames remain in my view for a long time. So much shit is floatin' through my mind. All the whens and hows.*

*By the time the cops haul my ass into the downtown Atlanta precinct, I think I have my thug armor securely in place and I'm prepared to ignore their bullshit interrogations until my state-appointed lawyer shows up. Once again, I don't say shit when Officer Asshole nearly rips my arm outta socket and bangs my head on the doorframe as he drags me out the back of the patrol car.*

*"Sorry about that," he lies with a cocky-ass grin.*

*For a moment I'm wishing for just two minutes alone with this muthafucka without these goddamn handcuffs. I betcha his ass wouldn't be grinning after I got through. My thoughts are clearly reflecting in my eyes and the cop quickly chest bumps me, tryna initiate some shit.*

*"What's that look about, nigga?" Asshole growls in my ear and then chest bumps me again. "What? You think you can beat my ass?" Another chest bump. "C'mon, nigga. If you feel froggish—jump."*

*I snap. "Alright, then. You take these muthafuckin' handcuffs off and I'll show you how I get down."*

*"Is that right, muthafucka?"*

*Before I can even think about responding, this asshole lands a punch square across my jaw that reels my mind back so far, I swear I can remember the taste of my momma's* breast milk. Blood bursts from my bottom lip as my knees buckle and then kiss the concrete. While I'm dazed for a coupla seconds, Officer Fat Bitch finally rushes around the patrol car and pulls at her partner.

"C'mon. Now stop horsin' around. The piece of shit ain't even worth it. Let's just get him in and take him to the interrogation room."

I spit out a mouthful of blood as I listen to their bullshit good-cop bad-cop routine. I've seen better actin' on the comedy channel. But I gotta hand it to Officer Asshole. The muthafucka got one hell of a left hook.

"Get yo ass up." He snatches me back onto my feet and I'm dragged into the precinct lookin' busted and disgusted.

Every head and set of eyes cut toward me as I perform my awkward perp walk, but still I somehow manage to keep my head up. That is 'til I catch sight of my man, Alonzo, sitting at a cop's desk on the other side of the room. What the fuck? Was Alonzo a goddamn snitch?

A'ight. I'ma tell the muthafuckas everything.

In the interrogation room, I collapse into a rusted-out metal chair behind a peeling brown folded table. The muthafuckin' room smells like musk and Lysol, giving me an instant headache. I've lost count of how many times my ass has been up in this very precinct over the years, but every time I'm in here I'm amazed at just how bright the white walls are and how intense the quiet can play with your nerves.

"Want something to drink?" the female cop asks, still playing the role of the good cop.

"Water," I answer, and then watch her as she strolls out of the room to leave me alone with this black Dirty Harry wannabe.

Immediately after the door clicks closed, a nasty smirk slithers onto this mean muthafucka's face. I can tell by the gleam in his eye that he wants to whale on me some more but somehow he's keepin' his shit in check . . . for now. After a few minutes, I start wishin' that he would start hittin' me. Anything would be better than the silence. I shift around in my chair—and once I get started I can't seem to stop.

"You look uncomfortable," Asshole says, stating the obvious.

I ignore him.

"Maybe you got a lot you want to get off your chest?" he suggests, walking to the table, flipping one of the other metal chairs around, and then squatting down into the seat. "Maybe you want to tell me why you planted that bomb at the Walkers' estate?"

Silence.

"What's the matter? You couldn't handle that Sabrina Walker didn't want some out-of-work play thug? You figured if you couldn't have her then nobody could? Is that how it went down?"

I grind my teeth and feel the veins along my face throb, but to my horror a tear skips down the side of my face.

Asshole immediately starts laughing. "Awww. I got my ass a sensitive thug in here." He leans over the table. "What's the matter? You gonna start tellin' me your ass was in love or some shit?"

*My heart starts hurtin' again as this muthafucka just hit the nail on the head.*

*"So you're just a nigga Romeo that likes to play with explosives. Is that it?"*

*Silence.*

*"Or maybe you were targeting Mr. Walker?"*

*My eyes meet his.*

*"Yeeeeaaah. That's it." His shit-eatin' grin widens as he continues to read my ass like a book. "You were trying to get him out of the way, weren't cha?" He cocks his head, watches my reaction.*

*My guilt is blazing up from the soles of my feet and burnin' the tips of my ears. I used to have a better poker face than this, but tonight everything has changed. I'm a murderer now and nothing will ever be the same again.*

*"Let's start with something simple. Why don't you just tell me how you met Mrs. Walker?"*

*I lick my busted lip as the memory comes back to me in an instant. And before I know it, I'm spillin' my guts. "I met her at this club called The White Room. . . ."*

From the moment Alonzo, Crazy Larry, and I rolled into the parking lot of The White Room in Crazy Larry's black on silver Escalade, I knew that we had arrived at the spot. This huge white and glass building didn't look like no regular club, but like one of those fuckin' high-class museums. Real classy like. And the women? *Goddamn.* The suburbs were rollin' with some fine-ass bitches. Believable hair weaves, thousand dollar outfits, and enough bling to blind a nigga.

Alonzo and Crazy Larry wasn't playing when they said that this place had a better grade of women. Each and every one of them looked as if they had just stepped out of the pages of those glossy magazines I used to jerk off to in the joint.

"Well? Whatcha think?" Alonzo asked, whacking me on the back and cheesing like a muthafucka.

"I think my ass just died and gone to heaven," I said, following a long line of firm booties, hypnotized.

"Damn, nigga. Close your mouth."

Figuring that he had a point, I quickly snapped my shit shut and just moved with the flow of the crowd. Inside, I was again impressed by the setup. For the most part the place was decorated wall to wall with chrome and glass while mini-searchlights flashed every color of the rainbow from different corners of the club. The music was bangin' and the place smelled like cotton candy and pot all rolled into a heady aphrodisiac that instantly had my dick hard and my balls throbbing.

Me and my two-man posse continued to peep out the scene as we got our pimp walk on toward the bar. The place was jumpin' with old Michael Jackson hits. A real tribute to the music man we all just lost. I quickly ordered a Hennessy from the one-gloved bartender and then returned my attention to the dance floor.

*That* was when I first saw her.

An explosive vision in red and with curves that put every chick that ever graced the defunked *King* magazine to shame, I spotted the woman that I most definitely wanted to pump a whole mess of babies out of. She had long black, wavy hair that a nigga could just picture winding his hands around and the smoothest, prettiest peanut butter complexion I'd ever seen. I knew instantly that this red angel wasn't like none of those ghetto chicks I was used to fuckin' with. This woman just oozed so much style and class that I had no doubts that those fat diamonds dripping from her ears, neck, and wrists were the real deal.

No shit, baby girl had a nigga wantin' to bust out a pen and some paper to write some poetry or some shit.

"I told you to close your mouth, nigga," Alonzo shouted over the music. "I don't want nobody thinking that I brought Forrest Gump up in this muthafucka." He laughed.

I snapped my mouth shut and blindly reached for my drink from the bar. One thing I refused to do was pull my eyes from my red angel. As Michael Jackson's "P.Y.T." blasted from the speakers, baby girl sent tongues waggin' with her firm ass rollin' in perfect harmony with her slim hips.

"She's the shit, ain't she?" Alonzo said close to my ear. "I know you wanna hit that."

I heard amusement ringin' in his voice. "What hood with you? You know this chick?"

"Hell, everybody up in here know her. Remember that big-ass crib I told you I've been workin' these past few months?"

I nodded.

"Her and her man stay up there. Money out the ass. Their gangsta ain't no joke."

"Oh, she got a man, huh?"

"That shit surprises you? She probably been bankrollin' niggas since she bought her first training bra."

I shook my head as I watched those hypnotizin' hips bounce, wiggle, and roll. "You ain't gonna tell me no *one* man can handle all of that."

Alonzo laughed. "Probably not, considering Mr. Walker got a good twenty years on her fine ass."

"Gold digger?"

"Aren't they all?" Alonzo drained the rest of his drink and then quickly hollered for a refill.

I smirked. "What's her name?"

"Off limits," he said.

"Funny," I said, unamused. At the same time, Lady in Red glanced my way as if she heard me. In an instant our gazes locked just as the music shifted to MJ's "The Way You Make Me Feel." We both smiled at the same time, and in my mind I convinced myself I just might have a chance with this woman who was so clearly out of my league.

"You don't want to go there, man," Alonzo warned. "Messin' with that woman ain't nothing but trouble with a capital T."

"Well, what do you know about that?" I said, emptying my glass in one gulp and then slamming the glass back down onto the bar. "I *love* trouble."

"Alright. Don't say I never warned you."

As I moved toward the dance floor, I performed a casual head rock while my eyes dragged slowly over Red's curves. A few other ladies tried to holla at me, but I didn't hear a damn thing they were sayin'.

Red's smile grew bigger and my eyes locked on her pretty pink tongue as it glided across her full red-tinted lips. She was definitely feelin' me. She was practically transmittin' nasty images into my head.

The nigga she was dancin' with flashed me an annoyed look, but he might as well step before I embarrass his ass. The weak punk even made an attempt to reclaim her attention, but she dismissed him with a flick of her hand and started groovin' toward me.

My cock was so hard and heavy that, shit, I just wanted to slam this fine-ass black Barbie doll up against a wall somewhere in here and fuck the shit out of her.

"Dirty Diana" started bumpin' and this chick started rubbin' her ass against me, puttin' a big smile on a nigga's face. I wrapped my arm around her tiny waist and started matchin' her grind for delicious grind. I knew right then and there my ass was caught up in everything from the smell of her hair to how her body felt up against mine. We rocked those same dance moves for at least two songs—to the point that I finally had to say something.

"You're gonna fuck around and I'ma send your ass home pregnant." I was hoping to win a smile or a sexy laugh outta her, but instead she stopped dancin' and looked back over her shoulder at me. I knew immediately that I'd fucked up by the way disappointment flickered across her face. Unbelievably, she went from actin' like a starved sex kitten to a prim and proper lady within a blink of an eye.

Without saying a word, she turned from me and started walking off the dance floor.

"Hey, wait."

She whipped back around with an expression that clearly said, *Fuck off.*

I didn't get a chance to respond before she jerked away and then disappeared into the crowd, leaving me looking like a love-struck fool in the middle of the dance floor—my dick still hard as hell.

# Chapter 2

*O*fficer Good Cop finally rolls back into the interrogation room with a small Styrofoam cup of water. She instantly glances at her partner. The question of whether he'd gotten a confession from my ass is written clearly in her deep chocolate gaze. It's then that it occurs to me how I've royally fucked up by talking.

"I not saying another muthafuckin' word 'til my lawyer gets here."

"Your lawyer?" Asshole chuckles. "You got something to hide, Delvon Jackson?" His dark gaze is shooting hollow points at the center of my fuckin' forehead.

I shift in my chair again. I have a graveyard of secrets and right now it feels like these two muthafuckas are about to dig up a lot of caskets.

Officer Good Cop sets my water down. I'm just stuck lookin' at it 'til she finally remembers to uncuff me. When those tight-ass silver bracelets are removed, I quickly start massaging my wrists. My freedom won't last. I know this. I can feel it. And when I close my eyes and picture Sabrina wrapped in my arms, I know I deserve whateva's comin' my way.

"Forget the fuckin' lawyer," I mumble.

The two cops share a knowing glance.

"I'll tell you what you want to know." My eyes mist.

"Alright," Asshole says, crossing his meaty arms. "Did you set that bomb tonight?"

The room becomes as quiet as a tomb, givin' me a moment to spit out the truth. But I can't do it. It's too hard.

"Alright," Asshole says after it's clear I'm not ready to confess just yet. "How about we go back to when Mrs. Walker left you standing on the dance floor with a hard-on. Why don't you tell us what happened next?"

Thinking about the early days lightens the burden on my shoulders and even loosens my tongue.

I cough, trying to clear my throat. "Can I get a cigarette?"

A muscle twitches down the side of Officer Asshole's jaw, but after another long silence, he reaches into his top pocket and withdraws a pack of Salem Menthols. The good shit.

Seconds later, I take a strong hit of nicotine and immediately feel my nerves settle.

"Is there anything else we can get for you, Mr. Jackson? Maybe you'd like for us to rub your feet or order you something to eat?" Asshole suggests.

I pick up the sarcasm and just barely stop myself from

*flipping the cop off. "I visited The White Room every night for the next two weeks, hoping to get another peek at my high-class shawtie." I shrug. "I searched high and low but no dice. If it wasn't for my man, Alonzo, I would have thought that I had imagined ever meeting her in the first place. . . ."*

As usual, The White Room was jumpin'. But this time I wasn't feelin' it.

"There are plenty of other women up in here, ya know," Alonzo yelled above the music and the jovial crowd. His arms were wrapped around this sexy Keri Hilson look-alike. I noted that my dawg's eyes were drooped so low, he practically looked like he was asleep. No doubt I probably looked about the same since we both got fucked up on the drive out there.

"What?"

"Don't play dumb, nigga." Alonzo laughed. "I know who you're lookin' for." He shook his head and pulled his hot bitch closer. "Your nose is always wide open when it comes to pussy, man. It's a damn shame and somebody needs to confiscate your playa's card."

I propped my arm up on the bar, almost tipping over my drink. "You don't know what the fuck you're talking about."

"Uh-huh. You keep tellin' yourself that."

I swiped a quick glance at the fine bitch clingin' on every word Alonzo said. Our eyes met for a brief moment and I knew that I could steal the bitch with hardly any effort if I wanted, but surprisingly I wasn't interested. My mind and heart were set on hooking up with just one woman and one woman only.

"Say, do you still work out at the Walker Estate?" I asked, deciding to go at this shit another way.

Alonzo bobbed his head, either enjoying his high or the hand job his trick was giving him under the bar counter.

"Think you could get me on?"

Alonzo's eyes fluttered just a bit higher.

"C'mon. You know I have to pull a W-2 just like you to keep my parole officer off my back."

"I hear you. I hear you." His eyes drifted again.

"So you'll get me on?" I pressed.

A half smile cocked a corner of Alonzo's mouth. "I'll see what I can do. No promises."

It took another week of pestering Alonzo, but I finally landed an interview with the landscaping company that handled the Walker Estate. The first time I rolled through the iron gate, I thought that I was caught up in an episode of *Lifestyles of the Rich and Famous*. The grass wasn't just green, it was that emerald green shit. All the hedges were like works of art and the flowers were beautiful as fuck. But nothing, absolutely nothing, could've prepared me for my first sight of the mansion.

The bitch was off the fuckin' chain for real. I'd spent time around rappers and ballers—so it wasn't my first time around niggas with money—but goddamn. These bougie niggas weren't playin' with their hustle.

"Forty thousand square feet," Alonzo whispered back

over his shoulder as he led me to a stone building that oper-
ated as both the groundskeeper and landscaping company
offices. "Fifteen bedrooms and twenty-two bathrooms. Can
you believe that shit?"

"What the fuck you say these people did again?" I asked
Alonzo as I strolled behind him, struggling not to leave my
mouth hangin' open.

"I ain't been able to figure all that shit out yet." Alonzo
stopped at the door and then surveyed the wide estate.
Whateva the fuck it is, the nigga got bank.

Taking in all that shit, my confidence took a major fuckin'
hit. It made me reconsider the whack game I was gone try
and spit at Mrs. Walker. Shit. Why the fuck would she ever
consider fuckin' around with me?

"This is the guy you were tellin' me about?"

I looked up as this big-ass Rick Ross–looking muthafucka
rolled through the door. There was nothing about homie that
said *landscaper*. In fact, I thought the man looked like he
was more suited for bustin' niggas' heads open in the back
of dark alleys or some shit.

"Yeah. This is my partna I've been tellin' you about,"
Alonzo said, grinning and bobbing his head. "He and I go
waaaaay back."

I shifted, uncomfortable beneath my potential new boss's
intense scrutiny. In my short twenty-two years, this would
be my first legit 9-to-5 job. But hell, how hard was it to drive
one of those cool riding lawn mowers?

"Your man here tells me that you're fresh out the joint. Is
that right?"

"Yeah." I cleared my throat. "I, uh, just got out a few weeks ago."

"What did you get locked down for?"

I hated this part. My business was my business and I always hated nosey muthafuckas.

"You wanna speak up?" the boss man asked, crossing his arms and lookin' like he was ready to dismiss my ass.

After a shrug and a coupla scratches to the side of my head, I just laid it out there. "Drugs. Cops found a roach in my car's ashtray."

"You got a temperament problem?"

I clenched my jaw. "I ain't say all that."

"Didn't have to." The boss man walked across the room to a huge desk and then plopped into a chair that squeaked out in protest.

My gaze cut toward my boy, Alonzo, who quickly stepped forward and went to bat for me again.

"Hey Tommy. You know I'ma vouch for my man here. He's gonna toe the line and do a good job. My word is bond on that."

Tommy looked me over again, not even bothering to hide his dislike or distrust. Finally, he shifted his eyes back to Alonzo. "A'ight. Trust that I'm gonna hold your ass responsible if this muthafucka fucks up."

Alonzo instantly relaxed and broke out a smile. "Ain't no thang. My man's gonna make you proud. You'll see."

I nodded. "Thanks, man. I appreciate it."

"Don't thank me," Tommy said. "Thank your man Alonzo

there. If it wasn't for him, I wouldn't give you the time of day."

The truth stopped me cold, and for a few brief seconds me and my new boss were locked in an intense staredown. It took everything I had not to cuss this asshole out. Shit. He didn't know me or my circumstances. There was no way this big, greasy muthafucka hadn't been on lock before and now he was sittin' there tryna judge me?

"C'mon, man," Alonzo said, tugging on my arm. "Let me show you where we'll be working at today."

I decided to let the shit go and turned from the big man to follow my boy out the office.

"What the fuck was all that about?" Alonzo hissed once we were outside.

"What?"

Alonzo rolled his eyes. "Man, I got a sweet setup here. Promise me you're gonna be on your best behavior."

"What the fuck you think I'm gonna do—run off with the hedges?"

"Whateva, nigga. C'mon. We gotta put down some fresh mulch out back."

"Yessir, massa. I git dat for you real quick."

"Don't start that shit. You wanted this job, now you got it. So quit your bitchin'."

"Look at you. All official and shit," I teased as we marched across what felt like a goddamn football field.

"What—you gonna diss a nigga 'cuz he takes his job seriously now?" Alonzo said.

"C'mon, man. It's a bullshit job. Playin' in the dirt and shit."

Alonzo shook his head and kept marching onward.

"What? You for real?" I laughed. "Nigga, I thought you were just out here for the W-2."

"Ain't nothing wrong with a little hard work," Alonzo mumbled.

Hard work was puttin' the shit lightly. After an hour of slavin' away beneath the Georgia sun, I was ready to just say fuck the dumb-dumb and roll up out of there. But just at that moment, the back glass doors opened and Mrs. Walker stepped out onto the scene.

I was hunched over on my knees and spreading mulch around a line of newly planted trees when I glanced up and sucked in a stunned breath. What baby girl looked like at the club the other week was nothing compared to what she was bangin' today. I took my time drinking in everything from her pretty pink painted toenails, to her sun-kissed bronzed skin, and most certainly to the cotton candy pink bikini that clung to her curves like a second layer of skin. God didn't make them no finer, and my cock was seriously testing the hell out of the seams of my pants.

I watched, hypnotized, as she strolled down the stone stairs and then strutted her fine ass over to the property's large pool. Just when I thought my afternoon fantasy couldn't get any better, I got a glimpse of her backside and saw her two perfect brown buns accessorized by a single pink string.

"Goddamn," I mumbled.

Alonzo chuckled. "Ain't she something?"

"Something ain't the word for it." I glanced toward the back door. "Where her man at?"

"Mr. Walker?"

"Is there another?"

"Not to my knowledge." Alonzo shrugged. "But I ain't her babysitter."

My gaze boomeranged back to the lovely vision making herself comfortable on the lounge chair. "Hold on. I'll be right back." I stood, but before I could take a step, Alonzo grabbed my arm.

"Whoa, nigga. What the fuck do you think you're doing?"

My head snapped back. "What? What's the problem?"

"The problem, nigga, is that you can't just go makin' your moves on the boss man's woman and shit while you're on the job. What the fuck? Are you tryna get your ass fired on the first day?"

"Man, you know I don't care about this bullshit job. I'm tryna holler at shawtie for a hot minute."

"Shawtie?" Alonzo's face twisted. "Nigga, look where you at. She ain't no ghetto dime on ho patrol. And whether you care about this job is irrelevant. I vouched for your ass and you ain't about to screw me over again."

"Again?"

Alonzo just gave me a hard look. "She's off limits while you're on the job."

I thought my dawg was crazy, but there was no reason to escalate this to a full argument. Alonzo did go to bat for me so I was gonna have to be a little more sly with my shit. "A'ight, man. A'ight." I stole another glance toward the pool

and watched as Mrs. Walker took her time drizzlin' sun-
screen all over her body. The tease had to know that she had
all us niggas up there droolin' over her fine ass. All of them
too scared to make a move.

Not me.

She glanced up, caught my gaze from across the way.
Even from the distance, I saw her surprise . . . and then interest.

I smiled and tipped my head.

She dismissed me by lowering her expensive sunglasses
and then lay back on her lounge chair.

"She wants me," I said, wiping my arm across my sweaty
brow. "I just know it."

"You think all women want you." Alonzo laughed, returning to work.

I smirked. "They usually do."

# Chapter 3

"So is that when you started stalking Mrs. Walker?" Officer Asshole asks, interrupting my story.

I shake my head and roll my eyes. "Do you want to hear this shit or not?"

Asshole clenches his jaw and leans over the folded table. "You're tryin' my patience, boy. Why don't you just get to the fuckin' point? You saw something that you couldn't have so you made sure nobody could have her. This fuckin' story is as old as time."

"That's not how it happened," I snap. I might get the fuckin' needle for this shit, but I ain't about to let this nigga with a badge turn what happened into just some other ghetto drama that rolls up in here on the regular. There was more to our story than that.

For a few long seconds, me and this asshole try to stare each other down. His partner is tired of our nonsense and places a hand on his shoulder. "Let's just let him tell the

*story." Her dark gaze swings back to me. "Go on. What hap-
pened after your first day on the job?"*

*I look at the two cops, weighing whether I should clam
up. But honest to goodness, I just have to get this shit off my
chest. I draw a deep breath, relax deep into my hard chair,
and just keep spillin' my guts. "For about a week or so I just
kept watching her from a distance. . . ."*

It was nearing the end of July. The humidity was so thick it
could choke a horse. But there was me and my nigga,
haulin' shit around like two fresh-off-the-boat slaves. Hell,
even at the Fed pin they didn't keep niggas out in heat like
that. At least Alonzo was doin' somethin' he claimed he
loved. I was out there hopin' to catch glimpses of the big
man's lady. At that point, I'd only seen Mr. Walker once.

Big dude. 'Bout six foot four, six five, something like that.
I wasn't no suit-and-tie man myself, but I can respect a nigga's
game who could wear that shit and wear it well. Mr. Walker
certainly did that. He stepped out the front door of that big-
ass house one mornin' lookin' like he belonged on one of
those *GQ* magazines. He was supposedly twenty years older
than his lady, but he sure the fuck didn't look like it.

James Walker was as black as shoe polish and looked as if
he could bench 250 to 300 in his fuckin' sleep. Though the
suit was smooth, his bling was subtle but still demanded respect. I'm talking cuff links, one or two rings, and a diamond
in his ear that was worth enough to feed everyone in the
projects for the rest of goddamn year.

I ain't gonna lie. I was one jealous muthafucka.

Still, whenever I asked about Mr. Walker's hustle, niggas clammed the fuck up as if damn Homeland Security was monitoring our fuckin' conversation. Even though I was intrigued about how this man was making his bank, I was more interested in his wife. The fly honey had to know she had all of us watching for those small glimpses when she would parade half-naked either out by the pool or marching by the sheer curtains in the upstairs bedroom.

I even caught her watching *me* a coupla times. Sure, she would play the shit off. But I could always feel her eyes on me when she thought my ass wasn't lookin'. Bein' that it got so hot, a lot of us worked with our shirts off. And believe me, I was out there flexin' every fuckin' chance I got. But after a coupla weeks of playin' this cat-and-mouse game, I knew that it was time for me to make a move—any move.

It was a Friday afternoon. Just minutes after she'd finished teasin' us to watch her play in the pool. I lied and told Alonzo that I was gonna head back to Tommy's office and see about us gettin' off work early. Instead I snuck off to the house, got in by the kitchen. I knew their gay cook wouldn't say shit because he was too busy actin' like he could flip a straight hood nigga like me. I told him I needed to use the facilities to see about some bullshit cut on my hand—which was a lie. He just swished his hips and pointed me in the direction of the downstairs bathroom.

Of course I just walked passed the muthafucka and skipped up the stairs. Now I ain't gonna play and act like my heart wasn't poundin' like one of those racehorses you see on TV. It was. All the time that I'd been peekin' this woman out, I still didn't know what the fuck I was gonna say when I got her alone. But fuck it. I was just gonna wing the shit.

I figured she'd be in her bedroom and I knew which room that was by the peep show she always gave. Still, I felt like an illegal alien strollin' down that expensive marble floor and past the white spotless walls. Most I could hope for was to be her nigga on the side 'cause I couldn't offer the chick nuthin' but a discount on some street drugs and a big dick.

And one thing I've learned is to never *ever* underestimate the power of a big dick.

I heard the shower long before I reached the master bedroom. When I was finally standing outside the door a whole list of reasons why I should punk out rolled through my head. The main one being that she might call the cops on my ass. That would severely fuck up my parole. But a nigga ain't never got nowhere being too scared to take a chance.

I opened the door, stuck my head inside. I was instantly hit with this sweet floral scent. Later on, I found out it was honeysuckle and jasmine. Her signature scent. Anyway, that shit smelt nice—even made my dick harder, if you could believe that. Now I probably should have turned away right then and there, but I could hear baby girl was singing in the shower. She sounded good.

I strolled on into the bedroom, closed the door behind me, and then took a good look around. That one room was bigger than my whole apartment. The walls were this soft buttery yellow and the carpet was so plush and soft, hell, I wouldn't have minded sleepin' on the damn floor. Then again, one look at that big-ass four-poster mahogany bed had me seriously daydreaming. My mind flooded with images of Mrs. Walker's legs hangin' over my shoulder, her titties bouncing up and down, and my dick buried so deep I was puttin' dents in her uterus.

I smiled as I walked over to the bed and touched the silk sheets. Shit. I ain't never fucked on anything other than good ole reliable cotton. Hell, I stood there for a long time, wondering about all kinds of shit. Was she a screamer? Was her pussy tight? Did she ever take it up the ass?

The shower had shut off and the singing stopped. In that moment, my mind cleared and my ass panicked. I needed to get the fuck out of there. But hell, there was no way my ass could sprint across the room and not get caught so I rushed toward the first available door, which turned out to be a closet. Hell, even *that* was bigger than my apartment.

The bathroom door opened and I stopped the closet from clicking closed—bettering my chances of *not* getting caught. It seemed to work. And as luck would have it, I had a damn good view of the Mrs. as she strolled over to this long kind of lounge chair, still patting her naked body dry. At that moment, my dick was so hard it coulda plowed through steel. Baby girl curved in all the right directions. And her titties. Goddamn. If I had to guess, I'd say she was a 38 DD. And those muthafuckas were real and sat at attention. The best part was how the nipples were puckered and looked as if they had just been dipped in a batch of milk chocolate.

My ass started salivating.

But the torture was just beginning. I stood there peeking out the closet, watching her take her sweet time putting lotion all over her body. At first I thought I was the only one gettin' hot, watching her cup and caress her breasts. But before long, I saw that she was turnin' herself on. Her caresses turned into gentle squeezing and then pinching and pulling of her nipples. She rocked her head back, her eyes appearing to roll to the back of her head as she leaned all the way back in the chair.

She left the lotion alone and instead reached for some type of oil. She drizzled some out all over her flat belly and even onto that cute little triangle of pussy hair. She set the bottle down and slowly started massaging the oil into her skin and even into her clit.

I reached for my dick and at first tried to massage my shit through my pants but then mentally said, *Fuck it,* and unzipped them. My hand was a sorry substitute when you considered there was some perfectly good pussy just a few feet away. She musta been thinking the same thing, because she got up from the chair for a few seconds and then returned with this long glass-looking dildo.

She gave the damn thing a kiss and then turned it on. It didn't hum—more like purred. She rubbed the tip of the dildo against her marbleized nipples and then started purring her damn self. The shit was sexy as hell.

I stroked my meat faster. I watched that damn toy, hypnotized and jealous like a muthafucka. When she pulled open her pussy lips I could see just how turned on she was by the thick, creamy cum that made her big-ass clit shine.

My ass started droolin', feinin' for some blackberry pie. A lot of brothas claim they don't like eatin' pussy but, to me, pussy was like a delicatessen. There are no two that taste exactly alike. Sure, there are some fishy ones, sour ones, and downright nasty ones—but there are some delicious ones as well. Some that would make you want to spend all your money, some that'd make you cry, and some that'd turn an illiterate muthafucka into a poet. And her pretty pussy looked like it was all of that and then some.

As she slid the dildo in, inch by slow inch, the damn thing started to sound like it was drownin'. One thing for sure, baby girl's moans started to sound out of this world. When her hips got into the game, it started to get damn near impossible for me to control my own moans and shit.

"Awww. Goddamn. Shit," she growled, breathlessly.

It was kinda surprising to hear that kind of language comin' out of her pretty, full lips. But the shit had me ready to bust a nut.

She turned up the speed. Her sex toy went from gurglin' to soundin' like an underwater jackhammer.

"Awww. Yeah. Shit." She tossed her head from side to side and started bitin' on her lower lip.

Then I fucked up.

Either I said something or gasped too loudly. But suddenly baby girl's eyes popped open and she sat straight up. Shuttin' off the dildo, she glanced at the bedroom door and then around the room. Clearly she was tryna figure out what she had heard.

I was tryna figure it out too while mentally kickin' myself. No doubt this is the kinda shit that would fuck up a nigga's parole. I decided to step back from the closet door. I didn't want to risk the chance of her seeing an eye peekin' at her from the narrow slit. But my foot hit some kind of purse or bag and the girl woulda had to be deaf not to have heard me.

She jumped up from the lounge chair. "Who's there?"

And just as if the devil had it out for a nigga, I heard Tommy blastin' my name from somewhere in the house.

"Yo, Delvon! You up here?"

I closed my eyes and swore under my breath. Just kill me now.

Her eyes locked onto the closet door.

Next I heard Alonzo's voice outside the open window. "Delvon! Where the fuck are you, man?"

In my mind, I could just hear the clickin' sound of hand-cuffs and, worse, the screechin' wail of my foster momma when she heard my ass was back in jail for some Peepin' Tom bullshit.

Her long curvy legs started toward the closet door. My heart dropped as if it were tryna escape by the wrong route. I coulda dove behind some of those clothes in there, but it woulda just delayed my ass bein' discovered by a few seconds—at most. Then two things happened almost at the same time. She pulled opened the closet door, gasped at seein' me standing there with my dick in my hand—and then the *bedroom* door burst open and Mr. Walker rushed inside.

To my amazement, she slammed the door in my face, turned, and pressed her weight against the door.

"Honey, what are you doin' back here?" There was a nervous quiver in her voice and I hoped to God he hadn't picked up on it as well.

"Forgot that damn insurance policy the agent sent over yesterday. Can you believe that shit?" He laughed. "Have you seen it around?"

"Umm, no. I haven't."

There was a long pause. "What the hell are you doin' parading around naked in the middle of the damn day?"

"I, uh—"

"Oh, what's this?" The sound of her handy dandy dildo purred back to life. "I leave for a couple of hours and you're already missing *big* daddy?"

"You know it." Her weight eased off the door as she moved toward him. There were a few kissing and whispering sounds. Jealousy crept up my spine.

"I wish I had time to play with you, my little angel—but duty calls."

She moaned her displeasure and then said, "I understand."

"Maybe later tonight." There was another kiss and then, "Ah, here's my folder. I better go."

I breathed a sigh of relief. At least I wasn't about to be trapped in the closet while listenin' to them fuck. I did, however, have to confront Mrs. Walker's wrath when she reopened the door. I was so busy thinkin' about all this shit that I never once thought to zip my dick back into my pants. Turned out to be the very thing to save my ass.

When the closet door jerked open again, Mrs. Walker

had draped on a silk robe and her eyes were blazing with anger. But she took one look at my hard-ass dick and everything about her went soft.

"What are you doin' in my closet?" she asked, her voice husky as shit.

I puffed out my chest and took a chance. "I came up here to see you." I took my time glancing down her body.

"Why is that?" She tightened her hold on the robe.

" 'Cuz I want to fuck the shit out of you." Now that confession was either brilliant or *real* stupid. I didn't know which one for a few *lonnng*, silent seconds. But maybe it helped that my dick visually started jumpin' in time with my fast-beating heart. Her eyes got big as fuck at that shit. Finally, slowly her hand loosened on her robe, allowing it to slide open to show me all that lay beneath. Big titties. Small waist. A pretty pussy.

She smiled. "Then what the fuck are you waitin' for?"

# Chapter 4

"*Give me a muthafuckin' break!*" *Officer Asshole thunders as he jerks up from his chair. "What the fuck—we look stupid or some shit to you?"*

*I toss up my hand. "Look, you wanted to know how this shit went down so I'm tellin' you. Maybe she hooked up with me because she was one of those desperate housewives or some shit. I don't know. But that's how our shit started. I was feelin' her and she was feelin' me," I bark.*

*Even Officer Good Cop starts to shake her head. "I've met Sabrina Walker, and none of this shit you're sayin' sounds anything like her. The woman is a pillar to the community. Affluent. Well-educated."*

*These two are seriously pissing me the fuck off. "Look. I don't know nuthin' about all of that. I just know how she was with me. A'ight?"*

*Neither of these muthafuckas look like they are buying this shit, but what the hell can I do about it? I'm spittin' the truth. Shit. At this point, I ain't got nuthin' to hide. I know I'm gonna go down for this shit.*

*Asshole just starts pacing the room, like that is all that is keepin' him from ringin' my fuckin' neck.*

*"Go on," Good Cop says. "What happened next?"*

*"What do you think happened? I fucked the shit out of her."*

I don't know much, but Mrs. Walker had the sweetest, tightest pussy I had ever had the good fortune of fuckin'. And I mean that shit. That sweet honeysuckle pussy clamped around my big dick like a warm velvet glove. The moves she had on the dance floor a few weeks before wasn't shit to what she laid on me in that big, silky bed. The woman was actin' like she hadn't had no good dick in years.

And talk about *wet*.

Fuck!

My toes stayed curled the whole time I was hittin' it and splittin' it. And baby girl was tearin' up a nigga's back with her long red nails. I didn't care. Nothin' was gonna stop this nut. As hypnotizing as her jigglin' titties were, they were nothin' compared to how passion and bliss covered her beautiful face. She was a lady and a freak all rolled into one. She proved that shit when my tongue bathed that beautiful, tight booty hole of hers a few minutes before I squeezed the head of my cock in there.

She tensed, tightened up, and I damn near came right then and there. "Relax, baby. Relax," I urged, hissing through my teeth.

She tried, but I was a big muthafucka, determined to see if she could take it all in. She took a little more than half before she started screamin' into the pillow.

"Wait. Wait," she pleaded. "I need to catch my breath."

I chuckled and she started laughin'. But to make sure we stayed in the groove I reached down and around and slid my fingers up and down her soppin' wet clit. She quivered and that tight ass opened up just a little more. After that, we just wild out.

"Oooh!" Sabrina quivered and shook.

"Look at you," I taunted. "You ain't so high and siddity now, are you?" Our bodies started slappin' together. She was straight takin' it to the balls now.

"Awww. Shiiiiit. Jeeeeezzzus!"

"You've been teasin' me for a hot minute. Haven't you?"

*Smack! Smack! Smack!*

"Haven't you?" I asked again, though I knew she was strugglin' to breathe. "You like teasin' niggas? Is that it?"

"I . . . I . . . I . . ."

"Goddamn, baby. You got some tight-ass shit." I clenched my teeth together, feelin' my nut rise. But I didn't want that shit to end just yet. "Flip yo' ass over." I whacked her on the ass.

She definitely knew how to follow orders. She flipped over and wrapped her legs around my waist so I could go back to work. Pussy juice was everywhere.

"Hell, yeah! Shiiiiitt!" I was startin' to sound like her.

"Awww. Yeah. Don't stop!" She grabbed my ass.

"I don't plan on stoppin', baby." To make my point, I

picked up my hips' tempo. "Give me some of these titties." I dropped my head and waxed and polished those fat nipples like it was a part-time job. She was quivering and tremblin' all over the damn place.

There was something about the way her moans and groans changed up that clued me in that she was on the verge of comin'. I pounded away with no remorse. "I want you to say my muthafuckin' name," I told her, and then realized that I probably needed to tell her what it was. "Let me hear you say, 'Delvon, this is some good dick.'"

"D-D-Delvon . . . t-this is some gooooooood dick," she panted.

"Damn right it is, baby. And you can have this shit anytime you want it."

"Oooooooooh!"

"You comin', baby?"

"Yeeeeeaaaaah!"

"Then come on." Then out of nowhere, her nails dug so deep into my ass I thought I was goin' to need a doctor to have them removed. But given that her pussy put the death grip on my dick, we both came at the same time.

I fell over to the side of the bed like a falling tree and straight up went to sleep. Me! Asleep! Pussy ain't never done that shit to me. I've always been able to hit and run with no problem. But that damn time, I swear I felt like I followed Alice down that rabbit hole to Wonderland.

When I woke, the sun was settin' and Mrs. Walker was still passed out her damn self. She even had a cute li'l snore that put a big ol' smile on my face. I watched her for a little while, thinking that she looked like a beautiful brown angel. Honest to God, it kinda took my breath away. Shit. I coulda just laid there all evening and all night just watchin' her.

A few minutes later Sabrina's long lashes fluttered open and I smiled and winked at her. "Hey, you."

She gasped and sat up. "What . . . ?" She glanced around the bedroom, noted the setting sun. "Oh God. What are you still doin' here?" She sprang out of bed.

I tried to act like her reaction didn't bother me, but I guess it did sting a bit. "I fell asleep."

She started raking the sheets off the bed while I was still in the muthafucka. "Well, you're up now. So get out."

I blinked and just stared at her ass. "Oh, it's like that?"

She tugged at the sheets up under me, hinting for me to get my ass up.

"A coupla of hours ago, you weren't actin' like you wanted my ass to go. You were booty clappin' all up and down my dick."

She turned away from the bed, jerked open the night-stand drawer. Next thing I knew a few bills came flyin' my way.

"What the fuck?" I finally jumped out of the bed. "What— you think I was fuckin' you for a coupla of dollahs? Is that it?"

"Weren't you?"

"Awww. So that's the real drill around here? You lure a nigga from out the yard, whup it on him, and pay him for his time?"

"Don't be ridiculous."

"I'm just goin' by what I'm seein', ma. So what's hood with you?"

"What's *hood* is that James should be on his way home and I don't feel like dying today—call me picky and shit—but that's exactly what's gonna happen if he walks in here and smells the funk in these damn sheets."

I cocked my head and stared at her.

"I've never done this shit before," she admitted. "Ask any of them niggas out there. You're the only one."

I heard her and I wanted to believe her but . . . damn, we were fuckin' before she even knew my name.

Finally she dropped her gaze. "You just caught me at a weak moment. The shit will never happen again."

Now that shit snapped me out of my daze. I didn't wanna hear no shit like that. The pussy was too good and she was too beautiful. "C'mon, now. No need for that kind of crazy talk," I said, steppin' to her, slidin' my hand beneath her heavy breasts. "We both had a good time, didn't we?"

She looked like she was torn between tellin' the truth and throwin' my ass up out of there.

"Look, ma. I ain't tryna fuck up your situation here. I know how to keep shit on the D.L. if that's what you're worried about. I'm feelin' you. That's all." When our eyes locked, I held my breath. One fuck and my ass was sprung. I knew it and I was scared as shit that she knew it as well.

"You need to get out of here," she whispered. "It won't be good if James finds you in here."

I bobbed my head, bent down, and scooped up my pants

from off the floor while she went back to stripping the bed. When she picked up the two hundred-dollar bills, she stopped and looked up at me. Probably was wondering if I wanted the money or not.

"Don't even think about it," I told her. "I was with you because I wanted to be with you. Simple as that." To my surprise a big-ass smile spread across her lips. Was that all she needed to hear?

Through the open window, we both heard a car pullin' down the driveway. In the time since her man left, she'd done nothin' but fuck and laze around all afternoon. His loss. My gain.

"You better get out of here," she insisted.

"Not until you tell me your first name and when we're gonna hook up again."

Her eyes grew wide. "I don't think that's a good idea."

I hopped back onto the bed.

"Delvon, are you crazy?"

I smiled. "I love how you say my name, Mrs. Walker."

She blinked at me.

"What?"

"Nothing." She shook her head and grabbed my arm and pulled. "Get out."

I didn't move. "Not until you say what I want to hear," I told her.

Outside, the car door closed.

We stared at each other as if tryna call each other's bluff.

I won.

"It's Sabrina and I'll meet you tomorrow night," she said. "Meet me in the lobby of the Sheraton Hotel in Marietta at seven o'clock."

I climbed out of bed and smacked her on the ass. "Don't have me waitin'."

# Chapter 5

"So this is how your supposed affair got started?" Officer Asshole spits, his black eyes hard and intense.

I shift in my chair while tryna keep my emotions in check. "It mighta started off as an affair . . . but it turned into something much more than that."

Asshole tosses up his hands. "Aww, fuck. Give me a break!"

The Good Cop just stares me down. "Are you sayin' you were in love?"

"We were in love," I correct.

Asshole laughs again.

"What—you think a woman like Sabrina Walker couldn't love a nigga from the streets? You think that she was too good for that shit?"

"Yeah," Asshole says, meetin' my gaze. "I do. In fact, I think you're just makin' this bullshit up. I think that when you started working for the Walkers, you developed an obsession with Mrs. Walker. A deadly one."

*"Naw. Naw. You got it all wrong."*

*"I doubt that."*

*We launch into another staredown, leavin' it up to the Good Cop to ride to the rescue once again.*

*"Say we believe you—what happened next?"*

The Sheraton was off the chain. After the first time, we started meeting there once to three times a week—whenever she could get away. To be honest I don't remember the exact time our fuckin' transformed into lovemakin', but it did. Shit. The way she made me feel whenever she was in my arms—man, I ain't never felt nothin' like it. She never asked me for nothin'—and yet I always wanted to give her whateva I had. That wasn't much. I mean, shit. The woman already had everything she could possibly want. So I just made sure that wheneva she was with me, I put my heart and soul into what went on between the sheets.

I told her everything about me. Shit I ain't never told nobody else. About how my Momma Gina, who ain't really my real momma but who was one of my daddy's around-the-way chicks, took care of me when he hit the bricks and married some ho out in Las Vegas. She didn't have to; she coulda just dropped my nappy-headed ass off at Family Children Services and kept it movin'.

But she didn't.

Her heart was too big. It still was. Momma Gina loved me like I was one of her other six kids. And despite the grief I'd given her over the years—my droppin' out of the ninth grade, my dope slangin', my car jackin', and a little of everythang else in between—she still loved me. By the time I was finished talkin' my ass was damn near in tears.

Sabrina just looked at me with those lovin' eyes of hers, pulled me into her arms, and sexed me so good I wanted to give her *my* last name. Yes. I was sprung and just flat out didn't give a fuck.

Lookin' back, Sabrina was a li'l mo' guarded. She always acted like if she told me too much there would have been serious consequences. The mystery was kinda a turn-on. Usually you can't stop women from tellin' you all their business, their best friend's business, their momma's business.

Sabrina was real cool about everything. Hell, she was just as vague about what her husband did for a livin' like everybody else I ran across. Hell, maybe I should be afraid of this muthafucka. But each time I looked at his wife, I convinced myself that she was well worth the risk.

In return for what I did for her, Sabrina showered me with gifts. She never made the mistake of just straight offerin' me money, but she certainly upgraded a nigga. My gear became the flyest shit on the block. She was coppin' me gold chains, diamond rings, and even hooked me up with a dope-ass Range Rover. Hell, you couldn't tell me my shit stunk.

Niggas on the block was hatin'—tryna to find out what the fuck I was sellin' on the side. My P.O. started askin' questions, but as long as I was still reportin' to my 9 to 5 and paid my fee, he left a nigga alone.

We connected. And for the first time in my life I can say that my ass was truly happy. Lookin' back that should have been my first clue that the shit couldn't and wouldn't last. Nothin' really does.

Just before everything changed, Sabrina and I switched it up and met at this li'l hole-in-the-wall hotel on my side of town. I don't know. Maybe she wanted to see the hood up close and personal. I just thought she wanted to see a li'l more of where I came from. Maybe it was just me, but I thought the shit was kinda . . . sweet.

After we had finished funkin' up some *cotton* sheets, we laid there clinging to each other—hot, sweaty, and satisfied.

"I wish that we could go away together," Sabrina said, lazily twirling the few hairs on my chest with the tips of her fingers.

"Where would you like to go?"

Sabrina sighed. "Somewhere far, far away. A place where nobody knows our names. Where they don't ask too many questions and we don't have to tell any lies."

I frowned. "What's the matter, baby?"

She shrugged. "Nothing."

It sure didn't sound like nothin'. In fact it sounded like a whole lot of something. "C'mon. Surely by now you know you can trust me." I kissed the top of her head. "What's weighin' you down, baby?"

Silence.

"C'mon. Tell me what's on your mind. Why do you want to go someplace where nobody knows your name all of a sudden?"

Sabrina shook her head against my chest. "Trust me. You wouldn't understand."

"Try me." There was another long silence but I was determined to wait her out.

"It's . . . James."

I immediately tensed when she said his name. I hadn't meant to, but jealousy was a muthafucka. "What about that nigga?"

"See. I knew I shouldn't have said nothing." She started to turn away, but I held on to her.

"What? No. It's cool. C'mon. What about him?"

Sabrina glanced up at me. "I think he's startin' to suspect somethin'."

"Then fuck that nigga then. You know that you got me." Even as the words came out of my mouth I knew that shit was whack as hell. How the fuck was a woman like her eva gonna adjust to the hood life—which was all I could eva offer her.

Sabrina was quiet. Clearly a sign that she was thinkin' the same thing.

"You know. Just forget I said shit." I pushed her away, rolled, and sat up at the side of the bed.

"Don't be mad," she whispered. "It's not like that. I'd love nothin' more than to run off with you," she assured me.

I didn't believe that shit for a minute—but I wanted to believe it. I glanced back at her over my shoulder. Loved how she rocked that fresh fucked look. Yet there was so much pain, misery, and even fear reflectin' in her eyes. "What's really hood with you, ma?"

Sabrina was quiet for so long, I thought that she wasn't gonna answer my question. But then she surprised me.

"I'm thinkin' that maybe we should end this before some-one gets hurt."

I clamped my jaw shut and lifted my chin high. But I still felt like I was goin' into cardiac arrest. No matter how I tried to act like that shit didn't hurt, I was sure that she could read my ass like an open library book.

"Delvon . . ."

She reached for me but I sprang out the bed like it had suddenly caught fire.

She tried again. "Baby, try to understand."

"Fuck that. Why we gotta stop? Ain't nobody onto us."

Sabrina rolled over, climbed out the other side of the bed, and started grabbin' her clothes. "It's for the best, Delvon. If we stop it now nobody will get hurt."

"Hurt? What the fuck are you talkin' about? How's any-body gonna get hurt? We've been real careful."

"I think some of the workers at the house have been whisperin'."

"That's bullshit and you know it." I grabbed her arm. "What's the *real* reason?"

Sabrina tried to pull her arm back, but my grip tightened.

"Delvon, let go. You're hurtin' me."

I looked down and saw how I was manhandlin' her and immediately released her. "I'm sorry about that. I didn't mean . . . I just tryna understand this shit. I thought we were . . . I thought we had connected."

Tears sprang to Sabrina's eyes and then skipped down her beautiful face. "Oh, baby. Of course we connected. That's why this is so hard. I'm feelin' stuff I ain't got no business feelin' and . . ." She stopped and tried to get it together, but she failed miserably. "Delvon, he'll never let me go. He'd kill me first."

"C'mon—"

"No. He's told me that more times than I can count." She sniffed and backhanded a trail of tears. "I *know* he means it."

Her words set off warning bells in my head. "Has this nigga been hittin' on you?" Just the idea of that big gorilla-lookin' muthafucka poundin' on her got my blood heated. I tried to absorb this whole conversation, but everything was just happening so fast.

"A'ight. A'ight. Let's just sloooow the fuck down," I said, reaching out and gently pulling her into my arms. "I'm sure we can work this shit out, baby."

Sabrina just shook her head. Her tears were streaming faster.

It broke something in me to see that curvaceous brick-house transform into something as delicate as those flowers I spent most days planting around her estate. Suddenly all I wanted to do was hold her and protect her. In my head, I was dreamin' of taking a two-by-four up against James Walker's head and whalin' on him 'til either I got tired or the police came and hauled my black ass back off to jail.

Together we sat back down on the edge of the bed, where she remained locked in my arms 'til the cryin' stopped and the kissin' began. As far as I was concerned I never wanted to see those tears again. Right now, I might not be able to do much about her situation, but I could make damn sure that she felt good whenever she was alone with me. That was the only chip I had in this fucked-up game. And no matter what she was sayin' right now, if I played this chip right, she would keep comin' back to me time after time.

I eased her back onto the bed and situated myself down in between her legs. Sabrina's body was flawless. There wasn't a scratch or blemish anywhere on her glowing apple-butter brown skin. I was addicted to more than just the feel of her; I was addicted to the taste.

As I peeled open her sweet, wet lips, Sabrina hooked her legs over my shoulder. Even though I just wanted to dive right in, I held back. I wanted to take my time with her. I gently stroked her stiff clit with the pad of my thumb while I planted kisses along her inner thigh.

"Ooooh," Sabrina panted.

"You like that, baby?" I asked, and then stroked her again.

"Ahhh. Yes." She started playin' with her titties. Pullin' on them and pinchin' them until they bloomed like rosebuds.

I smiled and went back to savor the meal that was before me. I teased her with my thumb and fingers for a little while. I always loved to see how many she could take. And she could take a lot while writhin', moanin', and even some times strugglin' to catch her breath.

That was when it was time to lay it on her. I glided my tongue so deep I wanted her to think it was a long pink cock. I knew I'd hit the jackpot by the way her legs damn near tried to cut a nigga's head off. But that shit didn't stop me.

I was gonna make her nut up like she ain't never nutted in her life.

And judgin' by her reaction I was achievin' my goal.

"Ahhh, Delvon. Wait, baby," she pleaded after her third consecutive orgasm.

But there wasn't gonna be no more waitin'. On her next nut, she screamed so loud and so long, I just knew that someone was gonna call the hotel management on our asses.

And I was right. A few seconds later our room phone rang, but we let that shit go to voice mail. "On your knees," I told her after unlockin' her legs. I stroked my dick while waiting for her to get into position. My ego inflated at watchin' her try to control her wobbly arms and legs.

"You know I'ma 'bout to fuck the shit out of you, right?"

Panting, Sabrina nodded and turned her perfect round ass up at me. I gave it a good smack, got off seein' my bright red handprint on her left cheek so I gave the other one a good smack.

Sabrina sucked in a startled breath and then wiggled her shit back at me.

I laughed at her eagerness. "You ready for this shit, ma?"

"I'm ready for anything you wanna give me, baby," she purred, lookin' back over her shoulder at me.

She was such a tease. But I did her one better by just runnin' the tip of my cock down her big ass cheeks and watched how she tried to push back on a brotha. To let her know who was runnin' the show I gave a coupla more smacks.

"C'mon, baby. Give it to me," she begged.

"Give what to you?" I reached down and fingered her exposed clit some more.

"Stop playin', baby. Put it in." She scooted back only to get smacked again.

"What? This?" I asked, slipping three fingers into her tight pussy. "Goddamn, baby, you're so wet." Her pussy made a loud squishy sound when I slid in the fourth finger. "Aww. Shit. You're ready for me, ain't you."

"Y-y-yes!"

Hell, I was ready too. Pre-cum was already drippin' from the tip of my dick and I couldn't wait a moment longer. I quickly removed my hand, gripped my shit, and in one long, hard stroke I went for mine.

Sabrina screamed out again while the walls of her pussy quaked all around my shit. I slammed my eyes closed and tried to hold still so that I wouldn't turn into one of those one-minute brothas that bitches loved to bitch about. A few painfully long seconds later, the tremblin' subsided and I was cleared to get my stroke on.

For a high-class broad, Sabrina knew how to put in work when it came to the bedroom. Sweat slicked her back and poured down all around her neck. She was in it to win it. What amazed me was that despite my big dick and the number of times I'd fucked her with no mercy, Sabrina still had a tight-ass pussy. And what she could do with her muscles damn near brought tears to my eyes.

"Look at you," I said, fuckin' without remorse. "Look how I got you wide open. How you gonna tell me you gonna leave this good dick?"

*Smack. Smack. Smack.*

"Answer me, girl."

"OOOOOH, GAWD!!!"

*Riiinnng! Riiinnng!*

Damn manager was tryna call again.

"Answer me, Sabrina. You tryna give up this good dick?"

"I . . . I . . . I . . ."

*Riiinnng! Riiinnng!*

"What, you want me to stop?" I immediately stopped pumpin'.

Sabrina gasped and then tried to back up on the dick again. I smacked her ass so hard my hand stung. "Answer the muthafuckin' question. You want me to stop fuckin' you?"

"No, baby. No. C'mon, stop playin'."

I started deep strokin'. "You love this dick, baby?"

"Oooh, yeeessss."

"So I can have this pussy any time I want?"

"Ooooh."

I whacked that ass again. "Answer my muthafuckin' question. CAN I HAVE THIS PUSSY ANY TIME I WANT?"

"Yeesss, baby. Yeeesss."

"All right, then." I picked up the pace and started hammering away. Pussy juice squirted back and splattered all up and down my leg. "Fuck yo goddamn husband. This pussy is my shit. You hear me, baby?"

"YEESSSS!"

"Tell me whose pussy this is!"

*Bam! Bam! Bam!*

Someone was bangin' on the door. "Y'all keep it down in there!"

"TELL ME WHOSE PUSSY THIS IS!"

"It's y-yours, baby."

*Bam! Bam! Bam!*

"That's what the fuck I thought!" I grabbed hold of her hips. "Now let's show these muthafucka just how loud I can make your ass scream!"

# Chapter 6

"As entertaining as I find your fantasy love life," Officer Asshole growls, "when the fuck are you gonna get to what the fuck happened tonight?" He looked over at his partner. "I mean, shit. He wants us to believe that everything was just hunky-dory between him and Mrs. Walker." His eyes cut back over to me. "What about that big fight you got in with Mr. Walker down at Sambuca? According to the complaint he filed, half the people at that restaurant stated that you were the one who started it."

I hold up my hands. "Wait a minute. That . . . that was because I thought I saw him hittin' Sabrina."

"You thought you saw?"

"It was dark and . . . and from a distance it sorta looked like her. But . . ."

"Give me a fuckin' break."

"I'm tellin' you the truth." I switch my attention to the Good Cop. "How the fuck was I to know the sonofabitch had a chick on the side?"

"According to the complaint Mr. Walker filed, he said he was at Sambuca with his wife."

"That's bullshit," I spit.

"Maybe he was," Asshole interrupts. "You said yourself that the woman sorta looked like her. Maybe she just wore her hair differently or some shit?"

"Naw. Naw," I insist, irritated. "I said only from a distance they looked similar. Up close the woman had brown hair, not black. Her breasts were smaller and she even had like this mole just above the corner of her lip."

Asshole and his partner glance at each other.

"What?"

"Well, I'm glad you took the time to notice the woman's breast size."

I shift in my chair. "Look. A few more things went down before that night. I mean, I was really fucked up 'cuz . . . 'cuz . . ."

"Because what?" the Good Cop asks, cockin' her head at me. "She went through with it, didn't she? She dumped you."

I clamp my jaw tight and draw in a deep breath. Even now that shit still fucks with me. After feelin' their curious gazes on me for a hot minute, I resume my story. . . .

After our day at that ratty-ass hotel, I had to say I was definitely smellin' myself. I showed up on the block, cheesin' like a Muppet on *Sesame Street*. All my boys were givin' me grief. Especially my niggas Crazy Larry and Alonzo.

"Damn, nigga," Crazy Larry boomed, slappin' me hard

on the back outside Momma Gina's apartment building. "Where the fuck you been? I ain't seen your ass out here in a hot minute."

"Yo, man. I've just been workin'. Ask my man, Alonzo, here."

Alonzo didn't bother crackin' a smile. "More like hardly workin'."

"What the fuck is that supposed to mean?" I challenged him. "You know my ass been on the job each and every day."

"Oh, you're workin', all right. Workin' on gettin' yourself killed by fuckin' with the boss man's woman."

Crazy Larry cracked up. "Are you shittin' me?"

"Naw, nigga. Gone with that bullshit." I tried to wave off his comment, but Alonzo wasn't havin' it.

"C'mon, man. You ain't foolin' nobody. I done seen you with my own two eyes sneakin' off to the house. And it ain't like that bougie bitch is quiet when you're bustin' that pussy. We all would have to be fuckin' deaf not to hear what's goin' on."

I started to get heated listenin' to my dawg spit my business out on the street like he was doin'.

Alonzo finally cracked a smile. "Don't get all mad at me because your ass is sloppy with your bullshit. Niggas talk and it's just a matter of time before one of them start talkin' to Mr. Walker."

I looked at my man hard. "You threatenin' me?"

Suddenly his eyes were just as hard as mine. "Now why would I do somethin' like that?"

Images of me bustin' a nut all over one of Alonzo's baby

mama's ass flashed across my mind. Did this nigga know what went down before I got locked down? Why was he mind fuckin' me right now?

Crazy Larry cracked up. "Damn, Delvon. Pussy has always fucked you up." He gave me a good whack across the back.

I flinched and broke eye contact with Alonzo.

"You gonna keep fuckin' around and somebody is gonna take your damn thug card away. You're a disgrace to the movement, man. And I mean that shit." Crazy Larry whipped out a fat blunt from his shirt pocket and then jammed it into the corner of his mouth. "Y'all niggas need me to give you a few minutes to kiss and make up?" He eyeballed us. "Y'all look like y'all ready to knuckle up or some shit. I know that shit can't be happenin' 'cuz y'all been niggas like foreva."

Neither one of us said anything.

"So y'all shared some pussy before. Ain't that what niggas do? Share and share alike?" He lit his blunt and took a deep toke off the muthafucka before passin' the shit to me.

*Fuck. Did everybody know my ass hit it with Cherry?*

Alonzo tried to squash the shit. "Look. Whateva, nigga. Just don't say I neva warned ya. You're in over ya head and don't even know it."

Crazy Larry passed Alonzo the blunt. He took one good hit and passed it to me. "I'ma catch up with you niggas later," he said, and then he was out.

I watched him go as Crazy Larry shifted his attention to

me. "Here my ass been thinkin' you been slangin' some bomb shit you didn't let us in on, and this time, you just scored your ass a sugah momma." He cheesed at me. "My nigga!"

We exchanged smiles and dabs and for the rest of the afternoon we just blazed trees. But in the back of my head I kept wonderin' about what Alonzo meant that I was in over my head. What did this nigga know that I didn't know?

The next week, my shit fell apart. I strolled up in Tommy's office on Monday and I was surprised to be handed my walkin' papers.

"What the fuck is this?" I asked, confused as fuck.

"What does it look like?" Tommy didn't even bother to look up from his desk. "It's your last check. Thank you for your time, but your services are no longer needed."

I blinked at his bulky frame hunched over his desk. "Just like that? I'm fired? What the fuck for?"

"You're fired because the boss said to fire you. No further explanation is needed."

My mind reeled. Did that simple muthafucka find out I've been creepin' with his wife? Had Alonzo made good on his threat? What did James do to his wife when he found out? Sabrina's hauntin' words came back at me full force and I was overcome with the need to see her—touch her— make sure that she was alright.

"We'll see about this," I said, waving my pitiful check at Tommy. I jerked around and headed to the door.

"And exactly what the fuck do you think you're gonna

do?" Tommy asked. "You think you're gonna roll up to the big house and confront a man about his own damn woman? Shit, boy. You are dumber than you look."

Angry and ready to take on the world, I jerked back around but was surprised that big man was up out of his chair and was practically inches from my face.

"Don't kid yourself, partna. Security has already been alerted and you're not gonna get anywhere near Mr. Walker's woman again. You've had your li'l summer fling. Now the shit is over. You can either walk out or leave in a body bag. Those are really your only two options."

The hairs on the back of my neck jumped up and I knew without havin' to look that there were a coupla more niggas standin' behind me. This muthafucka was prepared. Regardless, I still entertained the idea of whoopin' his ass. But that bullshit move would have landed my ass right back in jail. I couldn't get Sabrina back if my ass was sittin' behind bars.

After an intense staredown, I threw my hands up. "A'ight," I said. "You win. You win."

Tommy's expression didn't change and his black gaze followed me as I backed away from him. When I turned to head for the door, I was stunned as fuck to see that one of Tommy's henchmen was Alonzo. So much for our asses bein' boys and shit.

If Alonzo had any remorse for what he was doin', it sure as shit didn't show in his face. But you better believe I was mentally preparing to pay this nigga back for that foul shit. Once I was outside, I cast a look toward the big house, hopin' I could catch a glimpse of Sabrina in the upstairs bedroom window, but it was too far and I knew I was already stretchin' Tommy's patience.

Then I don't know what came over me. I raced toward the house—but I didn't get twenty yards before a line of niggas sacked my ass.

"You're a stupid muthafucka," one of them laughed, throwin' a coupla unnecessary punches at my gut, chin, and then head.

Shit, the muthafucka musta had bricks for hands because I passed the fuck out for a coupla minutes. When I came to, I was all crammed in the passenger side of my SUV and my boy Alonzo was drivin' me back to my hood. I came up swingin'.

Alonzo swerved and nearly ran off the highway. "Nigga, what the fuck is wrong with you?"

I got in a good lick upside his head and the car finally rolled off the road and dipped down into a grassy knoll. At that moment, I didn't give a fuck. I just wanted to whup his ass for that foul shit back at the Walker Estate. After the car stopped, Alonzo came back at me though.

"What the fuck, nigga. I'm the one that pulled those dudes off your dumb ass," he hollered, gettin' a good swing in my already-achy ribs. Every bit of air left my lungs and I swear to God I saw stars circlin' my head.

Alonzo was still heated. "I *told* your ass what was up. Now you done got my ass fired 'cuz you can't control your dick." He turned and punched the steerin' wheel. "What the fuck did you think was gonna happen—that the nigga was just gonna let you keep fuckin' his woman? Damn, dawg, you're lucky your ass still breathin'. That muthafucka got connections all around this city. And you gonna drag my ass into your shit. Like I ain't got enough problems."

"Nigga, I don't want to hear all of that shit." Awkwardly, I tried to sit up, but I was startin' to feel a little bit more pain. "Goddamn it. I think those niggas busted my ribs."

"I repeat, *you're lucky your ass is still breathin'*." Alonzo jerked his gaze away like he couldn't stand the sight of me. "Look, Delvon. I've put up with a lot of bullshit from you. Mainly because we're boyz and our asses go waaaay back. But this . . . fuckin' with James Walker . . ." He sat silently, shakin' his head. "I don't know about this. I gotta feelin' he ain't just gonna let the shit go with just a simple beat down."

I shifted uncomfortably in my seat. "*Who* is this nigga?"

Alonzo finally looked back at me. "Powerful, nigga. That's all you need to know."

Back at the crib, I paced so much I was sure I was wearing a hole into my apartment's cheap carpet. After my talk with Alonzo I grew more alarmed for Sabrina's safety than my own. I wanted to call her and check to make sure that she was alright, but all while we were creepin' Sabrina was never comfortable about givin' out her number. She kept sayin' that she knew too many folks who got busted when their man checked their phones. So she always called me, and even then her number would come up as *unknown*. Contacting the Walker residence was out of the question because their shit was also an unlisted number.

So I had no other choice but to sit and wait for her to call me.

*If* she called, I kept tellin' myself.

After a week had flown by, I knew somethin' had to be up. No way she could just up and quit me like that.

Then the second week rolled by and all my boyz started talkin' shit about how I was pussy-whipped and how I needed to return to the ole regular ghetto pussy strollin' up and down our block. But I wasn't tryna hear none of that.

Sabrina was the only woman for me.

I'm not a stalker. I've had a few hos who had trouble lettin' go in the past. I used to laugh at their asses. So I was tryin' real hard to convince myself that my drive-bys at the Walker Estate wasn't really stalkin'. I just wanted to see for myself that Sabrina was okay. After working a whole summer on the estate, I knew the weak security areas. I waited until nightfall one night and crept onto the property from the south end of the property.

I just wanted to see her.

I was smooth as shit, duckin' security and makin' my way up to the house. When I got about a hundred yards away, I could hear voices. Loud voices. They were arguin' or some shit. Sabrina musta really been upset because she really didn't sound like herself. Then again, she was shoutin' at the top of her voice.

I tried to get closer to see what the fuck was goin' on. Then I saw Sabrina rush by the upstairs window, but it happened so fast, I didn't really get a good look.

"I'm leavin' you!" she shouted. "So say good-bye to all

your li'l fancy clothes and toys. I'ma 'bout to take all this shit."

"C'mon, now, Sabrina. I done told you that bitch didn't mean nothin' to me!"

What the fuck. Did this nigga get caught dippin' too?

"You had the bitch up in my house," she shrieked. There was a loud crash and I assumed she was throwin' shit at the dude. I smiled because my baby was showin' a little fire.

"Hey, who's over there?" A voice thundered from my right.

"Shit." I jumped when a flashlight swept in my direction.

"Hold it right there!"

Fuck that shit. I jumped out of the bushes and got the fuck on, but it was hard work with what still felt like a coupla busted ribs. I tell you what, those big husky-lookin' mutha-fuckas had some speed on them. They damn near caught up with my ass.

When I got back out to the crib though, I realized that nothin' much had changed. I still didn't get a good look at Sabrina. Maybe it was time that I face that we were really over.

But then, two days later, I was doin' another drive-by of the estate.

And a couple days after that as well.

The funny thing was, it was just by chance I caught a glimpse of James Walker at Sambuca. It was sort of a fancy joint in the heart of downtown that catered to jazz lovers. Alonzo and I got a job down there, bustin' tables. For me the gig was to make sure my P.O. stayed off my back. He wasn't too happy to hear I'd got laid off with the landscapin' company.

Then my parole ended—but I kept the job anyway. It wasn't too bad.

Of course now I was back to hustlin' on the side. A minimum wage job don't pay shit nowhere. But like I was sayin', it was just by pure chance I saw James Walker there one night. At first, I thought I was just bein' paranoid. I first saw him comin' out the men's bathroom. I did a double take, nearly caused a four-waiter pileup when I tried to rush across the restaurant.

"Hey, watch where you're goin'," someone yelled behind me. I just yelled, *Fuck you,* in my head and kept it moving.

James was at his table and was helping a woman up. *Sabrina.* I smiled until I saw how hard her husband had gripped her by the arm. They started movin' toward the front door of the restaurant. But from where I was, it looked more like he was shovin' her. I don't know. Maybe because it was so dark, I got the whole thing screwed around in my head, but I kept rushin' after them. I shoulder bumped and knocked into a few people and when I finally made it out to the valet, I saw the Walkers arguing.

Mr. Walker's hand went up and . . . I don't know. I reached out, grabbed him, and threw a punch with my whole weight behind it. Damn, that felt good to see that muthafucka kiss the concrete like that. But my satisfaction only lasted half a second before a small army knocked my ass down as well. My ribs were screamin' at the body blows Walker's henchmen rained down on me.

"Who the fuck is that muthafucka?" Walker shouted above me.

The niggas stopped punchin' and kickin' long enough to jerk my head up so they could get a good look at me. Hell, I was havin' trouble seein' them as well. My eyes were swellin' up on the spot and my mouth was full of blood. But then when my vision focused, I was confused.

The woman on Walker's arm *wasn't* Sabrina.

# Chapter 7

"So who was she?" Asshole asks.

I draw a deep breath, shrug. "I don't know. Maybe it was that sideline ho they were arguing about."

The Good Cop shakes her head as she scans the complaint James Walker had filed regarding the incident. "Says here that he was there with his wife."

"He's a liar," I bark.

"So we're supposed to believe you, a killer, over him?"

"Look, I'm tellin' the truth," I insist. "Sabrina Walker meant the world to me. I loved her."

"Yeah. You loved her so much, you killed her."

"She wasn't supposed to be there!" I jump up and slam my fist on top of the table.

Asshole doesn't even flinch. He just slowly climbs to his feet; our gazes lock. "Sit down."

Tears sting the back of my eyes and I fight like a bitch not to let them fall. But it's too hard. I can't stop Sabrina's image

*from floatin' in my head. Her smile. Her laugh. Her amazin'
body.*

*A sinister grin slithers onto Asshole's face. "Don't make
me tell your ass again."*

*Reluctantly, I plop back down into my seat, feelin' as if
I've just aged ten years. "Why the fuck should I care if you
muthafuckas believe me? Y'all gonna do whatcha wanna do
anyway." I cross my arms. "Maybe I should wait for a
lawyer."*

*The cops exchange looks again before the Good Cop
presses. "Why stop now? This shit has gotta be gettin' close
to the end. What happened after you attacked Walker out in
public?"*

*I sniff and sit up in my chair. "Everything got compli-
cated real quick. . . ."*

While Walker's goons were beatin' my ass, I guess someone
in the restaurant called the police. For a split moment, I was
actually happy to hear from those muthafuckas. Then reality
set in and I knew I had to get up out of that muthafucka.
Shit. A nigga just got off parole. I wasn't tryna go back on.

Walker and his goons apparently were thinkin' the same
thing because they seriously broke the fuck out and left me
squirmin' in a pile of my own blood. One of the dudes at
valet tried to restrain me for the cops, but at least I won that
battle. Only problem was that I worked there and everybody
didn't think twice of droppin' dime on a brotha.

Hell, the police beat me to my own damn crib. I had no
choice but to lay low and wait them muthafuckas out. By the

next mornin' my ex-P.O. was blazin' up my cell. But I let all those calls go straight to voice mail. I didn't want to hear none of the shit he was talkin'. He didn't have any power over me no more. I musta stayed walled up in my apartment for a week.

Every time somebody would knock on the door, I treated them like Jehovah's Witnesses. Then out of nowhere, Sabrina showed up. Actually came to my hood blinged the fuck out. Shit. I was surprised she didn't get jacked, comin' into the hood lookin' like a million dollars.

When she knocked, I was just gonna ignore her like I'd done everybody else. But when she called out my name— fuck, it was like my heart stopped. Baby girl still had me whipped. I jerked open the door and sure enough, there she was. She was dressed head to toe in soft pink with very real diamonds draped around her neck and drippin' from her ears.

It was like I'd died and gone to heaven.

"Can I come in?"

I blinked and to my surprise she was still standin' there. Sexy as shit. It wasn't a muthafuckin' dream. "Sure. C'mon in."

Sabrina finally smiled and then slowly entered the apartment.

I ducked my head out into the hallway to see if anybody else saw her. There were a coupla li'l niggas playin' out there. But nothin' too serious. I went back into my apartment and shut the door.

Sabrina took her time, walkin' and lookin' around the living room. "An interestin' place you got here."

I instantly felt self-conscious about my shit. "Well, you know. It'll do for now." I shrugged.

She turned and looked me dead in my eyes. "I've missed you."

Shit. That was all I fuckin' needed to hear. I crossed the room and pulled baby girl into my arms. My chest was on fire when I crushed her body up against mine, but I didn't give a damn. The only thing that mattered was that my baby girl was back.

I swear her thick lips were sweeter than I remembered, her body even more intoxicating. I couldn't help but feast on her mouth while I also pulled and tugged that damn silk shirt from off her body. I felt like a crackhead finally gettin' a hit.

"Oh, baby. I can't tell you how much I've missed you," Sabrina panted, ripping my muscle T-shirt as if it were made from paper. She nibbled at the corners of my lips, raked her fingers down my back.

I reached down and cupped both of her ass cheeks and gave them a good squeeze. My ego blew up when she quivered and gasped. Hell, I couldn't wait to get back to the bedroom so instead I directed her over to my cheap-ass pleather couch. I was more than ready for some freak-nasty sex. But the moment she dropped back against the couch my gaze snagged on an army of black and blue bruises that covered her from her neck down to her torso.

"What the fuck?" I reached above the corner of the couch and clicked on the floor lamp. The bruises looked worse under the light. "What—did that muthafucka beat you?"

Sabrina quickly snatched up her blouse again and attempted to cover herself.

I jerked the blouse away and stared stupidly at the damage her deranged husband had inflected on her. "I'm gonna fuckin' *kill* him."

Sabrina's gaze snapped up. "Do you mean it?"

Her response surprised and thrilled me at the same time. There was so much hope and desperation shinin' in her eyes. *She's serious*, I thought. I dropped down to my knees and stood in between her legs as I held her gaze. "Fuck, yeah."

Suddenly my mind went wild at the possibilities we could have together if Sabrina's husband was out of the picture. We could lie in bed and fuck for days at a time. Hell, I could give her my last name and fill her belly with beautiful babies and hope that every one of them was a girl and looked just like her.

"Don't say it unless you mean it." She reached for the band of her bra and then pulled it up over her head.

My two best friends bounced and jiggled before me and I was instantly in a trance. My mouth watered like a muthafucka.

"I hate him," Sabrina whispered. "I have for a long time now." She leaned forward to kiss the tip of my nose and brush those perfect titties against my chest. I reached out, squeezed and pinched her nipples until they were the size and feel of marbles.

"Oooh, shit, baby. Bite them."

She didn't have to ask me twice. I bent my head and

sucked those babies into my mouth and fuckin' went to town. Sabrina gasped, moaned, and squirmed. Fuck, it felt like old times. I finally eased her back onto the couch, dipped my hand down in between her legs, and found her pussy wetter than a muthafucka. My dick was so hard it was about to poke a hole in the couch. But I wasn't goin' to just straight rape the girl. I had to take my time and make this shit last all night.

I kissed and licked my way down her body, but I kept gettin' distracted by the ugly bruises that covered her once-perfect skin. I tried to stay in the moment, but my anger was provin' too hard to control. Sabrina may be that other nigga's wife, but in my heart she belonged to me.

Feelin' a new fire burn in my blood, I raised up off the floor, positioned my baby's long legs east and west, and plunged in balls deep with one stroke.

"Awwwww. Shit, baby." Sabrina reached out to press back against my thighs.

My eyes rolled to the back of my head while her vaginal muscles squeezed and pulsed, trying to adjust to my size. I had to wait, because if I moved too quick my ass was gonna bust a nut waaaay too fuckin' soon.

Sabrina sensed this and started playin' games by squeezin' and relaxin' her muscles on purpose. "You like that, baby?" she whispered.

My breath started trippin' over itself in my chest and my toes were curled so tight they started to cramp.

Sabrina just smiled and started rockin' her pelvis.

"Sssssssssss." I grabbed her hips and tried to regain control, but she was havin' none of that.

She set her own rhythm, bouncin' up and down while squeezin' tighter and tighter. "Ooooh, baby. I missed this dick sooooo much," she moaned. "This is the best dick I've ever had." Her pussy slurped and popped as if it was co-signin' what she was saying.

A goofy smile slanted my face as my ego blew the fuck up.

"Let me show you how much I missed you, baby," she said.

I released her legs and the next thing I knew I was flat on my back and Sabrina had resumed the top position without releasing her mean pussy grip. I was still tryna do every trick not to come too fast, but baby girl wasn't makin' it easy. After she would pull up slowly, she would slide back down and swivel her hips like the figure eight. My spine tingled and my back started to hunch.

"Daaaaammmmmnnn, baby. You feel so good," I moaned and hissed. "Sssssssssss."

"You like how I do this, baby?" she cooed against my ear.

"Hell, yeah." I grabbed her ass and then sent her to the moon when I dipped my finger into her tight asshole.

"Oooooooh." Sabrina tossed back her head and thrust her titties forward into a hungry nigga's face. I lapped those babies up and we were both fuckin' and suckin' in perfect harmonious bliss. But it didn't take long for a nigga to get greedy. I locked an arm around her waist and scooted to the edge of the couch, tipped her back, and made this awkward transition to the floor.

"I'ma 'bout to tear this pussy up," I promised.

"Do you, baby," she panted. "Give me all you got."

I whipped those legs up over my shoulder and pounded that pussy until it sounded like we were havin' a conversation. Sabrina whimpered and moaned, but she took that dick like a true sex solider and threw each thrust back at me with equal force. With the pain of my ribs and the pleasure of her pussy, I quite literally started seein' stars again. No way was I stoppin'. I didn't give a fuck if it meant my ass was gonna be carried out of there on a stretcher. We was gonna get this nut.

I threw my dick so hard and so fast Sabrina started inching up the carpet. It didn't matter to me. I was determined to chase that pussy all around the living room, if need be.

"Oooooh, yessss. Fuck me harder," she begged. "Show me how much you love this pussy."

Hell, was that ever in doubt? Look what all I'd been through because of that tight-ass pussy. At that moment, I don't think there was a limit to what I wouldn't do for it either.

"Aaaaaah shiiiit, baby. Aaaaah, shit."

"Flip your ass over," I barked. A second later, I was beatin' it up doggy-style. Sweat was pouring off me like a goddamn water fountain and my knees was burnin'.

"Ooooh, baby. That's my spot," she panted. "That's my muthafuckin' spot. OOOOOH. Shit. I'm comin'."

I grabbed hold of her shoulders. "Then come on, baby.

Give daddy whatcha got." In the next second, Sabrina screamed as her warm, creamy juices gushed down onto my dick. That was all it took for me to pop my top like a champagne bottle. I sprayed my nut all on her ass, back, and hair.

Afterward I collapsed down beside her. I was dizzy and strugglin' for air. A part of me was ready to accept the fact that if I closed my eyes I might never open them again. My chest hurt that fuckin' much. Sabrina curled up under my arm and I started to drift off as usual with her lush body pressed up against mine.

When I woke, the sun was no longer streaming through the narrow slits of the venetian blinds and the apartment had cooled a good ten degrees. I hoped and was pleasantly surprised when I looked to my right and Sabrina was still there. I smiled and tried to lean down and kiss the top of her head, but a sharp pain ricocheted up from my rib cage and I gasped and collapsed back onto the floor.

Sabrina stirred with a soft, delicate moan. I watched her open her eyes and take in her surroundings. I don't know, maybe I was expectin' to see horror or regret in her face. But instead she turned up at me and smiled. "I wish it could always be like this."

"It could be. Just leave that nigga." At least I was able to reach out and brush a strand of hair back from her face. Damn. She was beautiful.

A new wave of sadness filled her eyes and she tried to look away. I quickly cupped her chin and forced her to maintain eye contact.

"Look. I know he's a powerful nigga. I get it. But I'll protect you," I said. "I know it may not look like it right now. But me and my boys can put our heads together and we can handle this situation."

Sabrina shook her head long before I stopped talking. "He's never gonna let me go. He'll kill us both before that happened. I just know it."

"He's just a nigga," I insisted. "He can bleed and die just like any man."

"Then let's kill him," she said, her eyes lit up with a sudden bloodlust and eagerness.

In my past, I have been a liar, a thief, and a drug dealer. Now this gorgeous woman that I had no business wanting was asking me to snuff out a life. And my retarded ass was seriously thinking about it.

"Don't you want us to be together?" She shifted to hover over me.

I winced, but I didn't say a damn thing as she started to snake her way down my body.

"With him gone, we can be together. Forever. It'll be you . . . me . . . and the money."

I sat up on that shit. "The money?"

Sabrina nodded her head. "If we do it right, I'll inherit everything. Easily a cool hundred million."

"You're shittin' me."

Her lips sloped into a half smile. "I wouldn't do that, baby." She leaned forward and brushed a kiss against my mouth. "Not when the stakes are this high."

A hundred million? Shit, I couldn't wrap my brain around

that kind of money. Ten million, maybe. A hundred million—who the fuck was this muthafucka?

Sabrina resumed inching down my body. "Don't be scared. It's like you said. He's just another nigga that bleeds and dies like the rest of us." She took hold of my fat cock and kissed the tip. "We get rid of him." Kiss. "Lay low for a while." Kiss. "Then we'll get married anywhere you like."

I smiled at her. "Alright. I'll do it."

"Really?"

"Yeah," I said, loving the light now shining in her eyes.

"I love you." She slipped her mouth over the head of my dick and vacuumed sucked that muthafucka until I could feel my nut rise from the sac of my balls.

As her head bobbed up and down, I raked my hands through her thick hair while visions of Benjamin Franklin danced in my head. This nigga may have gotten the drop on me a coupla times before so it was definitely time to put this nigga to rest.

# Chapter 8

"Give us a fuckin' break! Now we're supposed to believe that Sabrina Walker conspired to kill her husband?" Asshole roars, jumpin' to his feet. "What kind of fools do you take us for?"

"Is that a real question?" I challenge. I pick up my cup and drain the rest of the water. "I'm just tellin' you how it all went down. I wanted Sabrina and Sabrina wanted me. It's really as simple as that." I swing my gaze to the Good Cop and even she looks like she is havin' a hard time swallowin' this one. "You got to believe me," I plead.

She drops her gaze and pretends to be interested in the thick folder splayed out in front of her, but I'm not fooled. She thinks I am a murderer and a liar. "So the money didn't play any part in your decision to try to kill James Walker?"

I shift in my chair. "Nah."

Asshole groans while the Good Cop cocks her head. "You wanna try again?"

"A'ight. Not initially," I correct, feeling both annoyed and defensive. "But mainly, I went along because I loved Sabrina."

Asshole tosses in his two cents. "Dangerous thing—your love."

Just like that, my eyes sting with unshed tears. "She wasn't supposed to be there."

"Then why was she?" the Good Cop counters.

I don't want to answer. I drop my gaze and review why Sabrina went back to the house tonight. I don't want to accept the truth—that she had changed her mind. That she ran home to call the whole thing off. That maybe . . . just maybe, she really did love her husband after all.

After my long silence, Asshole clears his throat to catch my attention again. I glance up, barely able to control the tremblin' of my bottom lip.

"What exactly was the plan?"

I draw a deep breath to pull myself together, but this last part of the story would no doubt haunt me 'til my dying breath. "If anyone in my crew knew how to make a nigga disappear it was my dawg Crazy Larry. . . ."

Crazy Larry was old school. He didn't carry no cell phone or pager. He'd always claimed that the white man had put shackles on niggas for more than two hundred years so he wasn't gonna willingly put one on now so he could be tracked at any time or any place. Despite that, most people knew how to *track* his ass. On the half basketball court, practicing his dunk and dreamin' about goals that had long passed.

Back in the day Crazy Larry used to be known as *Hoops* because of his A game. The usual sad story of a sports injury had him shifting careers to the military. He was part of the first wave of soliders sent to fight Bush's oil wars, and when he returned we all noticed that he wasn't quite right in the head. He'd do anything and say anything. His hustle since he got back, on top of slangin' some weed here and there, was dealin' guns. Small time. But it helped with the bills.

When I caught up with him, and Alonzo, I put it all out there on the line.

Crazy Larry just laughed in my face. "Nigga, what the fuck do you need a gun for? You tryna land back in jail?"

The mention of jail immediately had me checkin' over my shoulder every thirty seconds for police. "Don't give me a hard time on this shit, man. I need this."

Alonzo clucked his tongue and shook his head. I didn't even have to ask what he was thinkin'.

"A'ight. A'ight." Crazy Larry held up his hand and then smacked it against his chest. "You're my nigga. So tell me what you need. I got you."

"Look. I just need a piece with some serious firepower. Something I can just handle my business with and then get the fuck on."

"This a solo job?"

"Yeah." I coughed and cleared my throat. I was nervous like a muthafucka and was tryin' to hold any second thoughts of doin' this thing at bay.

Crazy Larry stopped bouncin' the basketball, planted it

at the side of his left hip, and turned to give me a quick glance over. "What's the job?"

I shook my head. "The less y'all know the better."

"True that. True that." He glanced over his shoulder for a quick cop watch himself and then leveled his black gaze on me. "But given our current economic situation a nigga might be lookin' to get in where he fits in, if you get my drift."

My brows jump and then crash together in the center of my forehead. "What? You?"

"If the money's right." He shrugged and looked to Alonzo. "Why not? Whatcha hittin'—a bank or something?"

"Count me out," Alonzo said, shakin' his head. "I already know I'm not going to like a damn thing you say."

Crazy Larry laughed. "Please. Nigga, it ain't like you got shit else to do. You lost your job at the restaurant."

"Don't remind me," Alonzo said.

My mind was whirling at this. I ain't never dropped a nigga. I could really use someone with Crazy Larry's expertise on something like this.

"Well, what's up, nigga?" Crazy Larry asked. "Are you gonna make me fill out a job application or something?"

"Nah. Nah. It's nothing like that." I shook my head and glanced around again. "Look, maybe we oughta go somewhere else and talk. I don't think we should discuss this out here and shit."

"A'ight." Crazy Larry resumed bouncin' the ball. "It's 'bout time for my two o'clock smokes anyway. Let's go talk some business." He turned to Alonzo. "Is you too good to have a smoke with us too?"

Alonzo only took half a second to think about it. He ain't never in life turned down some free weed and clearly he wasn't about to start today.

I can count on one hand how many times I've hung out at Crazy Larry's place. Mainly because he was the kind of nigga that hung out at other people's cribs. And, more times than not, didn't know how to take his ass home. Another reason was because this fucked-up nigga only had one piece of furniture. A raggedy-ass couch that looked like some shit he picked up at a junkyard. He ate, smoked, slept, and fucked on that muthafucka and he was proud of it.

"C'mon, niggas. Have a seat."

Alonzo and I plopped down on his shit and sank so low our asses were actually lower than our knees.

Crazy Larry caught me wincing in pain. "What's wrong with you, D?"

"My ribs," I told him. "They're still givin' me a li'l trouble. It's no big deal."

Crazy Larry whipped out a shoe box he kept tucked under his sofa and started rollin' a fat blunt. "So talk, D. What's hood with you?"

I quickly established that whatever we talked about wouldn't leave the room. My dawgs looked insulted that I even had to say that shit, but whateva. I was gettin' ready to talk about knockin' someone off. Serious shit. I didn't give a fuck about their hurt feelings.

"C'mon, man. Just lay it on us."

So I did just that. I told them about Sabrina showin' up at my place, about all the bruises on her body—the fact that I caught her man out cheatin' with another woman. All that.

"Shit," Crazy Larry said, blowin' out a long stream of smoke. "This sound like *All My Children*."

Alonzo and I frowned.

"What? Don't act like I'm the only nigga that watch that shit." He hit the blunt again, and then passed it to Alonzo.

"So what? Y'all gonna help me blast his ass or what?" I asked.

"Hell, naw," they answered in unison.

I was stunned, especially since twenty minutes ago Crazy Larry was practically beggin' for the job.

"Why the fuck not?"

"Because this is over some damn pussy," Crazy Larry said bluntly. "Pussy I ain't even had. What the fuck I look like doin' time for some dumb shit like that? I ain't your bitch."

"Preach on it," Alonzo encouraged.

"Ain't nobody said shit about gettin' caught."

"Nobody ever says shit about gettin' caught," Crazy Larry pointed out. "That don't stop niggas from gettin' locked down. And of course you gonna get caught. You ain't never killed nobody before, and shit, if the nigga turned up with a bullet you'd be at the top of the suspect list."

"C'mon now—"

"No. You c'mon and get the smell of that bitch's pussy outcha nose. She got you straight slippin', man."

I took my two hits off the blunt and then kept the rotation going. "Look, I ain't gonna beg you niggas. I just need some firepower and I'll be on my way. Unless you're gonna renege and not hook a brotha up."

"Don't do it, man," Alonzo warned, his eyelids droppin' low.

"Yeah. Pussy ain't never worth it. You, of all people, should know that by now. You're always fallin' for the wrong bitches. What's up with that shit?"

"I didn't come up in here for a goddamn sermon."

"Consider it on the house then."

Alonzo just sat there grinning.

I waited a second or two before playing my ace in the hole. "Sabrina says the nigga is worth a hundred million."

The blunt stopped halfway up to Alonzo's lips and their drug-heavy eyelids suddenly sprang wide open.

"Come again," Crazy Larry said.

"A cool hundred million." I grinned, looking at their astonished faces.

A wicked smile curved across Crazy Larry's lips. "Well, shit. We all gotta go sometime."

"So you in?"

My dawgs looked at each other and then shifted their attention back to me. "What's the plan?" Alonzo asked.

I had them. "We gonna make this shit look like an accident."

Crazy Larry bobbed his head. "Yeah. Yeah. The nigga just accidently shot himself in the head. I feel where you're goin' with this."

"Nah. The guns are for insurance. In case Walker's niggas

roll up on my ass again. Sabrina and I have something better in mind for her husband."

"So the bitch planning all this?"

"Can you ease up on callin' her a bitch? That's my lady, man."

My dawgs shared another look and then cracked up.

"What?"

"Nigga, consider your playa card permanently revoked." Crazy Larry high-fived Alonzo.

I gave them a few minutes to get their chuckle on before gettin' back down to business.

"Alright. Alright," Alonzo said, clearing his throat. "Let's hear the plan."

"Then let's hear about how we're gettin' paid," Crazy Larry added.

"We're gonna hit the house," I said confidently.

"What? A burglary?" Alonzo asked. "What about security?"

"That's what the guns are for," Crazy Larry said, trying to help out.

"No. I said *accident*, remember?"

Their eyes returned to me.

"We're gonna blow that muthafucka sky high."

"Explosives?" Alonzo said, looking like he was gonna back out again.

"How the fuck is a bomb an accident?" Crazy Larry asked, intrigued.

I knew by the look in his eyes this shit was right up his

alley. Fuck Alonzo. "No bomb," I said, focusing all my attention on Crazy Larry. "We're gonna tamper with the gas line on the fireplace in Mr. Walker's study."

Crazy Larry's eyes lit up. "That's fuckin' dangerous. I've seen what that shit can do on the news. Muthafuckas always look like an atomic bomb went off." He licked his lips.

"Yep. And thanks to Sabrina, I know everybody's routine around that muthafucka, too. We just need the guns for insurance."

"What kinda cheese you breakin' me off?"

"A solid 250K."

Crazy Larry whistled. "You know I'm startin' to fall in love with this bitch, too."

Alonzo just sat there and listened as we smoked and plotted to kill James Walker.

Sabrina met the news of my bringin' my dawgs in on the plot with skepticism and then proceeded to nag me to death about who they were and could they be trusted. I did everything I could to ensure her that I had everything under control and for her not to worry. But she did worry. It seemed like every fuckin' moment.

She was so nervous about the whole thing that a few times I was worried that she was just gonna call the whole thing off. She came close a coupla times leading up to the day.

But she didn't.

On the other end, Crazy Larry wanted to make sure that Sabrina was legit and insisted that she pay them half the money up-front.

She paid it. Fenced through my man's cousin's car dealership. That way it didn't look like she was paying for a hit, but buying a car that didn't exist—complete with made-up VIN numbers and tags. It was brilliant because if she ever wanted or needed the money back all she had to do was report the nonexistent car stolen to her insurance.

Everything was a go.

Except Alonzo meant that shit when he said that he wanted no part of the operations. That didn't faze us because our dawg was no snitch.

The week Crazy Larry and I went out to the Walker Estate, Crazy Larry drove this white van we bought and decorated as *Whiz Plumbers*. We even bought white overalls and tool belts. I hid in the back, since security would know my face and would possibly cause all kinds of unnecessary drama.

Once at the main house, one of the maids led us to the downstairs bathroom where we pretended to work on the pipes. Instead we were sneakin' over to Walker's study where we worked on the gas fireplace. When we left, the gas switch said it was off, but the faulty valve we installed leaked a steady flow of gas into the closed-door study.

We were all banking on a huge explosion when Walker came home from his Thursday night poker game and lit his customary Cuban cigar. For an alibi, Sabrina had arranged to be out on the town with some friends. That meant in twenty-four hours, Sabrina would be free and after a small window of time, I would change her last name from Walker to Jackson.

All we needed to do was just hold tight.

But by the next day, Sabrina started acting strange. She kept callin' me every five minutes—always with a new scenario of what could go wrong. It seemed like nothing I said reassured her. The constant calls in turn made Crazy Larry nervous.

"That bitch better not roll on us," he kept warning.

It felt like I spent most of the day just tryna get everyone to chill the fuck out.

According to Sabrina, James Walker's Thursday poker nights usually ended around eleven o'clock. We estimated forty-five minutes for him to get home and then assumed it would take approximately ten minutes for him to go to his study for a nightcap and a cigar.

My nerves didn't start hittin' me until 10:30.

At 11:00 Crazy Larry had pulled out his shoe box and was hittin' his stash pretty hard.

Alonzo was true to his word and was straight up M.I.A.

But at 11:20, our plans went to hell in a handbasket.

Sabrina called cryin'. She wanted to call the whole thing off.

"What the fuck are you talking about?" I roared into the phone. "It's too late now."

"No, it's not! We gotta do something!"

"What you gotta do is calm the fuck down." Swear to God I was seein' red.

"What? What she sayin'?" Crazy Larry asked.

"Nothin', nothin'." I climbed out Crazy Larry's low-ass couch and tried to walk out of his earshot, but he was havin' none of that. "That bitch better not be thinkin' about backin' out of this shit."

"No, she's not," I lied, and then turned my back to him. "Sabrina, are you there?"

She was cryin'. "If you're not going to stop this, then I will!"

"What the fuck are you talking about?"

"Delvon, I still love him," she declared.

My fuckin' heart stopped. "You what?"

"I know you can't possibly understand, but I do," she sobbed. "I'm sorry."

"Sorry?! What the—!"

"I'm going to the house and stoppin' this madness."

"Sabrina, you can't—!"

Dial tone.

"Fuck!"

"What? What the fuck is goin' on?" Crazy Larry's eyes bugged.

"I gotta get out there and stop her!" I grabbed my jacket and raced to the door.

"I fuckin' knew it!" Crazy Larry roared.

I didn't have time to deal with him. I had to stop Sabrina before it was too late.

But I was too late. . . .

# Epilogue

*Two weeks after my arrest . . .*

"*B*ut you were too late," my state-appointed attorney concludes with palpable boredom.

I nod. It was my sixth time tellin' this story in the past two weeks and my eyes still water at the memory of seein' Sabrina jump out of her Jaguar and race toward the house. If I'd been just one minute faster, I would have been able to stop her. Instead, she had ignored my cries and raced into the house anyway. The fire department said that they had found her lifeless body crushed under stone and plaster. But miracle of all miracles, James Walker survived.

"You know the cops checked out your story with your friends . . ." My attorney glances down at his yellow notepad. "Alonzo Young and Larry Whitman."

"And?" I ask, knowin' I probably got a mark on my head for being a snitch.

"And they're claiming they know nothing about any of this. And quite frankly, you've given us nothing to prove that they have any ties to this case. You're the one claiming to have been having an affair with Sabrina Walker. You're the one with the restraining order to stay away from the Walkers. You were the one seen initiating a fight outside a crowded and popular restaurant."

"What about the car?" I ask.

"What car?"

"The car Sabrina bought through Crazy Larry's cousin?"

My attorney exhales a long breath. "There's no record of any car. And you said yourself the car didn't exist. Quite frankly, all the evidence points to you being a lover scorned—or worse, an obsessed stalker."

"C'mon. You can ask any of those niggas workin' at that landscapin' company and they'll tell you the real reason why I got fired."

"What you think we're all doing—playing with our dicks? We did ask them."

"And what did they say?"

"They say they've never seen you come within a mile of Mrs. Walker. Said that she hardly ever came to the estate."

"What? That's bullshit!" I'm heated now. "What was the point of everybody lyin'? I'd already admitted to murder."

"No. The bullshit is streamin' from you." The attorney withdraws a folder from his briefcase. "You said that your affair with Sabrina Walker started in late July and lasted for the rest of the summer."

"Yeah, so?"

"Well, the police have talked to a lot of Sabrina Walker's family and friends and every one of them states that she was in Italy this past summer. Seems she and her husband had hit a rough patch and she took a few months' vacation to clear her head. When she came back, she and husband tried to patch things up. One of the evenings while they were out to dinner, you attacked them outside of Sambuca."

"How many damn times do I have to tell you guys that Sabrina wasn't there that night? James Walker was there with some other chick—probably his mistress."

My attorney glances back down at his notes. "A woman who looked like Mrs. Walker?"

"From a distance—but it wasn't her."

"Uh-huh."

"I get it. You don't believe me, either."

Another long exhalation. "Sorry. But nothing you're saying is checking out. Including this wild idea that Mr. Walker was worth one hundred million dollars when it's well known that Mrs. Walker was the wealthy one out of the two."

"What?"

"Sabrina Walker came from an affluent family. Many suspected that James Walker married her for her money. Not the other way around. At best, he's a two-bit hustler with a gambling problem. According to Sabrina's best friend, Mercedes Wilder, one of the reasons for the trouble in the Walkers' marriage was that her husband spent money like it was goin' out of style."

As I stare at the man across the table from me, I'm sure there must be something wrong with my hearing.

"I have it right here." He opens the manila folder in front of him and my eyes snag on a photo inside. "Who's that?" I reach over and pick up the picture. "Hey, I know her."

"Not funny."

"That's the chick that was with James Walker at Sambuca."

"I know. Mrs. Walker."

I frown. "That's not Sabrina."

My lawyer starts looking at me as if I've just grown a second head. "Of course it is."

"No, it's not. Don't you think I know who I've been fuckin' for the past few months? That's not her."

My attorney tosses up his hands. "You know what? I think I need to get you evaluated by a doctor and see if we can get an insanity plea."

"There's nothing wrong with me. That's not Sabrina Walker! You got to believe me!"

"Guards!" the attorney shouts, looking alarmed. "Guards!"

"No, wait. We're not finished talking."

"I think we are." He quickly tries to shovel his folder and notepads back into his briefcase.

I catch sight of a few more pictures and make a grab for them. Wedding photos, college graduation photos, and party photos, all with that same mystery woman. "Where did you get these?"

"From my assistant. We got copies of everything the police have."

I hear keys rattle in the door. The prison guards are comin'. Then finally I see her. "There she is. That's my Sabrina."

My attorney looks down at the picture I'm pointing to. "That's not Mrs. Walker," he says, frowning. "That's Mer-

*cedes Wilder. Sabrina's best friend. I just talked to her yesterday."*

*His words punch me solidly in the gut. I stagger back into my chair. "What?"*

*"She was at Sabrina's funeral. She was there comforting Mr. Walker and Sabrina's parents."*

*The guards rush in and instruct me to stand. I'm in too much of a daze to do anything other than stare at Sabrina—no—Mercedes' picture. Suddenly this wild puzzle begins to snap in place inside my head. She was comforting Mr. Walker.*

*She and Mr. Walker.*

*"Tell me something. How much will Mr. Walker inherit from his wife's death?"*

*My attorney shrugs. "I assume everything. Plus, from what I hear, he had just taken out a huge insurance policy a coupla months before his wife died. He stands to be a very wealthy man."*

*"Well, I'll be damned." I kept starin' at Sabrina's—Mercedes's—picture and something told me that she, not James Walker, was behind this master plan. The bitch got one over on me.*

*She used me.*

*They used me. She never wanted me to kill James Walker. Their target was Sabrina this whole time. Sabrina was the one with the money. Sabrina was going to divorce her husband and leave him penniless. And Mercedes . . . had to have been the backstabbin' best friend. I search my memory and try to recall if I ever heard anyone else refer to Mercedes as Mrs. Walker. Everyone on the landscaping crew, in-*

*cluding Alonzo, just called her Mr. Walker's woman. His
woman.*

*Had Alonzo known this whole time? Had he played a
part in setting me up? If so—why? Just as soon as I ask myself the question, I know why. Cherry. Hadn't I stabbed him
in the back, too?*

"Have you talked to Alonzo and Crazy Larry?" *I ask.*

*My attorney sighs.*

"What?"

"We've been unable to find your two best friends. I did
manage to locate Alonzo's mother. Seems their family has
come into some money and . . ."

"He's ghost," *I finish for him, and shake my head.*

*These fools tricked me into killin' a woman I didn't know
and confessin'.*

*I start laughing—and then I can't stop. This shit is just
too funny.*

# Put 'Em in Their Place

ERICK S. GRAY

*"You can't hang around the fire
and expect not to get burned. . . ."*

*T*he sounds coming from the lavish master bedroom were similar to those of a small wounded animal, but they were human. The loud cries echoed through the well-furnished three-bedroom suite on the fifteenth floor in the Upper West Side of Manhattan. The room reeked of heavy sex, and the only noise came from David Lovett as Cha rode him wildly, her manicured nails digging into his chest, her knees pressed against the bed like she was trying to win the Kentucky Derby. Cha had David straddled tightly, her thighs pressing into his rib cage with each movement, his back mashed against wrinkled red satin silk sheets. He cupped Cha's breasts as she bounced up and down on him, grinding her thick hips against him, her womanly walls clamping tightly around David's hard-on as he cried out and whimpered.

"Nooooo . . . oooh . . . oooh . . . oooh, damn, you feel so good, Cha! Don't stop . . . huh, don't stop!" he exclaimed, his face twisting up like he just sucked on something sour and unsweet.

They both were a sweaty mess; perspiration trickled from David's forehead, Cha's chest was clammy, and his nuts felt like he just dipped them in water, making him wish that he'd opened up one of the bedroom windows before his sexual rendezvous with Cha. The temperature in his bedroom was reaching 110 plus, but David didn't want to stop Cha from making it feel like she was about to tear his dick from his nuts, she was fuckin' him so hard and fast. So he tolerated the heat, because he was in a zone and didn't want to interrupt their crazy encounter, not for one second.

"You like it, huh . . . you like it when I fuck you like this?" Cha exclaimed, feeling David's eight-inch erection rooted in her like cement.

"Oh yeah . . . huh, ugh . . . ugh, don't stop, baby, please don't stop, baby . . . I love it!"

Cha gave him a bizarre look when he cried out *baby*. She hated when any man called her that. She was far from anyone's baby or boo, or honey, or whatever. To her, when a man started speaking like that, it meant that he was getting too attached to her, and that was the last thing she wanted.

Cha's main goal was to get herself some dick, sweat it out with David for a few hours, and leave without any remorse or attachments. But lately, David had been really needy and clingy. He'd wanted to take Cha out to dinner and Broadway plays for the longest time, and after their last crazy episode, David had wanted to cuddle with Cha and have her spend the night. He'd wanted to make her breakfast in the morning. Cha had quickly refused, gotten dressed, and rushed out of David's crib like it was on fire. She left David puzzled.

But the only reason she came back to him again was because the sex was good. David had stamina and he was good to look at. He stood about six two, with a stocky build to him, hairy, strapping chest, gleaming bald head, thick goatee, and wearing skin around himself like night itself. He was the type of man who looked good in anything he put on, from a pinstripe business suit to a pair of sweats, T-shirt, and track shoes. David was a very successful investment broker with an office in the downtown area of the city.

But to Cha, one of his flaws that she peeved about was that he was too gushy and over the top when it came to romance. He would always want to wine and dine Cha when she would come over to his place to see him. But all Cha wanted was a wham, bam, and thank you, ma'am . . . nothing else in between.

David wanted to give her flowers and candies, but Cha hated flowers. David wanted to talk about marriage, kids, and a family, and Cha despised the proposal and felt that now was not the time. She was only twenty-five and felt that there would be enough time in her life for that. All Cha wanted was to play and play hard.

But what definitely irritated Cha a lot was when David would be constantly trying to introduce her to his mother, who was in her early fifties. Cha would be damned if she met any man's mother anytime soon. There was no place in her schedule that said *Mother's Day*. She didn't play that card. But David was deeply in love with her, and the painful thing about their situation was that she wasn't anywhere in love with him. He was just a good fuck and that was that.

David gripped Cha's sweaty and naked hips as he gyrated his shit into her and cried out, "Cha, baby . . . I'm gonna come. Shit, don't stop . . . don't stop, baby! Oh, shit, I love you, baby!"

Cha cringed again, hearing David say the unthinkable, but she continued fucking him and allowed him to get his nut. David's body went rigid under her as she felt him bursting greatly into her as he gripped the sheets with force and let out a loud, piercing groan that she was sure his neighbors heard.

Slowly she stopped rocking her hips back and forth against him, like a speeding training coming to a halt on the tracks. She allowed David to savor the moment he was having with her. She glanced down at him and saw the look of content. She sighed and climbed off him. She was ready to get dressed, collect her things, and leave. She was so turned off by hearing him say, "I love you, baby."

She hoped he didn't expect for her to share the same comment, because it wasn't happening. David slowly rose up and looked over at Cha picking up her scattered clothing across the parquet floor.

"You ready to leave already?" he asked.

"Yeah, I gotta go," she replied dryly.

David looked upset. He wanted her to stay longer. He rested his sweaty back against the headboard and took a deep breath.

"Damn, Cha . . . you can sure make a nigga feel like shit. I swear your mother gave birth to the wrong sex, 'cuz you look like a woman, but damn, you sure think like a nigga," he complained.

"Yeah . . . well, you knew how I got down when we first started this affair seven months ago. There ain't no changing it. Just 'cuz we got half a year in don't mean I'm a different bitch," Cha proclaimed.

Cha began pulling up her panties as David watched with much admiration for her body. She was curvy and thick in the right places from head to toe, with no tattoos. Cha had a J.Lo ass and Beyoncé hips, with a smooth carmel complexion that was radiant like the sunrise itself. She also had rich, sensuous black hair that was shoulder length, with full lustful lips and piercing green eyes that would put any man in a sudden trance from her beauty.

Cha had style to her and wore nothing but the best, from Décor and Gucci to Donna Karan and more. The city was Cha's playground, and men from the powerful and wealthiest to the thuggish and blue collar were all in awe and mesmerized by her style and grace, even more turned on by how raw and street she could become.

Cha was straight out of Newark, New Jersey—Brick City. She came up in the projects and done seen a lot in her twenty-five years of life—from drugs and thugs to pimping and killing. But she was determined to get hers and let no one put her under. She had big dreams and wanted to be a success by the time she was thirty, and she was well on her way.

Cha was almost fully dressed when David decided to get

out of bed and approach her. Cha stood by the large bay windows, which had an astonishing view of the West Side, from the Henry Hudson Parkway, out to the Hudson River and the shores of New Jersey across the river.

Cha felt David's arms coming around her suddenly. She quickly turned around and pulled away from him. David looked clearly upset.

"Why do you keep treating me like this, Cha?" he asked.

"You do it to yourself, David. I told you, it doesn't go any further than this with us. I'm not looking for a husband."

"Damn, you could be a cold bitch sometimes," he said.

Cha ignored his comment and collected the rest of her things. She was very well satisfied with what she came for— some dick, a nut—and exhaled. But David was always looking for something extra with every episode. It never failed.

David stood in the middle of his bedroom, butt-ass naked, dick swinging with the condom still attached, staring in awe at Cha leaving him.

"So, when you gonna call me again?" he asked.

"When I feel the need to," she replied matter-of-factly.

What David felt for Cha burned so intensely in him that he was ready to jump out his fifteenth-floor window for her love and break every last bone in his body, because she was already breaking his heart.

Cha easily left his apartment without any remorse. The door shut behind her and she walked toward the elevator. It was the first day of summer and Cha was looking fine in a pair of skintight Seven jeans that highlighted her butt and hips, a black Columbian tee that accentuated her full-figure tits, and a pair of Dior light blue open-toe shoes, carrying her hand-stitched Chanel purse. Cha looked good and she felt good.

When the elevator door opened up, before she stepped in, she turned and saw David watching her by his apartment door. She gave him a warm smile, blew him a light kiss, thanking him for the evening, and stepped into the elevator.

"Niggas is pitiful," she said to herself with a sly smile.

Cha crossed Riverside Drive, heading toward her powder blue drop-top Benz with a chip on her shoulder. She knew her pussy was good, and she had many niggas caught up, but her attitude was that you get what you want and need from a man, and leave him before he does the inevitable—beat you, cheat on you, fuck you, and then leave you for the next younger and flyer bitch. Cha thought, why give them the power or benefit of the doubt? She was going to do her. She wouldn't get caught up in a man again.

Cha got in her car, and the first thing she did when she started it up was drop the top so she could show off, and then she put in one of her favorite tracks—"Take Me As I Am," from Mary J. Blige's *The Breakthrough* album. Cha was a huge Mary J. fan and had been to a few of her concerts, and she even got a CD signed by her. Cha felt that she and Mary were the same—beautiful, powerful, and creative women that the world misunderstood.

Cha moved her convertible Benz north up the Henry

Hudson Parkway. The traffic was good and she pushed her Benz to do seventy miles per hour, loving how the wind flowed through her hair with the sunset in her face.

Cha arrived at her sizable, trendy two-bedroom apartment in Inwood, on 218th Street near the George Washington Bridge. The neighborhood was mixed, polite, and quiet. Almost every tenant owned a dog. Cha wasn't too fond of animals. The apartment was expensive, but Cha had no worries, because everything was paid for through her trust fund set up by her father. Cha had enough money to last her until she became a grandmother—which she knew wasn't happening anytime soon.

Cha parked her Benz in her assigned spot and proceeded toward the lobby. As she walked, she checked her Black-Berry and noticed that she had five missed calls and four voice messages. She put the phone to her ear, pushed for her floor, and began listening to her messages.

The first one was from T.J., who was from Harlem.

"Yo, Cha, was good, ma . . . where you at? I'm tryna see if we can link up tonight, you know a nigga tryna see ya and shit . . . get at that, 'cuz I miss it, no lie. But yo, I'm gonna be deejayin' at the club tonight and I want you to come through. I'm gonna put you on the list, a'ight, ma . . . peace out."

She deleted his message. She met T.J. at the club he deejayed at on weekends two weeks ago and loved his swag, so she fucked him that same night in his truck while T.J.'s homeboy Rick took over the party. Cha figured, why waste time with the meet and greet, dating and bullshit. She wanted to know what T.J. was working with right away, before she even wasted her time going any further. But T.J. wasn't working with much. T.J. got his immediate thrills and Cha got a quick yawn and her pussy eaten out. She gave Tony her number because he worked at a poppin' club, and knowing T.J., she was always in for free.

She gave him some a second time and he was even more whack than the first. So she decided to string T.J. along and accept his calls here and there, maybe talk dirty to him, but whenever T.J. wanted to see her, there always was an excuse. Cha laughed, because it'd been two weeks and T.J. still didn't get it yet.

The next message was from Boogie. He was from Harlem also. But Boogie was a young nigga that Cha was fuckin. He was nineteen, but a cutie in Cha's eyes. Boogie was packing in the jeans and his swag was like Jim Jones, running the block and dodging the cops. Everything about Boogie was poppin', but his only downfall was, he was a young nigga and sometimes an immature nigga and he constantly lived his life on the edge. Cha knew that when dealing with Boogie, she needed to pack her .38 and keep it close. Boogie was always getting locked up or shot at. There was one incident when Cha was out with him—she picked him up from his block, and they drove off to do their thang. Two hours later when she was dropping Boogie off at his block, niggas done put two shots in her back window because they done seen Boogie in her ride. Boogie told her that he would handle it and paid for her window. For Cha, Boogie was that risky pleasure. He always kept Cha on her toes and he was fun to be with, and it turned her on—sometimes.

But Boogie's messages were always short and simple. "Cha, you know who this be, just get at me."

She loved him for that.

Cha walked into her crib, getting ready to listen to the third message on her phone. It was from Donny. She met Donny a month ago at a lounge in Brooklyn. She was partying and drinking with her best friend, Essence. It was Essence's twenty-sixth birthday and they wanted to be in Brooklyn, where Essence was born and raised. Cha met Donny on the dance floor and thought he was cute. But the problem with Donny was, he definitely looked the part, with his six-foot-three height and sturdy build, and he dressed the part in his urban attire—Timberlands, white Ts, fitted cap, and jeans, but Donny was far from the part. In fact, he was a meek sheep in wolves' clothing. The man was soft like Johnson & Johnson. He did not have one ounce of hood or thug in him. Cha wanted to break him off that night, but all Donny did was buy drinks, show pictures of his two daughters, and want to talk about things and issues that were truly irrelevant to Cha. Donny grew up on Long Island and went to prep school, and he only saw the hood when passing it in his Benz. Donny didn't have any swag to him, and the only reason why he got her number was because Essence egged her on, promoting him like he was campaigning for something.

"Cha, he's nice and he's cute—why don't you wanna see him? . . . You need to change up sometimes, girl, and he's buying us free drinks. Shit, if I wasn't married, I would definitely see that," Essence had said to her.

So reluctantly, because of Essence, she had given Donny her number, thinking, hey, maybe something good might come out of it. He might be packing lovely in his jeans. Shit, Cha had wanted to talk nasty and feel him up at the bar, but Donny shied away from any dirty topics, and when Cha had rubbed her hand against his crotch subtly to see what he was working with, somehow Donny slid his chair back from her slyly.

Their first night talking on the phone, Cha feel asleep with the phone to her ear, because the nigga was so boring. He had no edge to him.

Donny left his message saying, "Hey, Cha, it's me, Donny. We haven't talked in a week. I was just calling to see if everything was okay with you. We definitely need to go out. I know this nice Italian restaurant in the city and I definitely want to take you there one evening. I know that you're a busy girl, but feel free to give a brother a call sometime, okay? I'll look out for your ring so we can talk. Bye, Cha, hope you didn't forget about a brother. Bye."

"Boring . . . delete," Cha said to herself.

She shook her head and wanted to curse Essence. Donny was a definite turnoff and she knew the nigga wasn't getting any pussy coming his way anytime soon.

The fourth message made Cha shake her head in shame. She plopped down on her couch and wanted to put her face in the pillow cushion and scream.

"Why are niggas so pussy-whipped?" she quipped.

The fourth message came from David right after she had left his place.

"Hey, Cha, what's up. Look, I didn't like the way you left my apartment earlier. I mean, why a nigga can't get any more time with you? I wasn't trying to push up hard on you and scare you off like that, but I love the way you feel in my arms, baby. I'm just saying, I know we agreed to just be friends with benefits, but truth, I ain't feeling that shit anymore, Cha. I'm ready to cut every bitch off just to get with you, yo. And you know I'm a catch, baby. I can take care of us. . . . You ain't never got to want for anything, you hear me. And yeah, I know you be doin' your thang too . . . but just think about us for a moment, Cha. I ain't tripping out or anything, I just wanted to let my feelings be known towards you. Holla back at me when you get the chance."

Cha sighed heavily and said, "Nigga, you is trippin'. . . . I see a bitch gonna have to start rationing out her pussy."

She quickly deleted David's message and decided that she needed to sit in her tub for a long moment with a bubble bath and relax. Cha began shedding her clothing as she approached the bathroom and filled up her oval-shaped porcelain tub with soothing warm water and the bubbles to match. Then Cha lit some sensual candles around the bathroom and submerged herself into the tub with her Mary J. CD playing in the background.

She let out a relaxing sigh, which was followed by, "Niggas be crazy, keep treatin' these niggas like a passing breeze, you feel it once then move the fuck on."

Cha chuckled and closed her eyes while soothing in the tub. She had to work tonight. She wanted to relax before she went down to the Pink Pussy to make her some money.

The Pink Pussy was a gold mine for Cha. On a good night, she was able to make up to twenty-five hundred, and maybe fuck a nigga or two. And on a bad night, the least she would leave with from the Pink Pussy would be fifteen hundred.

Cha was the main attraction at the place. She danced buck naked in some stilettos, her figure having more curves than a winding hilltop road, and she had an ass more booty-licious than Jennifer Lopez. When Cha got up on that stage, she was raw and temptation at its finest. She would entice the men like she was an appetizer to their strong hunger.

Cha went all out, giving her audience one hell of a show with nine-inch dildos being pushed into her pussy, or pulling long, black butt beads out her ass, or pouring beer into her pussy and squirting it back out into the thirsty and open mouths of men who wanted to savor every drop of her. Sometimes she would get a man onstage and have him eat her pussy in front of the crowd, or give him the most tanta-lizing lap dance that he would never forget. And if she liked him, then he got lucky with some pussy.

Cha had the Pink Pussy by the balls; she felt that she owned that place. Her clientele of men and sometimes women ranged from the Wall Street players, big-shot business exec-utive or CEOs, judges, athletes, rappers, and drug dealers, straight down to the blue-collar workers such as police offi-cers, city workers, teachers, and students spending their tu-ition money for some ass or a show. After dancing at the Pink Pussy for three years, Cha was already a paid bitch and very well-to-do.

Cha continued to soak in the tub, enjoying the music

from Mary J. She closed her eyes and took a twenty-minute nap. She had plenty of time before she went to work. It was early evening and Cha wasn't due to be at work 'til midnight—that's when the Pink Pussy became crowded and popping.

Cha sped up to an open parking spot on Canal Street in the Bronx. By the look of things, the Pink Pussy was live. The block was flooded with cars, and a few men lingered around the club. Cha grabbed her small bag from the backseat. She sauntered toward the club with a fierce attitude, activating her alarm to her Benz.

The Pink Pussy was one of the liveliest clubs in the Bronx. There were some nights where anything went—fucking, sucking behind locked doors, where the girls shook their most tangible assets in their birthday suits. And Cha would be in the mix of the perversion with no regrets.

"Hey, Danny," Cha greeted him. "What's it lookin' like inside?"

"It's lookin' nice, Cha," he replied with a smile.

"That's what I need to hear," Cha replied, slipping Danny a fifty-dollar bill.

Danny nodded, letting Cha go inside without a search for any weapons. Cha concealed a .22 handgun and she had made an arrangement with Danny, the six foot four, stout bouncer who guarded the front door.

Danny gave her a wink and let her pass. Cha strutted inside to the blaring sound of Jamie Foxx's "Blame It." She loved the song and knew that the deejay needed to play it again once she was on the stage.

"What's good, Cha," Candy greeted joyously with a hug.

Cha smiled and replied with, "You know, Candy, tryin' to bank these niggas before the night is up."

"I hear that. It's money in here," Candy replied with a grin.

Cha looked up onstage and saw that Bubbles was dancing. She was buck naked in some fire red six-inch stilettos, swinging around the pole. Bubbles and Cha locked eyes for a moment, showing some contempt between the two. Cha sucked her teeth and mouthed, "Fuck that bitch!"

Bubbles and Cha had had beef for months now, ever since Cha fucked both her younger brother and her ex-fiancé. Bubbles was furious and when she confronted Cha in the locker room, they fought and Cha whooped her ass, pulling out Bubbles's weave and leaving some bruises.

But Cha wasn't worried about Bubbles anymore; she was about money and dick. Bubbles still had a grudge against Cha, because her ex-fiancé had proclaimed to her, "Yo, that bitch Cha got some good pussy."

Cha rolled her eyes and walked toward the changing room, strutting hard in a short miniskirt, open-toe heels, and a tight shirt that accentuated her breasts.

The club was filled with men. They were horny, antsy, and so eager to spend money and fill up on a bitch. Numerous men noticed Cha walking in and all eyes were focused on her for a moment instead of Bubbles, sparking Bubbles to catch an attitude and glare at Cha.

"Hating-ass bitch!" Cha uttered.

Cha walked into the twelve-by-twelve changing room that was cluttered with chatter and half-naked strippers. When Cha walked in, suddenly all eyes were on her. Half the bitches in the room hated on Cha because of her beauty and not-caring attitude, and the other half hated Cha because she'd fucked their men or someone close to them at some point in time.

Cha didn't care what bitches thought of her. She didn't come to the Pink Pussy to make friends. She came to the place to make money and get her freak on. And she did it well.

Cha rolled her eyes and sucked her teeth and knew that she had the .22 close by in case any one of them bitches decided to act up. But she wasn't worried; she was from the hood and had won many fights in her past—being not just a pretty face, but a brawler when needed. The only girls Cha was really cool with in the club were Candy and Apple. They were sisters from New Jersey and they both were always themselves around Cha. Candy was just as pretty as Cha and felt that there was no need to hate on the next bitch for any reason, because they all were getting money.

Cha ignored the chatter around her like she was encased behind a thick partition and started to change. She pulled out her first outfit for the night—a black microfiber and faux crocodile halter top and matching skirt with an asymmetrical back hem and a matching thong with a laced-up armband. Cha slid her manicured feet into a pair of sexy clear slides with coordinating glitter straps and platform filler. The shoes made her about four inches taller. She then oiled herself down slowly from head to toe and let her sensuous hair fall down to her shoulders, her pierced belly button showing.

In forty minutes' time, she was looking like a true diva ready to hit the stage and get money.

Cha secured her belongings in her locker and stepped out into the vivacious, dimmed club with a go-getter, Hollywood diva attitude. She knew men would give their right arm to see her perform, and their left nut to spend one fraction of a second with her.

"Ah shit, y'all . . . Cha is in the muthafuckin' building. Y'all niggas ready to get it poppin' up in here?" the deejay announced over the mic.

Cha quickly scanned the room, standing in her diva posture, hands on her hips, legs spread like she was posing for *Smooth* magazine. The deejay knew what song to put on for Cha to hit that stage and tear it up. The loud notes of Rick Ross's "Magnificent" switched to 112's seductive hit "Anywhere."

Apple collected her things and cleared the stage for Cha to perform.

"Go get 'em, girl," Apple said with a smile.

Cha returned the smile and strutted up the steps to the spotlight. The stage was sizable, with two long poles that stretched from the ceiling to the stage. Mirrors lined the walls of the club, so Cha could see herself in action from a short distance. Cha hit center stage, dropped her small bag to the floor, grabbed hold of a pole, and slowly twirled herself around it like a schoolgirl playing in the park, hearing her song blaring in her ear.

*We can make love in the bedroom floating on top of my waterbed . . .*

Cha continued to twirl herself around and then quickly pulled herself up the pole, having great upper body strength. While suspended over the stage, being close to the ceiling, Cha spread her legs widely, dancing seductively in rhythm with her song while balanced above her spectators. She then slowly brought herself down in slow-mo style. She was like a gymnast—flexible everywhere and able to do tricks that had niggas in awe. Cha then coiled herself around the pole like a snake, her skirt riding up her thighs, exposing her skimpy thong—both which were soon to come off.

*I can love you in the shower, both of our bodies dripping wet. On the patio we can make a night you won't forget. On the kitchen floor, as I softly pull your hair, we can do it anywhere . . .*

Slowly but surely, she peeled away her scanty attire and became ass naked. Cha's moves were so seductive, enticing, and on point. Her nude body was glistering in baby oil. It seemed like she was alone onstage, the way she made love to herself—the way she hugged the stage and licked her lips and touched her tits, the way she gyrated and ground her pussy and hips against the hard stage. Men loved the way she clutched the pole, like it was a long piece of hard dick, sliding herself up and down on it like a gentle massage. Niggas were hypnotized.

Every curve, crack, tits, and ass openly exposed to those who could not turn away. Cha's pussy was shaved and smooth like ice. Her ass cheeks jiggled like Jell-O, and men began tossing money at her, eager to see so much more and yearning just to lick the sweat from her body.

"Yo, I'm lovin' this bitch," a spectator shouted out with zeal.

Cha reached over to her bag of goodies and pulled out a long, black, nine-inch dildo for her to have fun with while everyone watched. She looked over and noticed Ely, the manager of the club and the boss's son, staring at her intently. She smirked and knew she had that nigga so hard.

Cha spread her legs for all to see and slowly pushed her large toy inside of her, grunting and crying out, "Oooh. Mmmm. Ummm . . . ummm."

With her free hand, she cupped her tits and licked her lips.

"Damn, ma, can I get in that too?" someone exclaimed.

A few laughed at the comment.

Cha went on to continue fucking herself rapidly. Her legs quivered with her eyes shut and her breathing deep. She arched her back and pushed the dildo farther inside of her. When she opened her eyes, she noticed David standing near the stage with a jealous look about him.

*Why the fuck is he here tonight?* she asked herself.

She just got finished fucking him a few hours earlier and now he wanted to be at her job, looking like he was about to regulate on her. But Cha had a surprise for him. She wanted to fuck with him and show David how wild and out of control she could really get. Cha scanned the crowd of men and looked for the perfect one to pull onstage with her. She quickly spotted a tall cutie clutching a Corona beer and sporting long braids. She reached out to him and he quickly climbed up on the stage with a broad smile.

Cha immediately began enticing him, licking and sucking on his neck and then fondling his package. The stranger was in awe. He clutched Cha's booty and had this blissful look about him.

Cha whispered in his ear, "You like me, boo?"

"Hells, yeah," he replied.

"Then show me how much you like me."

She pulled the man down to the floor with her. He quickly found himself in an enticing sexual position. Cha then pushed his head near her throbbing pussy, demanding him to eat her out. She got no resistance. He curled his tongue deep into her and began sucking and licking on her wet, sweet lips.

The crowd began chanting and roaring, excited about the act taking place. Cha panted and moaned, running her hands through his braids and then clutching them tightly as she wrapped her legs around his neck, strongly securing his head between her moist thighs. She wanted to take it further and upset David even more. She looked for another stranger to get onstage with her. With her pussy getting eaten out, she looked around and then gestured for a younger man in a throwback Giants jersey and fitted cap to get onboard. He did without a second thought.

The second stranger kneeled beside Cha with a lustful grin. Cha picked up the beer next to her and began pouring it all over herself—having it run down her nipples and down to her belly button, and then she poured more between her legs and near her pussy, making her look like a human waterfall. She then pulled the second man closer to her and had him lick the beer off her tits and from her pierced navel.

The crowd went berserk. Security stood close by, watching carefully in case something happened, but the smiles they had on their faces proved that Cha had everyone under control. The two volunteers were going in on Cha. The one eating her out looked like he was truly enjoying his job, and the second man ran his tongue up and down Cha's nude body, licking her clean from any beer residue.

As Cha massaged the man's head, she turned to look to see if David was still around. He was nowhere in sight. She guessed he got the hint. The show went on for another ten minutes, where Cha made one of the guys become shirtless, exposing his small gut and hairy chest. She had him lie on his back and straddled his face, pushing her wet pussy into his face.

By the end of her freaky episode, almost six hundred dollars was scattered all around the stage for Cha to collect. Both men walked off the stage smiling like teenage boys.

Cha collected her things and money and strutted off the stage a proud bitch. The other strippers in the club could only shake their heads in wonder or hate hard on her.

Before she could make it back to the changing room, a young man was pulling at her arm and asking, "Yo, can I get a private dance wit' ya?"

"Hold on," she replied.

Cha walked into the changing room with a stack of money in one hand and her outfit in the next. She dumped her clothes to the side, took a seat on the bench, and began counting her money naked while the other strippers just watched with envy. She smirked and loved every minute of it.

"You a wild bitch," Cha heard someone say.

She turned around and saw Ely standing behind her in a pair of blue jeans and a T-shirt. Ely was tall and handsome, having swagger like Jay-Z. He and Cha had an ongoing thing for months, and as always Ely wanted more. Ely was the manager of the Pink Pussy and ran through almost every bitch in the place. He had taken over after his father, Page, retired. Ely'd been running the Pink Pussy for more than a year now, and was good at what he did. But he was a slut and sometimes let pussy get in the way of business. When he first met Cha, he had a thing for her. They fucked a week after meeting, and Cha put it on him something serious—sucking his dick 'til his forehead caved in and had Ely nut in her mouth, swallowing his babies. Ely never had a freak like Cha and had pussy that good. He was a playa and always had the ladies chasing after him, so it was a shock that he was chasing after Cha.

"You know how I rock, Ely . . . don't be actin' like ya brand new to what I do," Cha replied.

"I'm sayin', you gotta have two niggas up on you like that . . . pouring beer down your shit. What the fuck was all that about?" Ely questioned.

Cha sucked her teeth and rolled her eyes. She put her money away someplace safe and was looking for the next outfit to put on. She wanted to ignore Ely. Ely had women sweating him left and right, but yet he always took time out of his busy schedule to question Cha about her freaky antics or wanting to fuck. Ely never questioned the other strippers about what they did onstage, but Cha knew that they couldn't compete with her anyway.

"Cha, let me talk to you private in my office," Ely suggested.

"Ely, I got a busy night."

Cha knew he wanted some pussy. Her freak show had turned Ely on more than he was willing to admit. She began changing into a different outfit, with Ely watching her every move. The other ladies in the background tried to pretend like they weren't all in Ely and Cha's conversation. They listened closely, pretending to be distracted by other things in the room.

"Nigga, you gonna just stand there and watch me get dressed?" Cha barked slightly.

"I just wanna talk to you for a moment," he said.

"Well, later. I got some nigga waitin' for a lap dance," she said.

"I see, well, I'll get at you later on."

Ely walked out of the room, leaving Cha to shake her head. Ely was becoming like David and she was becoming turned off. The dick was good, she had to admit, but his father was better. Ely's father, Page, was longer, more experienced, and more nasty with his bedroom actions. Cha had to admit to herself, if she had to settle down with a man, Page would have been the one.

The way Page would eat out her pussy and fuck her made Cha cringe with just the thought. But Page was a married man, with six kids, and grandkids, and reaching into his sixties. Throughout the years, they both had an understanding; it was just sex and nothing else. Page was always nonchalant and treated Cha's pussy like a bank robbery—you go in fast, get what you need, and be out with no turning back. Their relationship was so discreet and on the low that Ely never had a clue.

The night continued and a few strippers got onstage and tried to outdo Cha's last performance, but the majority couldn't even come close. Bubbles even took a bottle of wine and poured it on herself, emulating Cha's performance somewhat. But the men weren't that much rowdier or excited about it. Bubbles got money, but didn't collect half of what Cha made.

Cha made her way through the dense and dimmed room, stark naked except for her stilettos, and being the most chased-after bitch in the spot for a lap dance or reserved dance somewhere more private. Her hands were full with money. She was very frisky and flirtatious with the men and didn't hesitate to feel on a nigga's package to see what he was working with.

By two in the morning, Cha had earned more than twelve hundred dollars and the other strippers in the spot hated hard on her. When Cha hit the stage, niggas quickly crowded around and were ready to throw money at her.

As Cha twirled her naked self around the pole for the umpteenth time with T-Pain blaring in her ear, she saw Ely watching her heavily. She just smirked and kept on with her show. She sprawled out on her back and began playing with her pussy. She moaned loudly and went to work on her shit, having her index and middle finger thrust in and out of her wet pussy rapidly, causing her audience to drool and yearning to touch.

Her third show wasn't as intense as the first, but it was still eye catching. She continued on and was all over the stage like wet on water. When Cha stood upright on her knees, pussy throbbing, her breasts wet with perspiration and a pile of money between her legs, she caught eye of a familiar face staring at her from the crowd. She locked eyes with the man. He was very handsome with a distinguished look about him. He was tall, with salt-and-pepper hair, clad in a gray pinstripe three-piece suit and clutching about two stacks of cash in his bejeweled hands. His beady, dark-colored eyes met with Cha's light green eyes. His goatee was thick with strands of gray in it, and his skin was dark like a moonless night. The stranger didn't get rowdy and scream out obscenities like many others around him. He just stared at Cha with this calm and collected look about him.

Cha thought that he had aged very well and had to be in his early fifties by now. It'd been almost twenty years since she last saw him and the contempt she had for him in her heart was fresh like fruit being grown from a tree. But seeing him again didn't distract Cha. She moved and ground her body to the beat in a seductive rhythm, having niggas in a state like *Whoa*.

The man moved closer to Cha, his eyes fixated on every part of her. Next to him stood a young, dark male who looked to be in his early twenties. He wasn't dressed as snazzy as his friend, but he still looked nice in a pair of MEK jeans, a fitted V-neck white T that highlighted his strapping figure, and a blue Yankees cap fitted over long braids.

Cha kept her composure and hatred of Ya-Ya, the man in the suit, concealed behind a lustful smile. Cha never thought that she would see him again, but he was there in the flesh. Cha approached him slowly and Ya-Ya showed a look about him that said he didn't recognize her at all. But the last time he had seen her, Cha was only ten years old.

Ya-Ya removed a few bills from his stack and tossed them into the air, making it rain on Cha. The money came pouring down on her like a shower. Everyone watched on as Ya-Ya continued to toss more money her way.

The area around Cha was soon covered with bills. Ya-Ya leaned in close and began caressing Cha with his touch. He fondled her breasts and slid his hand between her thighs and felt how wet she was.

"I want a private dance with you," Ya-Ya said in an exact tone.

"Cool, give me like ten minutes," Cha replied.

"I'll be in the back by the bar. Don't keep me waiting too long, beautiful," Ya-Ya said.

Cha showed off a counterfeit smile and went on with her show. Ya-Ya retreated from the stage, while Cha rolled around in her earnings like a pig playing in mud. Ten minutes later, she collected all her earnings and her things and strutted off the stage still naked, her stilettos click-clacking against the hard floor.

The music was still blaring. She approached Ya-Ya. He stood by the bar with his right hand, Zulu, standing next to him. A large bottle of Moët was near his reach, and Ya-Ya held a half-empty glass in his hand. He eyed Cha with a sinful smile.

"Beautiful, come have a drink with me," Ya-Ya said, patting the empty barstool next to him.

Still in her birthday suit, Cha took a seat near him by the bar. She glanced at Zulu, and his strong, powerful presence held her gaze for a moment. She loved what she saw. Zulu stood about six two and had a build to him like a true African warrior. His well-defined arms were bulging through his shirt, and his skin was smooth and enticing like chocolate.

"Zulu, give us a minute," Ya-Ya ordered.

Zulu nodded and walked away without a word, like the loyal apprentice he was.

"So, beautiful, what is your name?" Ya-Ya asked.

"Cha," she replied with a flirtatious smile.

"Well, Cha, they call me Ya-Ya," he informed her.

But Cha already knew his name and knew his reputation. It was a name and face that were forever entrenched in her memory.

"Unique, and why they call you Ya-Ya?" she asked.

"You fuck with me long enough and you'll find out. But let me pour you a drink," he suggested.

Cha nodded.

Ya-Ya poured her a glass and his eyes stayed glued to her thick and curvaceous figure. He leaned in close to her and rested his hand against her thigh. The more Cha looked at him, the angrier she became. But she kept her composure and pretended that it was their very first meeting.

Cha downed the Moët and Ya-Ya poured her another glass. Ya-Ya slid his hand farther up her thigh and expressed a naughty smile.

"So, can I get this private dance with you?" he asked.

"It's fifty for the first fifteen minutes."

Ya-Ya pulled out two hundred-dollar bills and placed them on the counter.

"Then I want an hour with you," he proclaimed.

Cha downed her second drink, and then stood up from the barstool. She collected the money, grabbed Ya-Ya by his hand, and led him toward the VIP section of the club. She came across Zulu in passing. They locked eyes for a moment and Cha showed him a smile of interest. But Zulu held a deadpan gaze and nodded at his boss in passing.

Ely watched Cha's action from across the room, and knowing Cha's demeanor, she was going to do more than just dance with Ya-Ya. At the entrance to the VIP rooms,

Cha gave the bouncer on guard the two hundred and they were let through.

Cha tossed her items to the side once entering the VIP room. The place was shadowy and cordoned off from the club. The room was a comfortable size, decorated with rich burgundy-cushioned seating, dark curtains covering the entrance, and thick carpeting. Ya-Ya quickly removed his suit jacket and vest and tossed them over the armrest of the couch. He took a seat and stared up at Cha with a look of impatience and zeal.

Cha lingered over him for a moment, dancing provocatively to an R. Kelly track. She gyrated and shook her hips, nearing her shaved pussy to his face, and swung her breasts to his drooling lips and molested Ya-Ya where he sat. Ya-Ya reached out for her, yearning to touch her, but Cha playfully pushed his hands away, showing him that she was in control of the session. She toyed with him for a minute, rubbing and touching on his hard-on and then placing her nipples into his mouth. She allowed Ya-Ya to suck on her nipples for a short moment and then pulled her dampened nipples from his suctioned lips. She smiled and laughed.

Cha slowly straddled Ya-Ya, feeling his hard-on pushing through his pants. She ground her pussy against his lap and massaged his chest. She wanted him so aroused that it would hurt. She felt his dick poking her between the thighs. She felt his breath warm against her. She felt his touch tingling against her skin. Her hatred was replaced with being horny and wanting revenge. And Cha knew that sex would be the best way for her to get close.

She neared her glossy lips to his ear, her hand wrapped around his bulge, and she whispered, "For the right price, anything can go."

"And what's the right price?" Ya-Ya asked.

"Five hundred."

"That's a little steep for some pussy."

"I'll be worth it, believe me," Cha whispered, massaging his bulge with such an enticing touch that Ya-Ya squirmed.

Ya-Ya couldn't resist her offer. He reached for his suit jacket and pulled out a wad of bills. Cha took the wad from his hand and removed five hundred-dollar bills from the stack and placed the rest back into his jacket.

"Now do what the fuck you do, and do it right," Ya-Ya said to her.

Cha stood up and then lowered herself to her knees in front of him. She began unzipping his pants and pulled out his snake of a penis. She was impressed. It curved in her grip like a thick German smoked sausage. She put her lips to it and had her tongue coiled at the tip. She licked it nice and slow—sucking here and there, kissing it soothingly. Her suction on the dick started off slow and sweet. She ran her tongue from the base to the tip and then took all of him into her mouth—deep throating at her best.

Ya-Ya let loose a blissful moan, slumping farther into his seat.

"Oh shit . . . damn that feels so good . . ." he hummed.

Cha sucked his dick like a porn star, with her lips chewing on his nuts, sliding against hard, bulging, warm flesh, and feeling the veins in his dick against her tongue and mouth.

He was big. She sucked his dick rapidly, jerking him off simultaneously. Ya-Ya couldn't keep still. He pulled at Cha's hair. He cupped her tits. He panted out like a winded athlete.

"I wanna fuck you," he uttered.

Cha continued to suck him, feeling the tip of his big dick hit her in the back of the mouth. She loved how hard he was in her mouth. When she shoved all ten inches down her throat, it felt like she was about to choke on it.

Ya-Ya couldn't tolerate the blow job Cha was blessing him with and pulled her head away from his dick.

"You want me to come in your mouth?" he questioned.

"If it's what you want," Cha whipped back.

Ya-Ya smiled. "I like you."

Cha stood up and straddled Ya-Ya's monstrous dick and exhaled as his big dick crushed into her walls. She clutched Ya-Ya and started riding him,

"Shit, your pussy feels so good," Ya-Ya exclaimed.

Cha clutched him tightly, feeling her pussy being opened up like a giant hole in a wall. Ya-Ya thrust into her, causing Cha to run her manicured nails down the back of his neck. Her breathing became intense and her body quivered. Ya-Ya became naked from the waist down and turned Cha into the doggy-style position and slapped her ass red from the back. He was fucking Cha like a pro, having forty years of experience under his belt, and even though Cha had a lot of animosity toward him, the dick had never been better. It slid in and out of her like a large train running on open tracks.

"I'm comin'," Cha exclaimed, clutching the couch tightly, feeling her ass cheeks being spread wide.

Ya-Ya gripped her by her naked hips and fucked her like he was in his early twenties.

"Damn, I like you," Ya-Ya cried out. "Damn, you a fly, beautiful, nasty bitch. Oh shit . . . oh shit."

Cha chuckled.

Ya-Ya quickly pulled out and busted off on her back. He looked spent a little. He flopped down on the couch and pulled up his pants, trying to collect himself from the exhilarating episode he just had.

"Damn, nigga, can I get a little bit of help wiping your babies off my fuckin' back," Cha barked.

Ya-Ya tossed her a handkerchief. He looked over at Cha and smiled.

"You got a man?" he asked.

"I'm good," Cha said matter-of-factly.

"Nah, you ain't never good. . . . You always gonna want more or want better, that's how life is," Ya-Ya stated.

"Well, if you lookin' for a girl, I ain't the one," Cha mentioned.

"Who said I was lookin' for a bitch?"

"So what are you lookin' for?" she asked.

Ya-Ya stood up and walked over to Cha as she was getting dressed. "I'm lookin' for a bitch to have a good time with, and you look like a bitch that I can definitely have a good time with," Ya-Ya said.

"You believe that?"

"Cha, right?" Ya-Ya asked.

She nodded.

"You have a number I can reach you at?"

"Maybe," she teased.

"I don't need a maybe. I want a yes from you."

"You got a girl?" she asked.

"Nah, ain't no bitch out there wild enough for me. But you definitely come close," he stated.

Cha smiled.

"Let me take you out sometime," he offered.

"You think you can handle me?"

"Give me a number and we can continue this wherever."

Cha looked at him for a moment, and then gave Ya-Ya her number. He nodded and knew he would be giving her a call real soon. Cha walked out of the VIP area and back into the club, fixing her hair and five hundred dollars richer. Many eyes were on her as she counted the money and strutted like the true diva bitch that she was. She had made enough money for the night and all she wanted to do was go home and get some sleep.

Cha pranced into the changing room with this self-centered attitude. She clutched a stack of money and smirked at the broke bitches in the room that couldn't get their money up like she did.

Cha sat down and was about to change when Bubbles walked into the room. She paid Bubbles no mind and counted her money for all to see. She went through fifties and twenties with a smile. She then heard Bubbles mumble, "Bitch think she gettin' money, fuckin' ho."

Cha turned and chimed back, "Bitch, you got sumthin' to say, say it to my fuckin' face!"

Bubbles dropped what she had in her hands and stormed

over to Cha. Cha quickly stood up and stuffed the cash into her small bag, ready to fight with Bubbles.

"Bitch, don't get mad 'cuz your whack ass can't get money like me," Cha shouted.

"Bitch, you a fuckin' ho . . . fuckin' every nigga in the club like it's cute," Bubbles retorted.

"Bitch, don't get mad 'cuz you can't do me," Cha returned, coming up in Bubbles's face.

Bubbles's friend Cheney had to pull Bubbles back from Cha.

"You know what, bitch, how my pussy taste in your mouth, 'cuz when I was fuckin' your man, I had my pussy in his mouth every night, lovin' my shit . . . love it, bitch!" Cha exclaimed.

"Fuck you, bitch!"

"Bubbles, don't get fucked up in this room a second time . . . .a'ight. Step the fuck off, 'cuz I ain't the one!"

"You nasty, ho . . . it's all good, I got sumthin' fo' ya ass," Bubbles threatened.

Ely came rushing into the room. He glared at Cha and then looked over at Bubbles.

"Yo, what y'all bitches arguing about in here now?" he asked.

"You better tell ya girl to chill, Ely," Cha said.

"Cha, let me talk to you in my office for a minute," Ely said.

Cha looked at him with attitude. "For what?"

"Chill wit' the drama. . . . Just fuckin' change and come see me," he demanded.

Cha sucked her teeth and snatched up her belongings from the floor. Bubbles had cooled down a little, but the hatred for Cha she had in her eyes could kill. Cheney had her friend calm, but looked at Bubbles and asked, "Girl, what was all that about? I thought you been over that shit."

Bubbles was quiet. She just stared off into the distance. Cheney then noticed a few tears trickle down her friend's face. Bubbles seemed really hurt and upset about something, but she wasn't telling anybody what was truly bothering her.

Cheney stared at her friend with concern and asked, "Bubbles, you gonna be a'ight?"

Bubbles nodded, wiped her tears, and said, "I'll be a'ight."

"If you wanna talk, just holla at me girl, okay," Cheney mentioned.

Bubbles nodded.

Cha walked into Ely's pimp-decorated office with an attitude. Ely was seated on his desk staring up at the mounted flat screen on his wall, remote in hand. He had a porno playing. Cha sighed and rolled her eyes.

"What you wanna see me about?" she asked.

"Yo, what's up wit' all the drama with you and Bubbles lately? I don't need that shit in my club, Cha," he stated.

"So, you need to be talkin' to that bitch. . . . Fuck you comin' to me for?" she hissed.

"Yo, watch ya mouth, a'ight. I'm just sayin . . . chill wit' that shit," he slightly barked.

"We done here? I got moves to make."

Ely stood up from his desk and approached Cha in a smoother manner. "Cha, I ain't tryin' to beef wit' you. I'm just tryin' to keep the peace in my club and wit' you and me. You know I got love fa you."

Cha didn't want to hear him at the moment. She knew Ely wanted some pussy, but she wasn't in the mood to fuck him. She felt that he was being corny tonight. Cha was hearing Ely speak, but she stood in front of him with a distant look and an aloof style.

Ely held Cha's arms lightly and tried to make eye contact with her.

"We cool, right, boo?" Ely asked with concern.

She hated for a nigga to call her boo. She rolled her eyes once again and just wanted to leave the office. But Ely tried to play the pimp position. He moved behind Cha and wrapped his arms around her in a loving way. He then whispered in her ear, "So duke in the VIP, you fucked him?"

Cha pushed herself away from his unappealing hold, spinning herself around to lock eyes with him.

"Nigga, is you really serious?" she exclaimed.

"What you beefin' about?"

"You really gonna ask that . . . like it's really your fuckin' business," she said.

"I was just asking. . . ." he replied.

"Ely, you done fucked like half these bitches in this club . . . so why you asking about my business all the time? Huh? Go step to the next ho about her business, don't come to me wit' the jealousy shit. All we do is just fuck, nigga . . . it ain't nothin' else," Cha strongly proclaimed.

"You a trip, Cha. I was just asking," Ely replied.

"Don't be asking about who else I'm fuckin'. . . . Nigga,

it's my pussy and I like to throw it out, and right now, most y'all niggas is fumbling," she clowned.

Ely just looked at her. Cha picked up her bag and stormed out his office. She had had enough BS for the night. She knew if she didn't leave at that moment, she would murder someone.

Cha woke up later that following morning to the ringing from her BlackBerry. She stirred a bit and looked over at the time and saw that it was only eight in the morning. Her eyes were still groggy and three hours' sleep wasn't enough for Cha after that rough and crazy night at the club.

Cha was ready to curse out the sonofabitch that was calling her so damn early in the morning. She looked at the caller ID and her expression became even more frustrated when she saw that it was David.

"Ohmygod. What is wrong wit' this fuckin' nigga?" she cursed.

At first Cha was just going to let it ring, but knowing David, he would call back again and again. She answered the call with a serious attitude, saying, "Nigga, do you know what fuckin' time it is?"

"What you doing right now?" he asked, obviously ignoring her perturbed attitude.

"Sleeping, nigga, trying to forget about your punk ass," she barked, ready to hang up on him.

"Yo, let me come upstairs and eat out your pussy, like those niggas did you last night," he said.

"What?"

"I'm parked outside your building right now."

"Nigga, is you fuckin' serious?"

"Yeah, Cha . . . I ain't got to be in the office 'til ten. I got time to please you this morning."

"Nigga, fo' real, fo' real, you is going too fuckin' hard right now."

"Cha, why you keep dissing me? So you gonna let some stranger eat you out onstage with no problem, but you have a problem with a nigga you fuck with to come please you early in the morning," David proclaimed.

"Then please me by leaving me the fuck alone with your whack ass . . . fo' real, David," Cha chided.

She hung up and tossed her phone at the foot of the bed, letting out an annoyed sigh. She was upset and frustrated with herself for violating her number one rule—never let niggas know where you rest your head at, because they do what David just did, show up announced. But fortunate for her, David was the only man who had her home address, and it was only because it was coincident at the time.

Cha had met David a week before Thanksgiving. She met him through a mutual friend, and thought he was cute and gave him some pussy that same night in the backseat of his truck. And from that first experience, David was opened like the freeway at three in the morning. Their second encounter was where Cha made the mistake. She met David for drinks at a local lounge in her neighborhood. She had an okay time and wanted some dick. It was too cold to have sex in the truck, and since Cha lived close by, she invited David up to her place for another round of hot, sweaty, and panting sex.

When they were done, all she wanted was for David to be on his way and lock the door when he left. But David wanted to linger around, and that bothered Cha. She didn't want him staying the night, so four hours later, she basically told him, "Look, I gotta get up in the morning; you need to bounce, yo."

He understood and left without any complaint.

But now David would show up at her place sometimes, not often though, unannounced like he had the right to do so, and Cha wasn't cool with that. The nigga was borderline stalking, and Cha prayed that she wouldn't have to get a restraining order against him, or worse, let loose her .38 and shake his frame up with some hot ones.

Cha was mad that she was up and had to pee. Before she stepped out of bed, her phone rang again, and she knew it had to be David calling back. She was ready to toss her phone out the window and just get a whole new number— but she had a lot of important contacts in her phone.

She ignored the phone, letting it go to voice mail. She knew that David would finally get the hint. She went into the bathroom, stretching her muscles out, and took herself a long-needed pee.

Cha figured since she was up, she might as well shower and cook herself some breakfast. She took a long, hot shower and couldn't help but play with her throbbing pussy. She slid her hand in between her thighs and started finger fucking herself rapidly. She clutched the shower curtain tightly, making herself come like a gusher.

She came out the bathroom clad in her white terry cloth

robe. She set the pot for some coffee and began making her-self an omelet. Cha loved the quietness around her—there were no niggas calling out her name, her phone had stopped ringing, and for once her mind felt at ease. Cha then thought about Ya-Ya, and seeing him last night brought back that feeling of hurt and anger inside her. Cha knew that the aver-age bitch wouldn't fuck the nigga who murdered her father.

Cha felt that her life was like a roller coaster ride at Six Flags Great Adventure, there were so many ups and downs, twist and turns—she didn't know which way she would end up sometimes. She thought about the men and women who loved her, the men who stalked her, the men who would give their right arm for her, and the men who were so obsessed with the pussy—because it was so good—that niggas would choke and slap their mamas for a piece of ass. Cha was good at what she did, from sucking to fucking, and had been around the block from corner to corner. Many would call her a ho, slut, bitch, or prostitute, but Cha didn't give a fuck who judged her for her promiscuous ways; muthafuckas weren't paying her bills, or couldn't walk in her shoes. Cha was liv-ing comfortable and had been through the pain and fire enough times not to allow any nigga or bitch to upset her.

Cha knew that most of the judgment toward her came from hate and jealousy, especially from bitches who wanted to be her but couldn't come close to Cha on their best days. They couldn't understand how Cha could just fuck a nigga for months and have no emotional attachment to that man whatsoever. Bitches couldn't understand why niggas wanted to fuck with Cha, even on some relationship type of way, when she done fucked so many niggas on the come up.

The list went on, with David, Ely, Boogie, Rahmel, Tyrone, Tyson, Lotto, Page, Oops, Knocky, Vick, Olay, Eric, Ant, T.J., and so on. There were many names and faces. Cha would joke and rhyme out, "What these niggas want from this bitch? I got their tongues lickin' clit, tastin' sweat from my lips, bitches hatin' 'cuz they man lovin' a bitch, they way I ride that dick, the way I fuck and suck, got him fallin' in love wit' it . . . shoutin' out 'I luv ya, girl,' my freakiness got his dick leakin', his weakness got his pockets creeping, a real bitch ain't gotta blame it on the alcohol, blame it on the pussy, blame it on my tongue game, 'cuz I got niggas open like a book, blazed like haze, damn bitch feelin' threatened 'cuz ya man fading like yes-ter-day . . . just to put it quick, y'all bitches ain't fuckin' wit' my ways, y'all step ta dis and get this Newark bitch whippin' ya ass, shatter you like glass."

Cha loved to rhyme and thought she could become the next Lil' Kim.

When Cha was young, Ya-Ya was her father's right-hand man. The two of them held the block down and were two of the most feared men in Newark. Cha lived well, and Cha's father, Madison, treated her really good. Ya-Ya was always around the family handling business for her father. He was in his thirties back then and treated Cha like they were family.

Then one chillin' March day, while Cha was in her bedroom playing, Ya-Ya came by the house with a few men to have a talk with Madison. Cha watched everything from the top of the stairs in pajamas when Ya-Ya walked into her home. Ya-Ya went into Madison's den to talk. Madison looked really upset about something. Cha stood by the stairs keeping quiet and to herself.

She heard an argument ensue, and minutes later four shots rang out. Cha became startled. Ya-Ya suddenly rushed from Madison's den with the smoking gun in his hand. He ran out the door with his crew, never checking to see if anyone else was in the house.

Cha ran downstairs and raced into the den. She saw her father dead on his back, covered in blood. She rushed to him, grabbed his body in her small arms, and cried. His blood stained her hands, and her tears felt like they would fall without end.

Soon word on the streets was that Ya-Ya was the main man in charge of everything, and Cha and her mother, Evelyn, were in grave danger. Cha and her mother soon felt threatened by Ya-Ya's position in Newark. Cha once trusted Ya-Ya and now the streets were talking about Ya-Ya wanting to kill off Madison's entire family.

So with the help of a friend, Cha and Evelyn left New Jersey and moved to Baltimore. Newark became too dangerous for them. And Cha never knew what her father and Ya-Ya had been arguing about.

They soon fell on hard times. They didn't have Madison around to support them. Cha watched her moms whore herself out to the hustlers and ballers in B-more. They tossed her cash for sex, blow jobs, and other kinky activities.

As long as Cha's moms stayed on her back or on her knees, both ladies lived comfortable and had a place to stay and money to spend, but with dire costs.

But Cha also witnessed how niggas could get too controlling with her moms; some of the men were very abusive and felt just because they were splurging on Evelyn and putting her and her child up with a place to stay that they were property. If Evelyn looked at a nigga too long, niggas like John D would punch her in the eyes in plain public. Or if she didn't do what she was told right away, then niggas like Rude would smack her face and pull Evelyn by her hair out the room with her kicking and screaming.

Cha witnessed how disrespectful niggas got when they had control over a woman who knew she had nowhere else to go, or nothing to fall back on like an education or a degree, or the bitch was just too dependant on that man for support. The men Evelyn dealt with took full advantage of her situation daily. Cha wanted to be nothing like her mother and vowed that she would become her own woman, not needing a man for shit, and avenge her father's death someday.

Cha sat at the breakfast table smoking a cigarette. The sun was at its peak and Cha needed to get high; thinking about Ya-Ya had her ready to flip out. She picked up her Black-Berry and noticed two new voice messages in her mailbox. She knew it was David still stalking her. She shrugged it off and called Boogie.

Boogie answered after the third ring. "What's good, Ma?"

"Hey, Boogie," Cha greeted cheerfully.

"Cha, what's good, ma . . . you tryin' to see me today?" he asked.

"You know it. I need some of that from you," she said.

"No doubt, ma . . . you know I got ya."

"Stupid niggas got a bitch stressed right now, Boogie," Cha mentioned.

"You need me to handle sumthin' for you?" he asked with concern.

"Nah, you knows I stay packin' my gat, and a bitch can handle herself. But I definitely need to see you so you can handle ya business and I can handle mines," she said flirtatiously.

"I hear ya, Cha. What time you tryin' to breeze through?"

"In like two hours."

"Just hit me on the hip when you get close . . . a'ight?"

"Got ya, Boogie."

Cha hung up feeling a bit better. Boogie always knew how to lighten her foul mood with his thick nine-inch dick and kush weed that would give Cha a real monster high. She put on a sexy skirt (for easy access), a halter top, and some heels and walked out the door ready for Boogie.

The day was warm and sunny, and the only thing on Cha's mind was getting high with Boogie. Harlem was only a hop, skip away. Cha walked out the building lobby and strutted to her Benz parked across the street. She was unaware that she was being watched.

David was parked a few cars down, in his new gray Saab

with dark tinted windows. He decided to skip work and see
who else had Cha's time. It was apparent she was fucking
other niggas, and David was jealous that he wasn't the only
male figure in Cha's life. He was like a firecracker, ready to
go off when Cha mentioned other males' names around
him. But last night had David furious. He hated to see Cha
wild out like that on the stage. He wanted to intervene, but
thought against it.

David had his beady eyes fixated on Cha as she got into
her Benz.

"Bitch keeps dissin' me," he said to himself.

Cha slowly pulled out of her parking spot and sped off.
David did the same. He made sure to stay three car lengths
away. But Cha was unaware of his new Saab and it made it
easier for him to follow her.

Cha was in Harlem moments later. She pushed her car
down Seventh Avenue, toward 115th Street, and saw Boogie
standing in front of a bodega with his crew. Cha doubled
parked and stepped out her ride looking like a diva attract-
ing attention to herself.

Boogie smiled.

"You look nice, ma," Boogie greeted.

"I know," Cha replied, slipping into Boogie's arm for a
firm hug.

"I need to chill wit' you for a while, get shit off my mind,"
Cha continued.

"I got ya."

Boogie nodded over to his crew, saying he was leaving,

and walked over to Cha's Benz. Cha tossed him the keys, saying, "Nigga, you drive. I wanna be busy doin' other thangs."

Boogie smiled.

David was parked a few cars down observing everything. He watched closely the way Boogie and Cha interacted with each other—the way Boogie hugged Cha in his arms made David cringe.

Boogie drove off and David followed closely.

Boogie drove two blocks and Cha wasted no time to get her freak on. She leaned into his lap and pulled out his snake of a dick. She wrapped her lips around it and began sucking his dick as he drove up Seventh Avenue. David maneuvered his ride close to the Benz when they were stopped at a red light. He witnessed Cha's head in Boogie's lap, and a frown came across him watching Cha suck another man's dick. He tried to keep a low profile, but he wanted to jump out his car and snatch Cha from the Benz so desperately.

Boogie and Cha parked on the west side of Harlem, on Riverside Drive, ironically not too far from David's place. The two stopped at a local bodega and bought some blunts to roll the kush in and a few beers. Boogie rolled up a phat blunt, and the two just got high, drank, and watched the sun descend over the Hudson.

David spent the majority of his day following Cha closely and he didn't like what he was seeing. He was seething when he watched Cha from a distance straddle Boogie in the front seat of her Benz. Cha was just with David yesterday, and then she had niggas eat her pussy out that same night, and later that night he saw Cha disappear into the VIP section with a man for a long moment. And now David was watching Cha getting fucked again, little more than twenty-four hours after she fucked him.

David decided to call Cha and see her reaction. He quickly dialed her number. He watched from a parked bench. Cha picked up her phone, saw that it was David calling, and rolled her eyes, tossing her phone to the backseat to continue fucking Boogie.

She panted and ground her thick hips into his lap, feeling his cement of a penis rooted deeply into her. The sex was becoming intense, causing the car windows to fog up and making it difficult for David to peep at them from where he sat.

David called Cha again, and it went straight to voice mail again. He wanted to toss his phone, but shoved it back into his pocket and walked away. He had seen enough.

Cha felt Boogie nut in her and she gripped him tightly. She was high like a kite, and the way Boogie's big dick thrust in and out of her made the feeling powerful like electricity running through her body.

"Damn, ma . . . you got that good pussy," Boogie proclaimed.

Cha chuckled.

After their fuck, Boogie rolled up another phat kush and they got high a second time. Cha looked over at Boogie and said, "Yo, I needed that shit."

Boogie replied with a high smile, "I bet you did."

❀    ❀    ❀

Cha had just parked her car when her cell phone rang. She didn't know the number, but answered anyway.

"Hello."

"Hey, beautiful. It's Ya-Ya," he announced.

Cha rolled her eyes; she knew he would be calling. But she put up a front. "Hey, Ya-Ya, what's good?"

"I wanna see you," he stated.

"I see. When?"

"Tonight, let's go out," he suggested.

"Tonight . . . umm, I could do tonight. What time though?"

"I'll come scoop you up around ten. I know this spot uptown that you'll like . . . wear something nice," he said.

"I got you . . . you like your women classy, but also nasty," she stated.

"See, that's why I fucks with you. You read my mind. We think just alike," he joked.

"I'll be ready for you tonight. Don't keep me waiting, handsome."

"I won't."

Cha gave Ya-Ya an address, then hung up and sighed. She decided to skip the club tonight and put her plan into action with Ya-Ya. She strutted into the lobby and wanted to get some rest before Ya-Ya called. She wasn't stupid to have him pick her up from her actual place. She gave him a phony address and would meet him there.

Cha walked into her apartment, kicked off her shoes, and plopped down on the couch. She looked around her crib and enjoyed the silence. Cha had no pictures of her parents, her childhood days, or any indication of friends or relatives posted on her walls, or anywhere in her place. David asked her why one day. She told him that she cared to forget about her past and just wanted to move on. David tried to be understanding for Cha, but she just wouldn't let him get in close to her life.

Cha took a needed shower and changed into a long flowing skirt, a sexy halter top, and open-toe sandals. She pinned her hair up into a bun and looked amazing for the night. She grabbed a few personal things, including her .22, and walked outside feeling like a million bucks.

Cha told Ya-Ya that she lived a few blocks away, near Broadway. She parked her car in a garage and strutted to the false address she gave. She walked into the lobby with her Chanel purse tucked under her arm and waited. She stood patiently for about twenty minutes when she noticed a dark blue Yukon turning the corner with serious blinding high beams.

Something in her stomach said that it was Ya-Ya. She kept her eyes fixated on the truck and when it double parked near the lobby she was standing in, Cha was sure that it was Ya-Ya.

Ya-Ya stepped out his high-end truck clad in a stylish three-piece dark blue suit that matched his truck. He got on his cell phone and dialed Cha. Cha heard her phone ringing in her purse and quickly picked up.

"You outside?" she asked, already knowing that he was.

"Yeah, babe . . . I'm out here waiting for your presence," he said.

"I'll be down in one minute."

Cha hung up. She stood hidden in the lobby, out of Ya-Ya's view. She decided to watch him for a minute. Ya-Ya walked back to his truck and got in. The block was quiet, but parking was nearly impossible to find. Cha made him wait for about five minutes and then strutted out of the lobby with a smile. Ya-Ya got out his truck and greeted Cha with a hug and felt on her booty.

Cha winced a bit.

"You look nice," Ya-Ya complimented.

"Thanks. You clean up nice yourself," she returned.

"I stay in nothing but the best, babe."

Cha got into his up-to-date truck and heard Al Green playing. Ya-Ya nodded his head and said, "That's real music right there, Cha . . . something a real nigga can fuck to."

Cha smiled. "I hear that."

Ya-Ya admired Cha's attire for a moment and then drove off.

Cha and Ya-Ya arrived at the stylish soul food spot, Mendel's, on the west side of Harlem, near Jackie Robinson Park forty minutes later. They were having a nice dinner. The atmosphere was exclusive, the food superb, and the service on point.

"So, Cha, where you from?" he asked.

"Brooklyn," she lied.

"I got peoples in Brooklyn," Ya-Ya said.

"And you?" she asked.

"Newark, New Jersey."

"Never been," Cha continued to lie.

"It's a hard town, but I run business out there. Doesn't anything go on without my say so," he stated.

"So what is it that you do?" she asked.

Ya-Ya took a sip of wine, then answered, "A little bit of this, a little bit of that."

"You just straight about business, huh," Cha said.

"Business is always good. . . . Keeps an aging man like myself healthy."

"You look good."

"I'm gonna stay being good, too, because I like to fuck a lot. I need a woman that can keep up. No use for Viagra, either," he boasted.

Cha chuckled. "Straightforward are we now."

"Last night, I enjoyed it and I want more of it."

"Well, if you continue to play your cards right, then anything is possible," Cha teased, taking a sip of wine.

"My cards are always played right. I make sure I have a good hand."

Cha stared at Ya-Ya. She thought to herself, if the bastard only knew who she truly was, how would he react? She remained calm and wanted to pick up as much information on Ya-Ya as possible.

"So, Ya-Ya, who is Zulu to you?" she asked.

"Zulu is my son."

"Oh, is he now. He's a very handsome man."

"He's a soldier and the only man I trust with anything. But enough about him, we're here to talk about us."

"Agreed."

But Cha wanted to know more about Zulu. She definitely

wanted to fuck him and knew in due time she would. Seeing Zulu made Cha's pussy tingle. He had a strong, dark presence like her father, and there was something about him that was so enticing. She felt that there was some kind of unspoken bond with him when they locked eyes the night before.

"So, Ya-Ya, do you have any more children?" she asked.

"Zulu is my only child."

"Ya-Ya, Zulu, both very interesting names. . . . Can I ask why?"

"You ask too many questions," Ya-Ya said.

"I'm just a curious bitch." She chuckled.

"Well, I'm not the one to answer questions. My business stays my business."

"I understand. I don't want the mistake of prying into your business," she said with a smile.

"The only thing you need to pry into tonight is my zipper," Ya-Ya joked.

The male waiter came over with their tray of food. He carefully placed two hot plates of catfish, collard greens, and rice in front of the two. Cha was ready to eat like a cow.

"Anything else I can get you?" the waiter asked.

Ya-Ya shook his head no and shooed him away. Ya-Ya downed the rest of his wine and went digging into the steaming catfish. Cha did the same. Cha wanted to know a little more about Ya-Ya. But he was very discreet about exposing his business. Cha definitely wanted to know more about Zulu, though.

❖   ❖   ❖

Ya-Ya was leaned back comfortable in his seat, staring at the GW Bridge from a distance, while Cha had his hard-on hitting the back of her throat. Her deep throat was something fierce and Ya-Ya's legs quivered with every suck, lick, and jaw movement she put on the dick.

"Oh shit, suck that dick, Cha. . . . That's right, get nasty with it," Ya-Ya exclaimed.

Cha sucked him off 'til he came in her mouth. She didn't even attempt to spit it out the window. She swallowed everything in front of Ya-Ya. He smiled and said, "Damn, you a wild bitch."

"And you better not forget it," she replied with a naughty look.

Ya-Ya was still hard after his nut, so Cha hiked up her skirt and straddled his lasting erection. He held her close and moaned, feeling Cha come down on him slowly. She neared her lips to his ear and asked, "So, you still live in Newark?"

"Newark is business, New York is home," Ya-Ya answered, and then grunted as Cha gyrated her hips into his lap.

They went on to fog up the windows in his truck and Cha felt Ya-Ya explode into her. Ya-Ya wanted to pull out, but Cha insisted. He looked at Cha with some resentment, saying, "I'm not taking care of any damn kids. So don't try to trap a nigga."

"Don't worry, I can't get pregnant," she let him know.

"Why not?"

" 'Cuz I'm on the pill, and besides, I have a condition where I can't have babies."

"And what condition is that?" Ya-Ya questioned, feeling the last of his nut seep into her.

"I'm not tryin' to set you up, and you don't have to worry, okay?"

"Cool. But I forewarn you, don't fuck with me, because I can become a dangerous man," he warned, grabbing Cha by her arms and staring into her pretty face.

"The only fuckin' I'm tryin' to do is right now," she countered with a smile.

Ya-Ya leaned back into his seat and allowed Cha to continue pleasing him. He closed his eyes and she rode him until there was no more erection left.

Cha got out of Ya-Ya's truck right after midnight. Everything below her waist was sore. Ya-Ya was so thick and hung that every inch of him felt like a cemented tree rooted into her stomach. But overall, it was a good night. She got to know Ya-Ya a little better. She knew he was still in the game. She knew he did a small bid in Attica two years after her father's murder. She knew that he was married. She knew Zulu was his son. Cha was very satisfied.

Cha watched Ya-Ya turn the corner and then went into the parking garage to get her own car. She sped out the garage and wanted to sleep 'til noon when she got home. She parked her ride in the parking lot near her building and began walking toward the lobby. She had her keys in hand and felt a bit tipsy.

She entered her building, and when she got close to the elevator, Cha heard someone say, "Cha."

She was a bit startled when she turned and saw David appearing out from the shadows.

"What the fuck you doin' in my building?" she asked with anger.

"I want to have a talk with you," he said.

Cha suddenly reached into her bag for her .22, but before she could get a grip around it, David rushed her. The elevator doors came open and they both went flying in. David gripped Cha tightly by her wrists and forced her against the walls of the elevator. His body strongly pressed against hers.

"I just wanna talk. Why you want to shoot me?" he barked.

"Get the fuck off me!" she screamed, and struggled.

"Relax, Cha. I ain't gonna hurt you."

"Well, I'm gonna hurt you," she told him through clenched teeth.

"Bitch, if you don't relax, I'll make it worse. Chill out!"

Cha decided to chill, knowing David had the upper hand for now.

"Now give me the gun," he demanded.

Cha looked reluctant.

"Give me the gun, Cha. I just want to be safe. You can get me hotheaded, and right now I don't trust you with any kind of weapon in your hands."

David went into her purse and pulled out the gun. He then pushed for her floor and the elevator quickly ascended. Cha stood still and glared at David. She knew there had to be something wrong with him. It was more than just lust.

David stared at Cha from head to toe. He held her gun down at his side.

"You need help, David. Why this infatuation over me?" she asked.

"You're different, Cha. I don't know why," he responded.

Cha quickly hit the stop button to the elevator and it quickly halted between floors.

"What you do that for?" he barked.

"Because I can," she retorted.

David went to restart the elevator, but Cha jumped in front of him.

"We're not going up to my apartment. We either talk here or you gonna have to shoot me wit' my own gun," she dared.

"Cha, don't test me."

"You think I'm playing?"

David glared at her. "A'ight, we'll talk. First, why don't you love me like I love you?"

Cha rolled her eyes. "I don't love anybody. It's because I'm a selfish bitch. I take what I want from a nigga and leave. Too bad you can't do the same."

"I'm tired of this cat-and-mouse shit with you, Cha. For seven months, it's been good, and can't you see that I'm a good guy?"

"David, there are some things you need to know about me, seriously," she mentioned.

"What, that you can be a straight-up bitch? And you a ho. I know you're messing around with other men. Who the fuck was the nigga in the blue truck? And the young nigga in Harlem, the nigga look like he could be eighteen," David proclaimed.

"You fuckin' following me now?! Don't get mad at me

'cuz you seen things you shouldn't have saw and now your feelings is hurt. Nigga, you know I like dick."

"You like a lot of things," David said.

Cha flashed a naughty smile. She had an idea. She stared at David intensely and asked, "You wanna fuck me, David?"

She slowly lifted up her skirt. "Is this what the fuck turns you on so much, David? You wanna fuck me right here in the elevator, huh?"

David looked at her. He felt his heart racing. Cha raised her skirt up to her hips, showing David that she didn't have on any panties.

"You like what you see, huh?" She smiled.

"Why you always teasing me, Cha? My life is not a game."

"I don't tease. . . . You know you can have it right now if you want," she stated seductively.

David still held onto Cha's gun. The elevator was still stopped between floors. It was nearing one in the morning and the traffic in the building was almost nonexistent. And besides, there was a second elevator in the building.

Cha stood in front of David with her skirt up and an inviting stare.

"You wanna fuck me, or talk?" she asked.

"Why you play games, Cha?"

With her skirt still up and her hand near her pussy, Cha replied with, "Who said I was playing games?"

David sighed. The lust in his heart was burning through him.

"You know you want this pussy," Cha added.

And David did. He licked his lips and took a step closer

to Cha. He placed the gun on the floor and approached Cha with a ravenous attitude. He pulled Cha into his arms and lifted her against the wall, her skirt riding up her thighs. She was pressed against David and the elevator with her legs wrapped around him. He fumbled with his jeans and dropped them around his ankles, along with his boxers. He quickly guided his erection into Cha and cried out, "Oh shit! Oh shit! Damn, you feel so good."

David thrust into Cha, rocking her body against the wall, clutching onto her tightly, and trying to grip some part of the elevator for some support. Cha felt her insides being opened up—his dick moving in and out of her like liquid. David was strong and had no problem maintaining her against the wall as he fucked.

"You love me, nigga?" Cha exclaimed.

David grunted and thrust into her, replying, "You know I do."

"And you would do anything for me?"

"Hells yeah, Cha. . . . Oh, you feel so good," he continued to cry out, pushing into her.

With a devilish look about her, she said, "We'll see. We'll definitely see."

David quickly got his nut in the elevator and collected himself. He picked up Cha's gun from the floor and handed it to her with a "I'm sorry. I didn't mean to wild out like that on you. It just . . . you be having me going crazy."

Cha smirked. She fixed her skirt, touched up her hair, and pushed for the elevator to start. "You need to chill, David. I just got a lot goin' on."

"Like what?" he asked.

"It's none of your concern, David."

"You are my concern, Cha. If you got a problem, then I'm gonna have a problem," David said, trying to play nice.

Cha reached her floor. The doors opened up and Cha took a step out. She turned around to look at David, who had a content look about him. His pants were still unzipped and sagging, with his shirt wrinkled.

"I'll call you," Cha said.

David smiled. For one brief moment, David thought that he was finally reaching through to Cha. He figured that fucking her on the elevator, after almost holding her hostage, was her breaking point. But he was wrong. Cha had other motives for David.

Cha walked to the apartment with deceit on her mind.

The next two weeks were nothing but one freaky, nasty, orgy binge with Ya-Ya, David, Ely, and a few clients at the Pink Pussy. Cha was so wild with her ways that she didn't care whose feelings got hurt and who was watching. One night she would be in the VIP room with Ya-Ya getting fucked hard and fast doggy-style. The next night, she would be sprawled out on Ely's desk with her legs cocked in the air. And sometimes David would be fucking her and proclaiming his love for her. But all the sexual episodes just rolled off of Cha's back—she would fuck and suck niggas and then acted like it never happened shortly after.

But David's jealousy was becoming out of hand. He would come to her place of work almost every night and watch her like a hawk. When Cha got too close or too nasty with some-one, he would either stand nearby paying close attention or interrupt Cha with her work. He got into a fight with a few men in the place and was thrown out.

But David was the least of Cha's problems. Ya-Ya was one frisky and horny man. Their rendezvous were almost daily, and sometimes Cha would forget that he was married. He mentioned to Cha that he and Maria had been married for more than twenty years and they had only one son together. Cha had seen pictures of his wife and thought that she was a very beautiful woman. But Cha never had known about Maria from her father when she was young.

"My wife doesn't fuck like you, Cha," Ya-Ya had pro-claimed.

"Well, I can teach her a few things," Cha said jokingly.

Cha became close with Ya-Ya in the short time since she met him. Ya-Ya was showering her with gifts and dinners. He started to spend more time with Cha than he would with his own wife. Ya-Ya bought her clothes, gave her money and jewelry, and sometimes Ya-Ya would pay fifteen hundred dollars a night for suites in the city to impress Cha. He was a show-off and boasted his money like he boasted his penis size. Cha was just in it for the ride and wanted to suck him dry. She hated him for killing her father and wanted to break and destroy him so he'd know how her mother had felt.

Cha wanted to put her next plan into action—fuck his son, Zulu, and then meet with Ya-Ya's wife to get some ques-tions answered.

❊   ❊   ❊

Cha finally got her chance to truly flirt with Zulu when he came into the Pink Pussy alone one night. Cha smiled. Her pussy tingled seeing Zulu's strapping build in a wifebeater, tattoos covering his arms, and in a pair of denim jeans and fresh Timbs. His dark skin looked smooth like cool, and his braids were freshly done.

Cha licked her lips and walked over to Zulu in an eye-catching strappy matte dress with a deep V plunge front and super-low rear cut, and black stilettos. Zulu stood by the bar, and Cha eyes weren't the only ones fixated on him. He was tall and stood out. She walked over to him quickly before the next bitch was able to approach. But when Cha came close, a petite, bootylicious stripper named Scandal got in her way. Scandal brushed against Zulu with a flirty smile and asked, "Can you buy me a drink, sexy?"

Zulu looked at her and before he could answer, Cha chimed in, saying, "No, bitch, 'cuz he's buying me one."

Scandal glared at Cha. Cha returned the look.

"You got a problem, bitch?!" Cha continued.

Scandal knew about Cha's reputation and wanted no drama with her. She was there when Cha beat the shit out of Bubbles in the locker room a few months back. Scandal showed her frown and walked away.

"Anyway," Cha uttered as she grabbed Zulu's arm playfully, and continued with, "How you doin', sexy?"

"Cha, right?" Zulu questioned with a deadpan gaze.

"Yup. So can I get a drink?"

"Like what?"

"I'll take a shot of Nutcracker," she said.

Zulu gestured for the bartender.

"Let me get a shot of Nutcracker and a Hypnotic with Red Bull," Zulu said.

The bartender nodded and went to prepare the drinks.

"So what brings you here alone?" Cha asked.

"I'm just here to chill," he said, being short with her.

"Okaaay . . ." Cha dragged out.

The bartender set their drinks on the counter. "That'll be sixteen."

Zulu passed him a twenty. "Keep the change."

The bartender nodded.

Zulu slid Cha her drink and he downed his in a matter of seconds. Cha sat near him, wanting to move her hand up his thigh and feel his package. She knew by the looks of him alone, he had to be holding like his father. But Zulu was younger and even sexier.

"What you lookin' for tonight, some pussy?" Cha asked, being blunt.

Zulu shot her a frosty stare and said, "I'm not like my father. I don't pay for pussy."

Cha smiled lustfully. "Who said that I was charging you? Nigga, you can fuck me for free."

Zulu sized her up quickly. He liked what he saw. Cha had these hypnotic-looking eyes that could entice the Pope and lips that could make a fag want to kiss her. He signaled for the bartender again. He ordered another drink.

Cha moved her seat closer and felt him up subtly. His bulge was nice, and his full lips made Cha want her pussy eaten out.

"You wanna fuck me?" she whispered in his ear, squeezing his bulge while doing so.

"You can hang?" he asked.

"Obviously you don't know me like that," she replied, batting her eyes.

"And you don't know me," he countered.

"So, let's say we go somewhere private and get to know each other really well," Cha suggested.

Zulu looked at her.

"I don't kiss and tell," Cha added.

Zulu quickly thought it over and nodded. Cha smiled and was ready to see who fucked better—father or son. Zulu downed his second drink and then followed Cha through the crowd with a few eyes watching in vain.

"Just give up twenty for VIP," Cha told him.

When they got to VIP, Cha pushed Zulu down on the padded suede sofa and positioned herself between his knees. She wanted to see what he was working with. She unbuttoned his jeans and whipped out a striking piece of work. Nine and a half inches of hard, thick, pulsating flesh was in her hand.

"Damn," she muttered.

Zulu just smiled.

"I see why they call you Zulu."

Cha went to work on it immediately. She slobbered it down halfway and sucked on the tip of it like it was a lollipop. Zulu had his hand tangled in her hair and tried to force her to deep-throat. Cha almost choked on it, but she went in and felt his titanic dick in her throat. Her head bobbed up and down in his lap like a basketball on the court and she chewed on his nuts like they were candy.

"Damn . . . you goes in," Zulu moaned.

Cha sucked, licked, and tasted every inch of him below. Zulu gripped the armrest of the sofa like he was holding onto it for dear life. He was hard like steel. She loved the way his dick curved in her hand and swelled in her mouth. Spit ran down his shaft as Cha gave him better head than Superhead.

Having enough, Zulu removed his dick from Cha's clamped jaws and stood up. He took off his shirt, and his six-pack was jutting off his stomach and his arms were ripped. Cha got buck naked and positioned herself on the cushy sofa. She cocked her legs back, gesturing that Zulu come beat her pussy up.

Zulu gripped her thigh and slowly pushed his big dick into her, causing Cha to squirm and moan. Zulu pushed inch by inch into her pussy as Cha ran her nails down his back with a grimace on her face from the penetration.

"Fuck me!" she cried out.

Zulu did just that, and he did it hard and fast. He pounded into Cha like a drill tip digging for oil. He switched Cha into the doggy-style position, with her legs spread in a downward V, and thrust his length deep into her while pulling her hair roughly and cupping her tits, squeezing her hard nipples.

"I wanna put it in your ass," Zulu requested.

Anal wasn't new to Cha.

"Just be careful," she said.

Zulu quickly pulled out and eased his thick head into Cha's butt. It opened her up like birth. She bit down on her bottom lip and allowed for Zulu to continue.

"Oh shit!" she exclaimed, feeling her asshole spreading.

Zulu continued to ease every inch into her, feeling a bit of tightness around his thick dick. Cha clutched the sofa, but used her teeth to clamp down on it, as Zulu began fucking her in the butt. It felt like he was trying to push a pipe through a Cheerio.

"Oh shit!" Cha screamed out.

Zulu was a beast and a freak. He was enjoying the pain he inflicted on Cha. It turned him on. So he fucked her harder and pushed more dick into her butt. Cha had tears rolling down her cheeks; it was a bit painful, but Cha got some thrill from it. She wouldn't dare tell him to stop.

"I'm gonna come," Zulu exclaimed.

He gripped Cha's naked and sweaty hips and rocked back and forth. He continued to pull her hair and after a moment of just hard and nasty sex, Zulu came in Cha's ass. His legs quivered and his hold around her hair loosened. His breath softened and his body felt limp.

Cha stood up and was breathless. It was one of the best fucks she had had so far. Zulu wasted no time getting dressed. He put on his jeans and wifebeater. Zulu walked out VIP fully clothed, but Cha walked out VIP still naked with her hair disheveled. It wasn't a secret what just took place. Cha had all eyes on her. She walked straight to the changing room while Zulu went back to the bar for another drink.

David saw Zulu exiting from the VIP section. But when he saw Cha exiting from the same area butt-ass naked with her hair looking wild and her body language saying, *"Damn, I just got the shit fucked outta me,"* his eyes flared up.

Cha walked right by David, paying him no never mind. It fueled him even more.

Cha walked into the room, tossed her stuff on the floor, and sat down. She had to recoup herself from that episode with Zulu. She took a deep breath and just sat there. It was after midnight and for once the changing room was quiet. The other strippers were still trying to get money.

Cha thought about her father and she missed him dearly. She remembered the times they had. Madison used to take Cha to baseball and basketball games on the regular, and she was supposed to be on the come up with her father on the streets. Cha was happy until Ya-Ya changed that.

She wanted Ya-Ya to pay dearly for what he'd done to her family. And she was going after him for revenge through his family—with his son and his wife, Maria, with shocking news. Cha sat with vengeance on her mind and deceit showing in her eyes. Since day one, Cha had been spinning a web of lies, trickery, and betrayal. No one really knew the true Cha and what she was about. She had very few friends and many enemies. She quickly became the talk of the town, from corner to corner. She fucked with hustlers and pimps and killers and wimps, but all for a price.

Cha's mind went from vengeance to David. He was just a small insect tangled up in her huge web of lie after lie. But

David was becoming too unpredictable, showing up at her residence and stalking her from work to play. She gave him some pussy in the elevator to chill him out and have him think that she was breaking. But Cha was far from breaking. David was just a back-up plan for her revenge. So she teased his ear and gave him some pussy from time to time to keep him in check. She knew that David was pussy-whipped and used that to her full advantage.

Cha sat thinking. Then suddenly, Baby, Bunny, and Candy came storming into the changing room, screaming out, "They fighting! They fighting!"

Cha stood up. "Who fighting?" she asked.

"Stupid niggas gotta keep fuckin' up my money wit' dumb shit," Baby shouted.

Cha was curious to see what was happening. She quickly threw on a piece of clothing and ran out the changing room. She heard the commotion and soon saw David and Zulu fighting each other near the bar. Security was trying to break it up, but David and Zulu were tearing into each other like lions over prey. Bottles and chairs went flying and soon other men got into the tangle. It was ugly and chaotic.

"You and your father stay the fuck away from her!" David shouted. His lip was cut and he was bleeding from the forehead, and he had a serious gash across his abdomen. Zulu had sliced him open with a three-inch blade.

"Fuck you! You dead, nigga! You dead!" Zulu retorted, holding the bloody blade in his right hand.

Security was pulling them away from each other. Cha

wasn't even pissed. She had a smirk on her face. She really didn't care for either man. The ruckus soon settled down. The club cleared out of a few people. They dragged David outside while Zulu tended to the small cut across his face. Police and an ambulance soon rushed to the club.

Cha had seen enough. She shook her head and went back into the changing room.

"Fuckin' jerks," she muttered.

"What's this I hear about you being with my son? You fucking him too?!" Ya-Ya asked with intensity in his voice.

Cha chuckled.

"What the fuck is so funny?" Ya-Ya barked.

"I don't know, what have you been hearing?" Cha replied.

"He got into a little incident at the club the other night, and your name was all over it," Ya-Ya stated.

They were talking in Ya-Ya's sixty-thousand-dollar truck with a full moon casting in the night. Cha looked relaxed in her short skirt and tight shirt that accentuated her breasts. She was nonchalant about everything.

"My name comes up in a bunch of shit. It's nothin' new," Cha said.

"Well, who is this David and why is he stalking you? You fuckin' him too?" Ya-Ya asked.

"Why, you jealous?"

"You fucked my son and got him caught up with your stalker," Ya-Ya said.

"I fuck a lot of men, Ya-Ya. . . . So why you care?"

Ya-Ya became enraged and rushed Cha in the truck. He

grabbed her by the neck and slammed her frame into the passenger door.

"Bitch, don't double-talk me and don't fuckin' play games with me, Cha. My son is locked up now because of you. Detectives are questioning my fuckin' son because they found a kilo of coke in his trunk that same night. That fight with David put heat on him . . . heat that you started."

"Get the fuck off me . . . I ain't start shit!"

Ya-Ya squeezed harder, causing Cha to gasp.

"What games are you trying to play, Cha?" he asked.

Cha scratched and tore at his wrist, trying to free herself from Ya-Ya's strong hold. Ya-Ya looked into her eyes and didn't see that sexy and feisty girl he was fucking. He saw a different person. He let his hold go and asked, "Who the fuck are you, bitch?"

Cha let out a sinister chuckle.

"Wouldn't you like to know?" she replied, trying to catch her breath.

Ya-Ya reached under his seat and removed a loaded 9mm. He cocked it back and put it to Cha's head.

"Tell me why I shouldn't blow your fuckin' head off right now in this truck," he stated through clenched teeth.

Cha stared down the barrel of death. But she didn't flinch. She looked nonchalant in her situation.

"You're not stupid," Cha said.

"I've killed women for less disrespect. You wouldn't be the first," Ya-Ya made known.

The wild look Ya-Ya had in his eyes made Cha wonder if it was the same look that he had had when he killed her father. They locked eyes, but Ya-Ya didn't squeeze the trigger. He retracted the gun and warned, "Get the fuck out my truck. And if I ever see you again, you won't be as lucky."

But Cha felt some relief, knowing that it pained him that Zulu was locked up for a drug possession charge. If she had her way, she would have Zulu do life in prison. Cha wanted to tell Ya-Ya her secret, but her predicament prevented her from doing so. But Ya-Ya didn't let Cha leave his truck without some form of punishment. Cha was about to exit the truck when Ya-Ya called out to her. She turned and Ya-Ya punched her square in the jaw. Cha almost blacked out from the hit but held on to her consciousness. Blood spewed from her mouth as she stumbled out of Ya-Ya's truck.

"Fuck you, bitch! Pussy wasn't that good anyway. I've had better," Ya-Ya shouted.

The truck screeched off, leaving a trail of dust behind. Cha let out a cough. She was fuming and her head began spinning. She took a seat on the curb and regained her composure.

Two days later Cha knocked on Maria's door. Maria had been in Ya-Ya's life since Cha's father, Madison, was alive. She just wanted to see the woman and ask questions. Cha knew that she lived in an upscale apartment on the Upper West Side of the city. Cha lifted the information from Ya-Ya's wallet when he fell asleep one night after one of their freak episodes. She had quickly jotted down everything that she needed to know and placed all items carefully back into Ya-Ya's wallet.

Cha waited for a moment and then the solid oak doors

opened, displaying a beautiful Dominican woman with long flowing hair, a curvy shape, and smooth olive skin. She was clad in a long-sleeve, fire red sheer robe with chandelle feathers and silver tinsel. Maria held a martini in her hand and stared at Cha, asking, "And who the fuck is you?"

Cha smirked. "The bitch that is fuckin' your husband."

Maria sighed. "Who's not!"

"Can I come in?" Cha asked.

"Whatever," Maria returned, gesturing listlessly.

Cha stepped into the well-furnished apartment. She looked around and took in the polished hardwood floors and Italian décor exhibiting peach-colored walls, along with statues, marble-top tables, and a large Persian rug, which made the room very stylish. Cha was impressed. Maria had just as good taste as she.

"You want a drink?" Maria asked.

"Yes, I'll take one."

Maria quickly sized up Cha, and she was impressed. Cha stood in front of Maria with a figure just as curvy as hers and sensuous hair, wearing a short skirt, halter top, and open-toe shoes.

"At least my husband got good taste," Maria said while walking toward the small bar.

Maria began making Cha's martini. Cha took a seat on one of the stylish sofas that decorated the room. Maria walked over to Cha with her drink.

"So, how long have you been fuckin' Ya-Ya?" Maria asked.

"A few weeks now."

Maria chuckled.

"You seem cool wit' this. . . . Why?" Cha asked, a little baffled.

"Listen, sweetie, I stopped giving a fuck about who Ya-Ya put his dick into years ago. As long as that muthafucka keeps me in jewels and Gucci, and keeps cash in my hand, he can fuck the Queen of England and I wouldn't care. I get mines, too, so let's just say we're even," Maria proclaimed.

Maria then stared at Cha. She noticed the jewelry around her neck and the rings and bracelet. Cha was looking dazzling, and Maria knew that it was probably from her husband's money.

"I'm curious, though, where did he meet you?" Maria asked.

"The Pink Pussy in the Bronx."

"Fuckin' pathetic," Maria muttered.

"Excuse me. . . ." Cha questioned with a raised eyebrow.

"My husband . . . he never knew how to keep his dick in his pants, and if it wasn't for his wealth, I would have left the muthafucka. You must have definitely put it on him for him to buy you some shit like that," Maria said.

"His guilt, I guess," Cha said.

Maria chuckled. "Please, you give that nigga some good piece of pussy and he'll splurge on you. I got the muthafucka to marry me," Maria mentioned with a devilish grin, showing Cha the 14-karat white gold engagement ring that cost ten grand.

Cha took a sip from her martini.

"So what brings you to my door? He hit you, beat you, or dissed you for the next bitch?"

"I was just curious," Cha responded.

Maria took a sip from her martini. "You got heart. I know my husband been with plenty bitches and you're the first to ever show up at my front door."

"Well, I'm a different type of bitch," Cha said.

Maria smiled. "Well, cheers to that."

Maria raised her glass in the air and then downed her drink quickly. She then strutted over to the bar to mix her umpteenth drink for the afternoon.

Cha stared at Maria. She was just too comfortable with the situation. Cha didn't expect this type of attitude to come from Maria. But it was whatever. Maria was in her early forties and carried an indifferent attitude toward her husband's infidelity. She was too tipsy most times to care or was too busy fucking the next young nigga to bother.

Maria fixed her drink and looked over at Cha. She then said in a blunt and sudden change of tone, "Look, bitch, if you came here thinking that you gonna knock a bitch out the box and have me replaced, then you're barking up the wrong fuckin' tree. I've been with Ya-Ya for over twenty years now, and my name is on too much shit for that nigga to divorce me about anything or have a bitch try to come and take what's mine."

"Relax, I'm not trying to steal your husband away from you. I was just fuckin' him," Cha spat back.

"As long as we have that understanding, then we're good. So why are you here?"

"I just need some questions answered," Cha mentioned.

"About what?"

Cha took a sip of her martini. She took in a deep breath and asked, "Do you remember a guy named Madison?"

"Madison." Maria smiled. "You mean from Newark?" she then asked.

Cha nodded.

"How can I forget? Damn, it's been such a long time since I've heard his name," Maria mentioned.

She took another sip from her glass and walked toward the window. She peered out the large bay windows with a picturesque view of Central Park and the city. Her gaze held on a few pigeons flying from one perch to another. She then turned to Cha and stated, "It's been a very long time now. Why did you ask about him? You kin?"

"You can say that," Cha answered.

"What you want to know, young lady? I mean, it's been twenty years now since his murder," Maria said.

"I just want some questions answered. I want to know why he was murdered."

"It was over love, sweetie," Maria informed.

She then took a seat and was happy to oblige Cha's curiousness about her father's death. The martinis were flowing through her system and the love lost for her husband made Maria like Google.com.

"Love?" Cha questioned.

"Madison and I were having an affair. Oh, and he was so good and such a gangsta and a gentleman, unlike my fuckin' husband. The way that man used to touch me and fuck me made a bitch go wild. I was in love with him. But of course we had to keep our affair a secret. I was married to Ya-Ya and he was married to Evelyn. That bitch didn't deserve him. He was too good for her," Maria proclaimed.

Cha kept her calm and was nonchalant with Maria's statement about her mother.

Maria continued, "Our affair went on for years. My husband would be out whoring with his bitches and I had Madison. Yeah, I shared him with Evelyn, but I was content with that."

Maria took another sip from her glass, and when she noticed Cha's glass was emptied, she asked, "Would you like another one? There's plenty to go around."

"No, I'm good."

Maria shrugged and took another sip.

"But with Madison, it got to the point where I loved that man so much that it showed when I was around him. I couldn't be subtle about it anymore. When a woman is in love, sweetie, she'll risk even her marriage to be with that person. Ya-Ya became enraged when he found out about our affair. I begged him not to do anything stupid, but with his temper, there's no talking to him. The night I found out he murdered Madison, I never cried so hard. I was also two months' pregnant."

Maria took another sip of her martini.

"So you was pregnant with Zulu?" Cha questioned.

"Yes. But it wasn't Ya-Ya's baby. It was Madison's," Maria informed Cha.

"Excuse me?" Cha asked with a baffled and disturbed gaze.

"It was Madison's baby. Ya-Ya would be so busy out fucking and splurging with his whores that he rarely took interest in me like Madison did. But after his death, I told Ya-Ya about the baby and he never questioned about him being the father."

"So you mean to tell me that Zulu is Madison's son," Cha sputtered.

Maria nodded.

Suddenly, Cha's stomach began to churn and tears couldn't help but escape from her eyes. The news of her fucking her brother was just too overwhelming. She felt dizzy and sick.

"You okay, sweetie?" Maria asked.

"I need to use your bathroom."

"Down the hall, second door to your right," Maria pointed out.

Cha bolted for the bathroom, feeling the urge to throw up. She made a beeline for the toilet, dropped to her knees, stuck her head in the bowl, and hurled out chunks into the toilet. She lingered there for a moment, trying to get her head right, but the thoughts of Zulu being Madison's son and how she fucked him the other night were very traumatizing.

Maria knocked on the door and asked, "You okay, sweetie? You need a drink?"

"I'll be out in a minute."

Cha collected herself. She splashed some water on her face, took a deep breath, and walked out the bathroom. Maria was standing there.

"Is something wrong?" Maria asked.

"Everything is so fuckin' wrong," Cha returned.

Maria then looked at Cha very closely. She then asked, "What was your relationship with Madison again?"

Cha stood quiet.

Maria continued with, " 'Cuz you know he had a family, and after his death Evelyn and her child left Newark in a rush."

"He was someone close to me," Cha informed her.

Maria stepped closer to Cha. She studied her features and then it suddenly came to her. The recognition was suddenly there. "Ohmygod! It's you . . . you changed so much. Ohmygod. You look just like your father. But how . . . ?"

Maria was stunned by Cha's changes. All she could do was look and be baffled.

With a smile and chuckle, Maria said, "And you were fuckin' my husband."

After the shocking news Cha got, she went home. She needed a shower and wanted to get her mind right. She entered her dark apartment and switched on the lights. She was shocked by David sitting on her couch.

"What the fuck!" Cha blurted.

David's face was bandaged and he looked a mess. He stood up quickly and appeared edgy.

"Cha, you gotta help me," he pleaded.

"How the fuck did you get into my apartment?" Cha asked.

"I had a key made behind your back," he informed.

"You did what!?" Cha shouted.

"Cha, I'm in trouble."

"Fuck you, David. I'm tired of your shit! Get the fuck out my house now!" Cha screamed.

"I can't. . . . Some niggas are after me. They tried to kill me earlier," David mentioned.

"Too fuckin' bad," Cha retorted.

"Cha, I fought that nigga for you 'cuz I'm in love with you. And this is how you gonna do me?"

"David, I didn't ask you to fight with him. I said chill . . . but you're dumb, and too emotional, like a bitch," Cha stated.

"I'm a bitch, huh!" David spat back.

Cha noticed that he was slowly reaching for something under his shirt. So she thought quickly. She saw the fire in his eyes.

"David, look, the only reason I'm treating you like this, is 'cuz I'm stressed. I admit, I do have some feelings for you, but the situation that I'm in won't allow for you and me to be together," she lied with ease.

"What situation is that?" he asked.

"Ya-Ya."

"You gotta tell that nigga to chill. I ain't mean to get his son locked up. Now this nigga got a hit on my head," David said.

"It's spilled milk now. Ya-Ya's a fool and there ain't no talking to him. He murdered my father, David," Cha informed him, bringing him into the loop.

David showed a stunned look.

"What? Why?"

"It doesn't matter why. He killed my father twenty years

ago over some pussy. And I want him gone. Are you willing to make that happen for me?" she asked.

David looked somewhat reluctant. But she had his heart, and he was willing to do anything for her.

"What you need from me, Cha?"

Cha devised a plan. She figured she could kill two birds with one stone. She knew that David was desperate to do anything.

"This shit ends tonight," Cha said.

Cha had left Ya-Ya a mocking text message.

> Nigga, I just spoke to ya wife and she told me all your fuckin' business and I told her all ours. Nigga, don't you ever put ya fuckin' hands on me again. But you gonna get yours. Peace, you fuckin' killer.

Ten minutes after the message was sent, Ya-Ya called her phone.

"Bitch, I warned you. . . . Now you bring my family into this? I'm gonna see you, Cha, bet on that," Ya-Ya sternly warned.

"Definitely see me, nigga," Cha retorted.

"I told you, Cha, don't fuck wit' me!" Ya-Ya screamed into the phone.

"You a murderer and I hate everything about you," Cha exclaimed.

"Yeah, I'm gonna be a murderer a'ight, when I see you, you're a dead bitch."

"Nigga, come see me now," Cha dared him.

Cha gave Ya-Ya her real address. She wasn't scared. She wanted her father's death vindicated. She was ready to stare the devil in the face and confront him—even if it meant causing disturbance in her own home.

After she hung up, Cha's heart raced. She knew Ya-Ya wasn't coming to talk it out. He might bust into her home with guns blazing. She checked her .38 and then the .22; her clips were full. Now all she had to do was wait for Ya-Ya's arrival.

It was after midnight. Cha sat in the dark with a .38 in hand. She tried to ease her nerves, but she kept thinking about how many ways her plan could go wrong. It'd been more than an hour since she'd spoken to Ya-Ya. She wondered if Ya-Ya was still coming to confront her. But he was unpredictable.

Cha's apartment was still and hushed. It was getting late and Cha was becoming tired. She stood up and peered out her living room window. Cha became stunned when she noticed Ya-Ya's truck parked across the street. He was there, *but for how long?* Cha thought. She turned to get her gun from the couch, but shockingly Ya-Ya had kicked her door in and came charging with a .45 in his hand.

"Where you at, bitch?!" he screamed.

The room was dark, making it hard for Ya-Ya to see anything. His eyes quickly scanned the room searching for his victim. Cha remained low and hid behind the couch, her breathing soft and her mind racing.

"You wanna fuck with me, bitch! I'm about to put some hot ones in that pretty ass of yours," Ya-Ya exclaimed, slowly walking around the room. "You go to my home and you involved my wife! Bitch, you must be fuckin' crazy!" Ya-Ya continued.

Ya-Ya stared at the couch, knowing Cha had to be hiding behind it. He approached slowly, his gun trained at the furniture. He was ready to take her head off. He smiled and moved near.

"I know you're hiding behind the couch. . . . Come meet death face to face, bitch," he threatened.

When Ya-Ya took another step closer, Cha screamed out, "David!"

Unexpectedly, David loomed from the shadows of a back room. He had a .45 aimed at Ya-Ya.

"Get the fuck away from her!" he shouted.

Ya-Ya quickly turned. He was ready to shoot. But David fired first, and surprisingly nothing happened but dry fire. Both men looked stunned. But Ya-Ya quickly knew David's mistake.

"Check the safety, bitch," he informed, before raising his gun and shooting David in the shoulder.

David flew back and landed on his side. Cha hurriedly emerged from her hiding place and viciously struck Ya-Ya with a lamp across his face. Ya-Ya fell back and then stumbled over some furniture. Cha ran up to him and struck him a second time. The lamp smashed against his temple and the gun dropped with Ya-Ya hitting the ground. Cha picked up his gun and had it trained at the fallen Ya-Ya. He glared up at her and taunted, "Bitch, what you gonna do with that? You probably don't know how to use it."

Cha smirked. She then surprisingly pointed the gun at David. He looked up at her with a worried gaze. "Cha, what you doing?"

She fired, shooting David in the head.

"Bitch, you crazy!" Ya-Ya shouted. He was shocked and underestimated Cha.

"What were you saying?" she mocked.

"You just killed your man," Ya-Ya exclaimed.

"No, I didn't. You just did. You came into my apartment and went wild, killing David, and then you tried to kill me," she said.

Ya-Ya knew he was being set up.

"My father taught me how to shoot a gun a long time ago. He was teaching me everything I needed to know about the streets, until you murdered him," Cha let known.

"Who was your daddy, bitch, that I supposedly killed? I killed a lot of people over the years," Ya-Ya replied with no remorse.

"You're a cold-hearted sonofabitch. But my father was Madison," Cha stated.

Ya-Ya instantly knew the name. But he became even more baffled.

"Fuckin' impossible. . . . Madison can't be your father. He only had one child, and it wasn't a daughter. He had a . . ."

Suddenly, it registered to Ya-Ya. His eyes grew wide with shock. He studied Cha's features closely. He wanted to be in denial, but the truth was staring him right in the face.

"Lil' Chase . . . nah, it can't be," he questioned.

"In the flesh, nigga."

"You mean . . ." Ya-Ya felt sick and wanted to throw up. He just found out that Cha was born a man. She or he was kinfolk to Madison. It made Ya-Ya even more disturbed to think how many times he done fucked her, or him.

"You sick fuckin' bitch!" he screamed.

"It's amazing what thirty thousand dollars and a good surgeon can transform you into. I've been a woman for five years now . . . and as you know personally, it's all real and good from head to toe," Cha stated.

"Fuck you, freak bitch!"

Ya-Ya wanted to jump up and strangle Cha where she stood. He wanted to see her life slowly drain from her eyes with his hands clutched around her neck. But Cha kept him at bay with the gun.

"Yeah, you loved it," Cha mocked.

"I'm gonna enjoy killing you even more," Ya-Ya threatened.

"You killed my father and you ruined my mother. I sat and watched niggas like you fuck her, abuse her, and then throw her away like she was a piece of shit . . . like she was garbage on the streets. Niggas like you care nothing about a woman, but use her for your own personal gain, and do nothing but spread lies and disease. Year after year, I saw my mother's condition worsen, because of muthafuckas like you. And I couldn't do shit to help, I was just a young nigga. When I tried to help and stop niggas from hitting on my moms, I would get beat too.

"I hated to be a man. I hated my own skin, 'cuz I felt weak in it. I used to cry night after night. I wanted revenge, and the best way to get back at you niggas was to change into a woman. It was the one thing that made y'all niggas become stupid and weak over some pussy. It was the one way I could become close and vindicate my father's death and my mother's constant abuse."

"You're a sick fuckin' bitch!" Ya-Ya said.

Cha had tears streaming down her face as she expressed her anger and hatred for Ya-Ya and men just like him. She still held the gun on him.

"You ain't gonna get away with this, you tranny bitch!"

"You kicked in my door, shot David dead, and came at me with this gun, which also has your prints on it. You've been stalking me. We've been seen with each other around town and at the club. You purchased nice things for me with your credit cards. But I got tired of you, you're violent, so I tried to break it off. You wouldn't allow it, and you threatened me. So it brings you here to my place, where you saw David and shot him in a rage of jealousy. And me, I was just trying to defend myself. You also have many priors, and have a violent past. . . . Need I go on?" Cha proclaimed.

The look Ya-Ya showed said that he was defeated and outsmarted.

Cha continued with, "And you wanna know something about your son, Zulu . . . you're gonna love this, Ya-Ya, 'cuz I find it hilarious. Zulu wasn't even your son. He was Madison's . . . my fuckin' brother."

Ya-Ya had heard enough. He scanned the room for any

kind of weapon to attack Cha with. He noticed David's gun nearby. He rushed for it, but before he could get his hands on it, Cha shot him once in the chest. Ya-Ya fell back, clutching his chest. Cha walked up to him and stood over him.

With tears still falling from her eyes, she uttered, "I hope you burn in hell."

She stood and watched the life drain slowly from Ya-Ya's eyes. His breathing slowed and his body became still. He was soon dead. Cha knew that she had to quickly clean up. She hid David's gun, and when the cops came rushing into her apartment, Cha was curled against the corner crying her eyes out. She looked like the victim, and cops believed her story. She gave her testimony of what happened and there was no further investigation.

But after Ya-Ya's death, Cha was in a state of depression. Zulu was still locked up and the fact that she had fucked her brother made her skin itch. But her life had always been in turmoil and there was still a secret about Cha that only she herself knew—but if you got close enough, it could also kill. She was wild and reckless and Cha knew that she was living on borrowed time. She felt that her own death was near. She knew her past would catch up with her sometime soon.

A week after she murdered Ya-Ya, Cha's secret of being a man was still a secret. She hadn't danced at the club and wanted to quit. She felt lost now that Ya-Ya and David were dead. Cha took a deep breath and decided to do the daring. She got dressed in an eye-catching Lycra tube dress, with a rhinestone buckle, sexy open back, and revealing cowl front. She put on a pair of stiletto sandals that exposed her pedicure. Her hair and makeup were flawless. She got into her Benz and drove to the Bronx. She was determined that it would be her last night at the Pink Pussy.

Cha parked her Benz and moved through security with ease. Soon all eyes were on her. Word had gotten out about the fatal incident with Ya-Ya and David. Some looked at Cha as fault but didn't confront her. Cha walked through the loud and busy club like a diva ignoring everyone around her. Jamie Foxx's "Blame It" was blaring in her ear. She asked for Ely and was told that he was in his office.

Cha knocked.

"Come in," Ely shouted.

Cha walked in. Ely turned and was stunned. Cha looked amazing.

"How you been?" he asked.

"I had better days," she replied.

"So . . . what brings you back?" he asked.

"I quit."

"Why? You're my best dancer, Cha. I like you. What happened with David and that drug dealer, it was self-defense, right?"

"Ely, I have my reasons and there's something you need to know about me," she started.

"That you're a bitch," Ely joked.

Cha sighed. She walked closer. She just wanted to expose her truth to Ely. There was no reason to dance around it. She said to herself, no more lies.

"Ely, you need to really know . . . that I was born named Chase instead of Cha," she informed.

Ely looked confused. "Chase?" he inquired.

"You figure it out."

It suddenly came to him. "You're a . . ."

She nodded.

Cha just walked out of his office, leaving Ely stunned and speechless. Cha went to the changing room. She wanted to clear out her locker and be gone from the Pink Pussy for good.

The changing room was quiet, with the music being heard from the floor room. Cha sat in front of her locker. She began to cry. There was so much confusion, deceit, and death in her life. Everything hit her at once like a brick wall. She thought that killing Ya-Ya and finally avenging her father's death would make her feel better, but it didn't. She thought about David and his naiveness and ignorance. She felt that David was a threat by his stalking and wild emotions. Cha knew that killing David to set up Ya-Ya made her just as guilty as her father's killer. She could never justify her actions. David was just a pawn in her web.

Cha said to herself, *The lies stop now.*

She sat, pondering her life; her tears flowed down her cheeks. She was still, her gaze transfixed on the locker in front of her. It was like she was in her own little world—with everything around her nonexistent.

Cha took a deep breath and felt a sudden presence behind her. She knew it was a foe coming back to take out her own vengeance against her. Cha sat still. She didn't even bother to turn around and see the face of her enemy. For once, Cha felt some ease in her life.

"You gonna kill me here?" Cha asked, having no fear in her tone.

"I told you I would be back wit' sumthin' for ya ass, Cha," Bubbles exclaimed.

She stood behind Cha, with tears trickling down her face, and a chromed .357 in her hand. It was aimed at Cha's back.

"You ruined my life, bitch!" Bubbles added.

"I ruined many lives, Bubbles. It's nothin' new."

"You had to go and fuck Christopher. He was my fiancé. I loved him!" Bubbles screamed. "And now 'cuz of ya trifling ho ass, I got HIV."

Cha knew she had the disease. But she didn't care. She thought if a nigga wanted to be trifling and fuck with her, especially without a condom, then they deserved what they got. And Christopher, like so many other men in Cha's life, had made that same foolish mistake.

"I'm sorry, Bubbles," Cha apologized.

"Ya sorry, bitch . . . you know what you did to me!"

"Your fiancé is as much to blame," Cha said.

"I know . . . that's why I shot his ass dead," Bubbles confessed.

"Look, Bubbles, you do what you gotta do . . . but if you expect me to beg for my life, then it ain't happening. Chris came at me, and we fucked. He the one that should have protected himself. But like men, when it comes to pussy, they don't give a fuck who they're fucking or who they hurt. They just give a fuck about a nut," Cha declared.

"You're a sick bitch that needs to be put down."

"Then put me down," Cha said in a somewhat importunate voice.

Cha closed her eyes and was ready for the blow to hit her. Her tears continued to flow, but she wasn't scared to die. She felt that there was no reason for her to live. Bubbles clutched the gun tighter and stepped closer to Cha. She was dying.

But Bubbles hesitated.

"Bitch, just do it already!" Cha shouted.

The gun fired. Bubbles just stood there with the smoking gun still in her hand. She had shot Cha in the back of the head and her body dropped with a thud to the floor. A few people heard the gunfire and rushed in. A few strippers screamed and ran to get Ely.

Cha's body lay contorted and still. Ironically, like her father, she'd suffered the same fate.

# Kandy Girlz

NICHELLE WALKER

# Prologue

## Kandy Girlz Don't Cry

*August 28, 2008*

$\mathcal{M}$y flight took forever to get back into New York from London. I was so ready to lie down in my own bed I broke my neck running through the airport. My life became hectic once my modeling agency, The Kandy Girlz, took over the scene. I stayed involved in everything and hustled any- and everybody I needed to. Between my meetings and staying in the mix, I rarely had time for myself. I jumped into my Aston Martin and headed straight to my estate in New Rochelle.

I'm not complaining about being busy. It felt good having Money, Power, and Respect! Everybody who was somebody knew my name. I got whatever I wanted when I wanted it. I branded myself. I went from being a nobody to being that bitch everybody loved to hate. Even my haters could not deny my mean-ass swag. I was living the life every bitch craved and chased after. I branded The Kandy Girlz and hustled us to the top. Bitches begged me to be a part of my team because we were the only one getting that paper.

I made sure I built a solid team of fly exotic bitches from all over the world. I knew the game needed something new and I gave it to them. Life was good for me. I even had a man in my life, which I thought would never happen. I promised myself I would stay single and trick until my pussy dried up. I still can't believe DJ took me by surprised. I wasn't looking for love when we hooked up. I told him I just wanted to fuck and keep it moving, but he put it on me so good I had to double back.

DJ had me open. His long dick, good looks, and multi-million dollar contract with the NBA were all too tasty. DJ was tall and handsome, his dark skin stayed smooth, and he had body for days. He was definitely a keeper, but what I liked most about him was his respectful ways. I had never experienced a man like him before. DJ made me feel special. He always made me feel like a woman. I tried to fight my feelings for him but I fell in love with him rather quickly. The feeling he gave me was overwhelming, I had never been touched, kissed, loved, caressed, or acknowledged by a man this way before.

Whenever DJ needed me, I'd stop whatever I was doing for him. I played my position with him well. I cooked all his meals, fucked his brains out, and sucked his dick off until he blacked out on the regular. DJ was a freak, so I let my friend Vanilla break him off from time to time. I was a G; I didn't give a fuck.

When I pulled into my gates, my sleep started kicking in. I just wanted to lie down. I opened my door and threw all my suitcases on the floor. I wasn't unpacking anything until the morning.

"I guess my boo is here," I told myself, because DJ had the music so loud I heard it in the front room. When I got closer to my master bedroom, I thought I heard a woman moaning. *That better be on the damn CD.* DJ had his Lil' Wayne CD up loud, but I knew that was a real woman's voice. DJ was fucking another bitch in my house. I swung open the door and flipped on the lights like I was Joey Greco.

"What the fuck?" I yelled as my heart dropped outta my chest onto the floor.

"Kandy," DJ yelled, surprised to see me. I was ready to draw blood. I pulled the covers back so I could see the bitch's face. I wasn't even surprised to see Vanilla. I been at this place with her before. Tricks never change.

"Kandy, I'm sorry. Please don't hurt me," she said, begging me for mercy. This was my fault; I let this confused bitch in my bed. She knew she didn't have my permission to be in bed with DJ today.

I looked at DJ. I was disappointed in him, and I couldn't believe I fell for all his lies. "So is this what we on now?" I asked him.

"Kandy, come on now. Why you tripping?"

"Tripping? Nigga, you just fucked this bitch in my bed."

DJ sat there acting like I was overreacting. "Bitch, get your shit and get the fuck out, and if I see you again, I'ma kill your ass," I said to the back of her head because she was hauling ass.

I stood there looking at DJ. I knew I should have never fell for the game.

"Kandy, don't act like we ain't fucked her before. I thought it was cool. Shit, you been gone two weeks."

"Would it be cool for me to fuck another man?"

"That's different. I got needs."

"So, you fucking any other chicks I need to know about?" DJ's ass musta got confused because I opened my bed up occasionally.

DJ looked at me. "Kandy, I have needs, so yes, when you're gone for long periods of time I fuck."

My heart completely stopped when he said that. I had no clue—everything had been so perfect between DJ and me. "Who else you sleep with at my agency?"

"Man, I ain't going there, Kandy."

"Okay," I said as I undressed myself and got into the shower. My feelings were hurt because I thought he was the one. *Dusty-ass nigga.* DJ shoulda checked my history before he tried to play me. I knew the game and I played it very well. DJ stepped into the shower behind me, kissed me on the forehead, and whispered he loved me in my ear. I wanted to break down and cry because I really did love him. However, I'd die before I gave him the satisfaction of thinking he'd hurt me. I sucked it up and smiled at him. *I'm gonna get you back,* I thought. *Kandy Girlz don't cry, we get even.*

# 1

## The Day My Father Died

*June 13, 2006*

*L*ife's a bitch. It's full of twists, turns, regrets, and emotions. Emotions are very tricky; they control what you think, how you feel, and what you do. I stopped dealing with emotions after my parents died. Why care about something or someone when at any time they can be taken away from you? After my father died it made me realize that nothing in this world is promised to you. No matter how great of a person you are you still end up getting fucked by emotions. I was a good girl growing up; I did all the right things and respected my parents. I followed all the rules. Well, most of the time I did. I was an honor student. At sixteen I finished high school, and secured me a first-class ticket into New York University.

Life was good for me growing up. Kane, my father, ran the whole South Side of New York. Money wasn't a thing for us. I definitely was spoiled and shielded from what it meant to be poor and desperate. My father had everything—fast money, cars, clothes, jewels—he was living the life and handed it all down to me.

I had it all—Gucci, Prada, Marc Jacobs, Kate Spade. I rocked all the flyest shit. I was a high-priced label whore, and whatever I wanted I got it. I only went to the hood to collect payments with my father. Other than that you couldn't pay me to mingle with hood bitches. I was above them hating ghetto roaches; they never liked me because I always looked like I just jumped off the pages of *Elle* magazine. I was fair skinned; my cocoa brown complexion was smooth like butter. I looked like my mother's twin; I took after her Coke bottle shape and her slanted light brown eyes. Some people thought I was mixed with Asian because my eyes were slanted and my hair was long and black.

Plenty of people would have killed to walk a mile in my shoes because I had it all. The funny thing about life, it sometimes fucks you. One day I had it all and the next day I was sleeping on the street homeless and broke. I woke up one morning and I was living in the real world. My parents were murdered and left me struggling trying to figure shit out. When my father died, I lost the money, power, and respect. The only option I was given was to move into a nasty ghetto group home in Queens. *I wasn't going back to live with the same bitches I couldn't stand.*

The first night I slept on the streets I lost all my dignity. I only had twenty dollars to my name. I couldn't believe I was poor. I sat up all night praying for God to wake me from the bad dream I was having. I knew I had to spend my twenty dollars wisely so I ate off the dollar menu at McDonald's. I always ordered one thing to budget my money, but this day I was hungrier than normal. I stepped into McDonald's and ordered me a double cheeseburger and a value fry. Once I paid for my meal I walked to the bathroom to freshen myself up.

"Kandy," I overheard as I left the bathroom.

I didn't want to turn around. I had an image, and people seeing me like this would be devastating. I kept on walking, trying to ignore them.

"Kandy," he insisted as he pulled the back of my coat.

I turned around and got embarrassed. *Fuck,* I thought. Andre was one of my dad's old workers. "Hey," I said, and turned back around trying to run off.

"What's up with you? Where you been—are you good?"

"Yeah, I'm good," I lied; I didn't want anybody to feel like I needed them.

"You sure? You know your dad was my nigga. If you need something you know I got you."

I wanted to say *I need you to save me,* but I couldn't fix my mouth to say it. "No, I'm good."

"Where you staying?" he asked.

"You ask a lot of damn questions."

"Na'll ma, I'm just saying I can drop you off."

"No, thank you. I don't know you like that." Andre worked with my dad daily. He used to give me the eye all the time, but the way I was looking I knew he wasn't checking me out.

"Come on, Kandy, don't front for me. I know you got pride and shit, but if you need a nigga tell me."

I looked out the window. The wind was blowing extra hard and I didn't want to be out in the cold another night.

"Well, you can get me a room. I really don't feel like going all the way back to Jersey."

"A'ight, ma," he said. I grabbed my food and followed him to his BMW. Andre opened his car door for me and I got in. His butter soft leather seats felt so good. I hadn't been around luxury in so long I forgot how good it felt. Andre got us a room at the Millennium in Times Square. When I got into the room I wanted to run around screaming, but I kept my cool. "I want to take a bath," I told him.

"Cool, ma, do you."

I hadn't taken a bath in weeks; I ran the water as hot as I could stand it to wash all the filth from my skin. I soaked in the tub for hours until Andre knock on the door and asked me was I still alive. I got out, washed my hair in the sink, and dried it with the blow dyer. I lotioned my skin with the lotion the hotel had, put on a robe, and came out.

"Damn, shorty, I thought you drowned."

"No, I just wanted to relax." I laughed.

Andre talked to me for hours about everything, but he failed to mention he had a wife and three kids. I didn't give a fuck about his wife; I needed somebody to take care of me. Andre was a looker, too; he was fine like Morris Chestnut and had body for days. My momma always told me pussy pays and I was finna find out. Andre kept on smiling at me; I knew what he wanted from me.

Andre was ten years senior to my seventeen, *but age ain't nothing but a number.* I was willing to do whatever I had to to get the good life back. I missed the finer things in life and if I had to suck and fuck him all night, that's what I was doing.

Andre reached in and kissed me and I started shaking. I had never had sex. I was nervous.

"Don't be scared, momma, I got you. I'ma take care of you."

"Okay," I said as I closed my eyes and let Andre have his way with me.

Andre sexed me all night and after a while it felt pretty good. When we got ready to leave he told me that he was going to take care of me. That I wouldn't want for nothing. That he would make sure I had whatever I wanted. *I'm your new daddy.* He smiled at me. I smiled back at him. I knew the game already, and I was ready to play it.

# 2

## Kept Woman

*A*ndre put me up in an apartment in New York City; I had the best of everything. He showered me with money, clothes, and a little bit of his time. Andre wasn't good at living a double life; he would constantly blow me off for his troll of a wife. I wouldn't care about that if he wasn't so controlling over my life. Andre wanted me on lockdown and waiting at his beck and call. I couldn't really trip. I knew the deal when I got with him. I just wanted him to be fair with the dick and his time. Andre was obsessed with me. He had me tracked like he was the CIA. I couldn't take a piss without him sending a search party.

Andre promised me that he would take me out of town to ATL for a vacation, but of course I didn't see or hear from him. Andre thought he had me open, but I knew how to pimp him for some time. I got dressed and went out with my friend Vanilla. Vanilla stayed two floors under me and Andre hated her. After I tricked up on me some drinks I made my way back home ready to lie down. My apartment was dark when I got back home. I hated to come home to darkness. I threw down my keys and removed my coat and looked through my mail. Once I flicked on the lights I saw Andre was waiting on me with an angry look on his face.

"Where have you been?" Andre yelled. I just looked at him, took off my shoes, and entered my living room. I knew he would be here; he always finds a way to get out if I carry my ass out the house.

"Did you hear me, Kandy? I told your ass about ignoring me."

Andre and I had been fucking around for a year now and he still got confused about my position with him. *Nigga, I'm not your bitch. I'm your kept woman. Get it right.* I cut my light brown eyes at him as hard as I could. *This nigga gotta lot of nerve,* his ass had been missing in action for three days. "I was minding my fucking business. Don't be coming up in here asking me questions when I was supposed to see you seventy-two hours ago," I yelled as I dropped down my Marc Jacobs bag on the table and turned on the TV.

"I know you were out with that stank."

"Is there a problem?" I asked him, because I didn't like the face he was giving me.

"It's eleven o'clock! Where the fuck you been? I've been waiting on you since six. I told yo ass about not answering my calls, didn't I?" Andre got up out of his chair and walked closer to me. I just rolled my eyes at him and sucked my teeth. I was sick and tired of Andre and all of his bullshit.

"Andre, save that drama for your wife. We just fuck. So if you want to fuck then go and get in the bed." Andre felt that because he was providing me with a roof over my head and ends in my pocket he could tell me what to do.

"Kandy, why you tripping? You know a nigga got feelings for you. You know you're the one that makes me happy. I've given you the best just like your dad, right?"

I looked at Andre. My dad didn't expect pussy every time he did something for me. I hated when Andre compared himself to my dad; he could never compare to Kane. All Andre was good at was trying to kick game, but my dad always told me the truth about men. He always told me, *It's a dirty game, baby girl*.

"So where you coming from again?"

"What," I snapped back.

"Stop playing games with me, Kandy."

"You are a married man, Andre. You come and go as you please, stand me up any time that you want. Why are you here again?"

"Come on, you know I want to be with you and stay here more. But you knew I had a wife." I never believed one word Andre said to me. My dad told me never to believe any words from a man who was cheating on his wife.

"Andre, please. You seem to get over here every time I leave the house just fine." Andre was not slick, nor was I dumb. I knew he had the doorman watching my every move.

"I came because I wanted to see you."

*More like worried I'm out giving my pussy away.* "So what's up? I know you got to get back home to your wife, so are we fucking or what?"

"I don't like you talking like that." Andre came over to me

and rubbed my face. I wasn't falling in love with a married man so I wore my heart on my sleeve. Andre was a temporary thing for me. I was getting me a new player so I could move on.

Andre pulled off my shirt and unsnapped my bra, unbuckled my pants, and advised me to remove them. I couldn't deny his dick. It was long, thick, and he knew how to work it. Well, at least he had me fooled since he was my first. Andre pulled off his pants, and his dick was standing at attention. I licked my lips and looked into his eyes. "What you want me to do to him?"

"You know what I want!"

"Do I look like a motherfucking mind reader to you?"

Andre smiled. He liked to get bossed around by me. "I want you to touch it."

"Oh, you just want me to touch it?" I grabbed his dick and rubbed it while I swirled my tongue around its thick head. "Is that all you want, poppa?"

"No, I want you to take care of him like you do."

I licked his balls, tea bagging them in and outta my mouth.

"Oh, get it, girl," he moaned as he took the back of my head and forced me down on his dick. I manned up like a soldier and took him straight down without gagging. "Woo shit, girl. You the best."

I liked making Andre weak like this. This was the only time he didn't act all hard and tough.

"I love you, Kandy. I'm coming!" he yelled as he fell back and put his hand over his eyes. "Oh my God, Kandy, I trained you well."

I smiled at him. I had sucked dick a few times before him, but a man always feels better when he thinks he was your first.

After Andre recovered, he bent me over and fucked me senseless for hours. I wanted him to spend the night, but he had to leave and go home to his wife. I wanted more than what Andre was giving me. The life of a kept woman wasn't all that great.

# 3

## *Vanilla*

Outside of Vanilla, I didn't have any friends.

Vanilla was a cool bitch and I called her a wigger because she thought she was black. Vanilla was shaped like a black girl, outspoken, and vulgar. She always said what was on her mind and that was what I liked most about her. I never really bonded with females because my mother told me they were all conniving whores. My mother hated the Kandy Girlz crew I formed in high school and found a reason not to like any of the girls. Vanilla was cool peoples. I trusted her.

Andre hated her guts. He constantly said she was a whore. I guess he thought she had me turning tricks with her or something. He tried to get me to stop hanging with her but I wouldn't. She was my friend and we had kicked it tight for the last year. He was always worried about the wrong things, and I was so sick of him standing me up. He would have me cook dinner for him, then call and tell me he had to go home. So one time I invited Vanilla up to eat so we could kick it and talk shit.

"Hey, bitch," Vanilla said as she walked into my apartment like it was hers.

"Hey, girl," I said as I handed her a plate of black-eyed peas and fried chicken.

"Girl, your ass can cook. Where your man at?"

"At home with his wife," I said as I sat down with my plate.

"Girl, you stupid. Why you staying faithful to that nigga?"

"He takes care of me."

"And so can the next dick. Andre ain't the only dick in the world with money. Besides, with your looks you could trick up on a baller easy."

"I don't know about sleeping around."

"Okay, but do you think you're the only side woman Andre has?"

"No, I don't."

"Good, I just want you to smarten up. You don't have to be faithful to no nigga that's not your man."

"You right."

"Fuck yeah, I'm right. My pussy pays all my bills."

I just looked at her because she was right. I had thought about dipping out on Andre plenty of times, but my dad always told me never to bite the hand that feeds you. "Well, I plan to leave Andre once I get enough money saved up."

"And how are you gonna find a way to save money when you shop like forty going north? The only way you can get rid of Andre is get you some new dick, trick to his wife, or control him."

"I know how to play my position with Andre; I'm not in

love with him. I just feed him all that so he can keep on taking care of me. I've seen enough to know the game."

"Honey, there's a difference in playing your position and mind fucking a man. I can mind fuck a man to the point where he feels he can't live without me. That's the trick to hooking a man—fuck him mentally. Get into his head so good that he will do whatever to stay with you."

"I hear you. I'll figure it out."

"Sure you will. You're a pretty girl, but sometimes you have to use what you got to get what you want. Thanks for dinner. I have to go catch me a date. I'll talk to you later."

Vanilla got up and left, but her words stuck in my head. I was tired of Andre. He wanted to control my every move and it was beginning to be too much. I wanted to make my own rules and do what I wanted to do. Vanilla was right—I had to use what I had to get what I wanted.

# 4

## Tha Backstabbers

*A*ndre was upset with me because I hung out with Vanilla the night before; he called, forbidding me from seeing her. I told him he needed to take that shit home to his wife. I was sick of him telling me what to do. I couldn't even go out the house by myself without his friend June following me.

"Kandy, I don't want you hanging around that trick."

"Andre, please stop it. Vanilla is good peoples."

"She's a whore and she's not your friend."

"Andre, that's enough. You're not going to be here long so I want us to enjoy our time together. Okay, poppa?" I rubbed Andre's shoulder gently. "I need you inside of me," I whispered softly in his ear, reaching in and giving him a kiss on his sexy lips. I got up and popped in a video I borrowed from Vanilla. She told me Pinky was the best in the porn industry.

Andre was trying to act hard but I knew he wanted me to break him off. "Come here," I demanded as I grabbed his shirt, ripping it off of him. "Give me my dick." I knew all the spots that drove him wild.

"Oh shit, girl," Andre moaned, running his fingers through my long black hair. "I like that."

"You like that, daddy?" I repeated as I took Andre's long dick deep into my warm mouth once again. I had Andre speechless. Vanilla was the furthest thing from his mind at that point. Once I felt him flinching up, I pushed his dick as deep as I could get it so I could receive all his juices in my mouth.

"Shit, girl," Andre said, grabbing me and forcing me down on his dick. I started moving my hips to the beat of "Rock the Boat" until I rocked myself into a mind-blowing orgasm. "Damn, your dick is the best."

"The best? You say that like you had something else."

I looked at him and rolled my eyes. Andre was so jealous it wasn't funny any longer. "Andre, would you chill out? You know this your pussy."

"Do you love me, Kandy?" I hated it when he asked me that question. How in the hell do you fall in love with a married man? I mean, I'm far from stupid. I knew I needed to gas his mind up so he could keep taking care of me until I left.

"Of course I do, poppa. You're my first, my last, my everything," I said as I sat in his lap and gave him a kiss. "I need you."

"Good. I don't want you hanging with that trick."

"Andre, she's my friend so get off it." Andre looked at me

like he wanted to hit me. "What's the deal with you and her? You fucked her or something?"

"What?" Andre yelled as he got up, pushing me out of his lap.

"Did you fuck her?"

"Man," Andre said, avoiding looking me in the eyes. I couldn't believe it. I thought Vanilla was my friend, all the times we kicked it together. I just couldn't believe it. "You're lying; you're just saying that so I'll stop hanging with her. I can't believe you would stoop so low."

Andre looked at me and didn't speak; he put on his clothes and started laughing.

"What's so damn funny?"

"Nothing, man. I 'bout to leave. You want something else?"

I knew Andre was lying. He would do anything to control me. "Yeah, some money?"

Andre took out a wade of money and handed it to me. "June is going to drive you from now on."

"What?"

"You heard me. It's my way or the highway, ya dig?"

That was it—I'd had enough of Andre. "I'm leaving," I screamed at him, pulling my clothes out of the drawers. I ran and grabbed my Louis luggage and started to throw my things in the bag. "You don't own me, Andre. I'm out of here." I called up Vanilla and told her I was coming to stay with her. I had options even if I had to turn a trick or two to get my money up. I was willing to do what I had to do.

"So you're going down to stay with your friend." Andre smiled.

I ignored his ignorance; I'd had it. Andre gave me a good life and his dick was the bomb; however, he didn't own me. Andre sat there watching me pack up my things. Once I had all that I was taking I looked at him. "I never meant anything to you anyway. You love your wife and you used me. I'm tired of being used."

I opened the door to let Vanilla in. I told her to take my two roll bags and I would carry the rest. Vanilla didn't say a word; she didn't like Andre just as much as he didn't like her. I was glad this was over for me; *I came in with nothing and am leaving with a fly wardrobe so I can't complain.* Once I got halfway out the door Andre came over and looked at Vanilla. "So you gone tell her or do I need to?" Vanilla looked at me and didn't say anything.

"Tell me what?" I asked.

"Oh, the cat got your tongue now? You always got so much to say any other day," Andre yelled. Vanilla stood there like a statue. I'd never seen her lost for words. "Go ahead and tell her how you been sucking my dick off."

I bucked my eyes wide open in disbelief. "What?" I asked, trying to make sense of everything. Andre pulled out his camera phone and showed me a video of him and Vanilla getting busy. My knees went weak; I didn't know what to say. All this time I had been fighting with Andre about her she had been stabbing me in my back. I fell back against the wall and grabbed my chest. "Why?" I asked her.

"Don't trip, girl, he's not your man. He has a wife. Didn't you say you're leaving him, so why you getting mad?" My mind blacked out and before I knew it I took Vanilla's head and slammed it into the wall. It took Andre ten minutes to get me off of her. Once he calmed me down I looked over and Vanilla was gone.

"You're a dirty nigga," I yelled at him.

"You're a kept woman, right? So deal with it." Before Andre closed his mouth good I punched him, busting his lip open. I went at him throwing my fist anywhere I could land a punch. Even though I was pissed and hurt I didn't cry. How could I expect anything more from a married man? Andre started kissing me all over my body and pulled off my clothes. "I'm sorry, I'm so sorry." he cried as he went down and started licking me like he never did before. My body went numb and I drained out all of his lies. Once he was done, I just looked at him. *I'm gonna get you back,* I thought to myself. *You will pay.*

# 5

## Envy Girls

*V*anilla moved out of our building and she better be glad she did. I was still pissed off that she played me. Andre was Mr. Nice Guy after all that shit kicked off, but no matter what he did or said to me, I would never feel the same about him. The little bit of respect I had was gone and I hated him. I still played my role with him, fucked his brains out, and collected my money. My plan was to take his ass to the cleaners before I left.

I tried to trick off but Andre had me on lockdown worse than he did before this shit happened. June took me everywhere I wanted to go and the doorman tricked if I snuck out. I played a guilt trip on Andre to let me go shopping since I'd been stuck in the house. Of course he sent June to be my babysitter. June was Andre's flunky, and he did whatever Andre asked him to. I knew June liked me; he always stared at me. If he wasn't so ugly and stanky I woulda fucked him just to get back at Andre.

June tried to talk to me on the way to SoHo. I just tuned

him out. I didn't care what the hell he was talking about. "You got two hours to shop," he said to me as I got out of the car.

"Whatever, Mr. Bentley," I said, mocking him being Andre's gofer. I grabbed my Gucci hobo bag and headed to Armani Exchange. Andre only gave me six thousand dollars; sometimes he could be so cheap. After I hit the bebe store, most of my money was gone. *I need to sit down somewhere,* I thought. My feet were hurting something serious. I walked pass a little handbag store that had the flyest snakeskin hobo bag on display. *Damn, I need that in my life,* I thought.

"Excuse me, but you're gorgeous," a voice whispered to me.

I turned around and it was a woman. I wasn't surprised— women stared at me all the time. I was blessed in the looks department. "Thank you," I said as I turned back around to finish window shopping.

"You ever think about being a model?" she asked me.

I turned back around and looked at her; modeling did come across my mind from time to time. I had plenty of offers on the table for me in high school, but my dad didn't want me to take them seriously. He wanted me to get an education and not worry about anything else. I ran with a crew of girls—we called ourselves The Kandy Girlz; it was my idea to form a clique of girls to model. We did local modeling shows on the weekend. "I've done it before, a long time ago."

"I'm casting for a T-Hood music video and I want you to be in it."

*T-Hood,* I thought. I knew who T-Hood was. I heard his music on the radio. But me being a video girl, I can pass on that.

"I'm sorry, I'm not looking to be a video girl."

That video girl shit was for them ghetto roaches.

"Well, it's not a video girl, it's being a model, and you can make up to ten grand a day."

When she said ten grand a day, I thought twice about the idea. *This could be my meal ticket out,* I thought to myself. If I could get paid like that on my own I wouldn't need Andre. I didn't want to fall for the game she was kicking, though. I didn't know her from a can of paint. Growing up in New York City, the one thing I'd learned, it's full of con artists ready to take their next victim down.

"How do I know you can get me in a T-Hood video? Who are you?"

She seemed offended that I questioned who she was. She removed her glasses and I took a good look at her. She was high yellow and had strong facial features; she was pretty, though. I'm not a hater, I can give her that. She was much shorter than me, skinny, but not white girl skinny. She still had curves like Kelly Rowland. I admired her bag; it was the same one I'd been drooling over in the window.

Rocking a bag like that, it was only two options—she either had a balling man or she was getting money. Her Christian Louboutin pumps matched fiercely with her stonewashed Seven jeans. Her perfume roamed the air. It smelled really good. If she wasn't who she said she was, she was a hell of an impostor, she definitely had me fooled.

"I'm sorry, what's your name?" she asked me.

"Kandy."

"Kandy, I'm Misty," she said as she handed me a card that read ENVY GIRLS. "I own Envy Girls. Everybody who's somebody knows who I am. I cast for all the major artist videos, TV programs, BET awards—you name it, I do it. You can Google me when you get in if you like. I don't play any games."

I knew she was serious. My dad taught me how to read a person before I went to school. "How much?"

"Well, for a new girl, since you'd be a extra, I normally pay a thousand to fifteen hundred dollars. But once you get your foot in the door and people start to request you, your pay will shoot up."

I knew everything in life was negotiable; the worst a person can do is say no. "Well, the only way I'll do it, I have to be paid at least two thousand dollars." I put my poker face on so she knew I meant business. She took a look at me and smiled as the valet driver pulled up with her car. Misty was rolling slick. She had a new candy apple red Jaguar with chrome rims.

"Two grand. Well, Kandy, this is your lucky day. I know I can make a lot of money off you. The shoot is tomorrow at 6 AM, not 6:05. If you're late you're fired. I do not tolerate lateness or bullshit."

"Okay, I will be there," I said.

"On time, Kandy," she said, then gave me the address. She jumped into her car and busted a U-turn in the middle of traffic. I laughed to myself reading her plate. ENVY ME, that was cute. I was impressed with Misty. I didn't know how old she was, but I wished I owned my own company. June pulled up and blew his horn at me like he was crazy. After I got in it dawned on me that I had agreed to show up without thinking about Andre. I knew he was going to trip about it. But one thing that no-good trick Vanilla taught me is sometimes you have to use what you got to get what you want.

# 6

## Guilt Trip

*O*nce I got home I came to my senses. Andre was never going to let me go around no rappers. *He thinks I'm his second wife or some shit.* I hated living like this. I felt like a damn prisoner. I did feel ungrateful at times—any woman would have died to live like this. My home was beautiful. I had all designer furniture, two closets full of clothes, and my shoe game was sicker than a chemo patient. But I wasn't happy; what good is it to have everything but no control? You're not doing what you want to do, living your life like you want to live it—it wasn't worth it to me.

I got up and started cooking dinner for Andre so I could butter him up. I didn't know if this was going to work, but usually when I pulled my guilt trip on him I got what I wanted. I needed to make up a lie, a good lie to get me out of the house without June following me. When Andre came in I made sure I had on some small lace boy shorts and a matching cami top. My red high heels stood out just like my Chanel red lipstick. I knew if I got him open and mind fucked him it would be easier for me to get out the house unwatched.

"Hey, daddy," I said as I took off his jacket and took his hand and pushed him down into his favorite chair. "How was your day?" I asked as I got on my hands and knees and took off his shoes.

"It was good. It's much better now that I'm with you," Andre said as he ran his fingers through my hair.

"I missed you, poppa," I said, sitting down on his lap.

"Hmm, you got it smelling good up in here."

"Yeah, I cooked all your favorites tonight—greens, candy yams, pork chops, and homemade corn bread." My mom taught me how to cook; she always said the way to a man's heart was through his stomach, and good pussy.

"You must want something."

"No, I just want to make you happy, then maybe one day we could be together. You know I want to get married and have babies too." Andre hated when I talked like that; he always felt guilty and I always got what I wanted out of him. "I mean, sometimes I feel like I'm not good enough for you. Like you don't love me. I know I'm young and I'm still learning, but I just want a man of my own. I want to have a family and a husband who comes home to me every night. My dad always told me never to settle for less and I deserved to have a man love me, like he loved me. Don't you think I'm worth it? You don't feel I deserve to have your love full time?"

Andre rubbed his head. I could tell he was stressed out; when we had conversations like this it always made him uneasy. I mean, really what could he say to me? He had a wife and three kids across town plus he fucked my friend. He knew he was living foul, but he's just like any other man—they want their cake and eat it too. I could tell he was looking for something to say to me. The thing about keeping a woman doing what you want her to, you have to have mind control over her and make her believe your lies.

"You know I love you, Kandy. I know you deserve to have a full-time man, and I want to give you just that. I will be all yours one day. Shit, it's just tight at home, you know. I need to find a way to let her know I'm leaving. But it will happen sooner than you think. I need you. I don't want to lose you. You're the only reason I'm out here hustling so hard, because I want to give you the best because you deserve the best. Don't give up on me—you know that I'll do whatever for you. You never have to ask me twice for nothing, right?"

I teared up. "But I must don't make you happy because you fucked my friend. How could you hurt me like that?"

Andre didn't say nothing. He just rubbed his face with both of his big hands. I was crying hysterically. He hated to see me cry. He wiped the tears from my eyes and gave me a kiss as I laid my head on his lap. "Look, baby, I don't know what to say. I was wrong as hell. I really fucked up. I hate I hurt you like that."

"Did you love her? Did she fuck you better than me?"

"No, you're the best, I swear on my kid's life you're better than any bitch I ever fuck with. What can I do to get you to forgive me?"

I had Andre right where I wanted him. "I'm sorry, poppa, maybe I'm tripping because I miss my dad. I need to go and see his grave. I want to go in the morning, please, I just want to talk to him."

"Yeah, I can have June take you."

I rolled my eyes at him and started pouting. "See, that's what I'm talking about. I can't do nothing on my own. You don't trust me. I can't even go and see my daddy in peace. You don't treat your wife like this." I started crying crocodile tears and turning red.

Andre looked at me and grabbed me and pulled me close to him. I tried to break loose from him. "Listen to me," he yelled, trying to calm me down. "I do trust you, I need you, and you're right, I do want you to do things for yourself. I just want to make sure you get back and forth safely."

*Wow, that's a good one.* Andre was a great liar but I wasn't buying it. "Are you sure?"

"Yeah, I'm sure; I want you to be happy."

I gave Andre a hug and kissed him softly on his lips. I stared into his eyes. *Sucker-ass nigga,* I thought. I wrapped my legs around his waist and kissed him gently on his neck. "I love you," I whispered in his ear while I licked his earlobe slowly. "I ain't going nowhere. You can trust me, I'll never hurt you." Andre hugged me real close to him. He could be the fool to believe I'm not going to get him back. I'm going to make him hurt ten times worse than he did me. *I will give him a dose of his own medicine.*

# 7

## Using What I Got

*I* got up early, took a shower, washed my long hair, and blew it out. I didn't bother to curl it since hair and makeup would be at the shoot. Misty didn't tell me how long the shoot was going to be for, so I really didn't know how I was gonna pull off being gone all day. I got myself together and took the elevator down to the lobby. The doorman looked dead at me in my face. I could tell he was surprised I was heading out so early. *I know he's the one snitching on me,* I thought. It was written all over his face. He couldn't even look me straight in the eyes.

"So you gone call him when I leave?" I asked him.

"Excuse me?" he said, bucking his big eyes open.

"Don't lie, nigga, you be calling Andre and ratting on me when I leave and come back."

"Shorty, I don't know what you're talking about," he said as he looked away. He was tall and thin, and his lips were dark black, probably from him smoking too much weed. His low-cut caser was lined perfect with his mustache and beard. He was a cutie pie, but I would never talk to him for real.

"You know what I'm talking about, you a little bitch. Running and tricking like a girl. How much he paying you?"

He looked at me and I could tell he was pissed at me for calling him a bitch. "Shorty, I ain't got nothing to do with your business. That's between you and your dude, so like I said before, I don't know what you're talking about."

His cell phone was laid on the counter so I reached over and grabbed it. He jumped out of his seat trying to take it back, but I blocked him. "So you telling me I won't find Andre's number in your phone?" I went through his text messages and the first message that popped up was from Andre at three o'clock last night asking him if somebody came by. "Right, you don't know what I'm talking about, you little snitch." I looked at him. I wanted to hit him in the mouth but I knew I couldn't take him down.

He sat back and looked all salty at me. "Man, shorty, it ain't personal, it's just business."

"Business. Well, how about I offer you something else to keep your mouth closed?"

He looked at me and smiled. "What can you give me? Shit, I make good money being your lookout."

"Well, what is it that you want?" I asked him as I walked around the desk, putting my stank walk into full effect. "I'll do anything that you want me to," I said in my sexy voice.

He cracked a smile. I knew he was feeling me. I mean, I am the finest thing on this side of town. "Man, shorty, I ain't trying to die messing with you like that."

"I won't tell if you don't tell," I said as I ran my fingertips up his legs, stroking his dick through his pants. He seemed uneasy like he was scared of Andre. "So you scared of a man that bleeds like you bleed?"

"I don't know, I mean, ain't no pussy worth dying over." He repeated himself like I didn't hear him the first time.

"What you scared of, pussy? Andre, he has a wife and he does not live with me."

"I ain't scared of him."

"Then you're scared of pussy. What, you a fag or something?" I knew that would boil his blood.

"I ain't no motherfucking fag."

"Hmm, I can't tell. You scared to come take this pussy, free at that. That says to me that you're a fag."

"Man, shorty, get the fuck out of here with that bullshit. I ain't no motherfucking fag."

"Well, prove it to me, DONALD," I said as I rubbed my fingers across his name tag. "I know a few fags named Donald. It wouldn't surprise me these days."

Donald was pissed. He looked at me like he wanted to beat my ass. He got up and told me to follow him. At first I resisted. I didn't know if he was taking me off so he could kill me or what. I looked at my watch and I didn't have that much time to spare so I followed him. Donald opened the door to a cleaning closet and told me to go in. I gave him the side eye. "You go in first," I told him.

"Oh, you getting scared now." He laughed.

"Nigga, please, I just don't know you like that, you could be a murderer."

"A'ight," Donald said as he entered the closet first, and I followed him, closing the door behind me. Donald turned on the light and looked at me. "Like I said, I ain't no fucking fag, girl. I don't give a fuck about your old man. I just don't want no trouble."

"Me, either. So if you be good to me, I'll be good to you. Now come show me how much you love pussy."

Donald grabbed me and pulled me close to him. I unbuckled his pants and let his dick loose, and his dick was long and thick like Andre's. I smiled at him as I licked my lips. I got mad love for the big dicks. I got down on my knees and looked him in the eyes and licked the head of his shaft slightly, scraping it with my two front teeth. He was wiggling and moaning and I hadn't even showed him half of my skills. I circled my tongue around his pee hole, letting my saliva fall all over his shaft. I took my free hand and stroked his long dick in a steady rhythm as my tongue stroked.

"Shit, shorty." Donald kept on moaning. "Do that shit, girl."

Once I knew I had him open enough I pushed his dick deep into my mouth, bobbing my head up and down like no tomorrow. "Oh fuck, girl, I can't take it." I started swirling my tongue around his dick as I bobbed even faster, making his leg shake. "I'm about to bust, girl." I pulled him out my mouth and slapped his long dick in my face while I jerked him off. Once his juices flowed all over me he fell back to catch his breath. Donald didn't speak to me; he just sat there and stared like he was shocked I could suck a mean dick like that.

I pulled a condom out of my Marc Jacobs bag and rolled it down his dick and ordered him to sit in the chair. I straddled myself over him, slowly pushing his long dick in me inch by inch. My body cringed because he was so thick but felt so good. Donald was the second piece of dick I'd had, and he was just as good as Andre. I've been missing out sitting up there being faithful to Andre's dumb ass. I needed to fuck different people more often so I could explore my options.

"Oh my God, you got some good pussy." He moaned as I rode him like a cowgirl. The more I moved my body the louder he screamed; then he started grabbing my ass and moving me back and forward. "If I was your dude I'd lock yo ass up to *fuck*."

"You gonna keep us a secret?" I asked, winding my hips like I was in a Hula-hoop contest.

"As long as you keep doing me like this." Donald closed his eyes and started to grind his hips, pulling me down hard on him. I knew he was coming and I wanted to make sure he wasn't going to open his big mouth again. I pulled myself off him. "You're going to tell on me, I can't do this," I said, interrupting his nut.

"No," he said as he tried to pull me back down on him. "I swear on my daddy's grave. I'm not letting this pussy go, I want this pussy."

"You sure?" I asked to confirm with him. Donald nodded his head, saying yes. I slid back down on him, bouncing up and down slowly so I could bring him to the best nut he ever had. "Oh fuck, girl, I ain't telling nothing," he moaned out as he came in me.

I got up and pulled my pants back up. I knew I had Donald gamed. He sat there looking at me dazed and confused. *I got him fucked up.* I knew if I kept breaking him off he'd be the least of my worries. Donald and I exchanged numbers and I told him I'd be out until late and to make up a lie to Andre if he called. I ran back up to my place and took a quick hot bath and headed out the door ready for my close-up.

# 8

## Camera Time

*W*hen I arrived at the shoot the address Misty gave me was for an abandoned building. *This bitch sent me off,* I screamed. I started to turn back around and jump back on the train but something told me to keep going. As I got closer to the building I heard loud music so I went inside. As I came through the doors I spotted two big bodyguards at the entrance with a sign-in sheet.

"I'm here for the T-Hood video," I advised them.

"What your name?"

"Kandy Johnson."

He looked though his list and found my name with *new girl* scribbled beside it. He looked up and smiled at me. "Fresh meat," he yelled out. I looked at him and humped my shoulder at him. "They're gonna love you." He laughed. "New booty on deck," he yelled up the stairs.

I was so embarrassed. I had never been talked to like that by a man. I didn't know if he was joking or not but he was out of his mind. "What is that supposed to mean?"

"No disrespect, ma, I'm just teasing."

"Well, I didn't find it funny."

"Excuse me for having a sense of humor. It's early. Look, I'ma keep it real. I was playing, but the next man may not be. Do you know what you are doing here?"

"I'm just modeling, that's it," I said as I rolled my eyes at his fat ass.

"Let me give you a piece of advice, sweetie—this industry is full of haters, snakes, and backstabbers. The snakes pick up on the weak and clueless easily. You have to be coldhearted and ruthless if you want to take the top spot. Remember, no-body's your friend but everybody's your competition. Closed mouths don't get fed and fucking might get you a name. Sometimes it might get you a spot at the top but there's al-ways a new girl with some new pussy to take it. Enter this game at your own risk. One thing for sure, you will never make it anywhere being scared or having a stanky attitude."

I looked at him. It was a lot to take in so quickly. I didn't know what to say back to him. I knew all about hustling. My daddy always said to me, *Pimp the game, don't let it pimp you.* "Thanks, I guess." I smiled at him and followed the line up the stairs. When I made it to the top, the room was full of women. It was mad competition in the room. I didn't have time to get nervous. *It's what it is. I'ma bad bitch so I ain't worried about these hos.* When I scanned the room there were only about five girls in the room who could even try to compete with me.

Misty came over my way with a smile on her face. "You made it, and on time. I'm impressed."

"Yes, I told you I would be here."

"Good. I just need you to sign these papers and go get your hair and makeup done."

I signed all the papers and gave them back to Misty. I followed the line of girls waiting to get their hair done and wardrobe fitted. After standing around for over an hour I got irritated because the line was still long as hell. *Is this shit ever gone move,* I mumbled to myself. Finally after another fifteen minutes a tall, slim guy stuck his head out from behind the curtains and peeped at the crowd. He came out and looked through the line. "No, no, and no," he said to all the girls before me. When he approached me he stared at me, making me uncomfortable. "Hi, I'm Kandy," I said, trying to be friendly.

"Kandy." He laughed. I looked at him and smacked my lips.

"Yes, Kandy."

"Well, Kandy, I like your eyes. I'm going to push you ahead of these bitches." I cracked a smile and was glad, but the other girls got mad and started yelling and fussing. "Don't pay them bitches no mind. They ain't running nothing but their mouths."

As I walked behind the curtains I got the ugliest mean mugs I'd ever seen. I didn't give a fuck about them hood rats—half of them gutter roaches shouldn't even got selected. Most of them hos looked tore down with crusty feet, black knees, and ashy skin. *I'm here to make me some paper.* I could care less about them simple bitches getting mad at me.

I sat down in the stylist chair. I advised her I just washed my hair before I came. "Good," she responded, yanking my ponytail out. After an hour of hair and makeup I was finally done. The makeup artist did some funky type of tricks with my eyes, which made them stand out more. I looked fly as hell. *Boy, Andre is gonna die when he see this shit.* I laughed to myself.

Misty walked by and stared at me; the way she looked at me made me feel funny. I couldn't place my finger on it, but she made me feel uneasy. "You look good. I knew I chose you for a reason. You're my new money maker." She smiled.

I followed Misty into a crowded room full of smoke, men, and loud music. T-Hood was seated at the head of the table; his demeanor was laid-back and chilled. He was a lot shorter than he appeared on TV; he looked at all of us and smiled. "I see you got some new girls," he told Misty. "Shorty with the slanted eyes is right. Who is she?" he asked.

Misty looked at me and smiled. "She's fresh meat. I found her yesterday."

"I want her up top with me," T-Hood said as he got up from the table and walked off.

I was excited; I looked at Misty. "Does that mean I will get more money?" I needed to know. All bullshit was set aside for me; my paper was my main focus at that point in my life.

"Yes, come with me," she said, and I followed her to the set. "Look, Kandy, this is your time to shine. If you do well here and stand out, this could put you on."

I knew what I had to do. I wasn't nervous at all. I had money to make and moves to make. When the video director came on the shoot he started yelling for us to do this and do that. He looked at me and told me to move sexier to the music, so I did. I moved my body like I was in Jamaica at a reggae dance club. When T-Hood got on the set I towered over him with my heels on. He pulled me close to him, and the director told me to lick his ear. I did as I was told and did it well. I was determined to make it to the top spot and get this money. T-Hood and I had mad chemistry on the set. I could tell he was feeling me by the way we moved with each other. Once the director yelled cut, he pulled me close to him and asked me to come back to his dressing room. I smiled at him and nodded my head yes. *Why the hell not,* I thought. *I'm finna do me fuck Andre, I'm leaving his ass anyway.*

Once I got dressed Misty came to me and handed me a check for five grand. "Thanks," I told her.

"No problem, cutie," she said as she ran her fingers through my hair. I did not like the way Misty stared at me. As I said before, women gave me compliments all the time so I was used to that. But with Misty it was different. She looked at me like she wanted me. It was kind of creepy.

"Okay," I said, trying to break the ice because I knew I had T-Hood waiting on me. "I'm about to go; I need to get home. It's getting late."

Misty looked at me as if I was lying. She frowned and rolled her eyes. "Right."

"Excuse me, do we have a problem?"

"Look, I know where you're going and it's not my business, but if you start sleeping around with these men you will get a name for yourself."

"What!" I yelled at her. This bitch had some nerve. She didn't know me like that to be coming at me sideways. "You're right, it is not your business, so keep your little comments to yourself." I pushed by her. I didn't know if I was more embarrassed and ashamed or more mad that she got out her body. She didn't know me like that to judge me. *Fuck her ass, I can do what the fuck I want.*

# 9

## Game Time

The closer I got to T-Hood's trailer the more Misty's words stuck in my head. I wasn't trying to create a name for myself. But hell, I was grown and I could fuck who I wanted to, and as long as he was paying I could care less who thought I was wrong. That judgmental bitch knew nothing about me and I wasn't letting these hos stop me from making moves. I had been on the set for hours. Time had slipped away from me—it was already eleven at night. I was surprised Andre hadn't called me. He usually called my phone every hour on the hour. He had to be tied up with something. I was pretty sure Donald didn't rat on me because he still wanted the good-good. T-Hood opened the door for me to his trailer. "Come in, ma, I been waiting on you."

I smiled at him and brushed by him. "You've been waiting on me? Please."

"I have, ma, you're beautiful, and I can see myself with a girl like you."

"You can." I knew he was kicking game to me. I really didn't care, I just wanted to get paid. T-Hood went on and on about how he takes care of his women and spoils them with the finer things in life. I knew the life of a kept woman—I'd lived it for the last two years. That life is for the birds. I wanted to control my own life and do what the fuck I wanted to do. I didn't want a man to give me nothing but cash money. I didn't need his love or time. I didn't give a fuck about these niggas, they weren't shit. *I ain't falling in love with 'em.* I just wanted my cut, the dick, and they can go wife up the next bitch. I didn't know what love was outside of my father and I wasn't trying to find out. I just looked at him lying through his teeth about what he wanted. He probably already had a bitch somewhere; these niggas think they're so smart. They think they can use you and throw you to the side when they want to, but not me. I'm playing with these niggas' emotions out here. I'ma get they ass first before they get me. I am living my life my way—it was game time for me and I was playing to win. Anybody who comes between me and my money would get dealt with, and that included Andre. I owed him one any-way. I was gonna get his ass in the worst way. *He will pay.*

I got into my role. "So you want to take care of me?"

"Yeah, baby girl," he said as he stroked my cheek softly. "I mean, I'm out here getting it, and if you rolling with me you can get it all." *Alright, Bow Wow.* I giggled to myself.

"Well, T-Hood I don't have time to waste. I got a man that stays across town and he puts me up in a condo in Man-hattan. So what can you do for me that he can't?"

He looked at me. I could tell he was thinking about what he should say. "Word you got it like that, ma."

"Yeah, I do."

"Well—" He paused. He went and pulled out a bag full of money and handed me some of it. "Whatever he can do I can give you more." My eyes glared up. The last time I seen that much money at one time I was with Kane picking up his drop money. I took the money and slid it into my purse. I pulled T-Hood's shirt off and his muscles were sick. You would have never known that he was this ripped up under those baggy clothes he wore. I pushed him down on the sofa and started to striptease for him. I moved my body to his latest song, which was pure trash. I took my leg and threw it over his shoulder and put my pussy in his face. He pulled my panties to the side and licked me from the front to the back. He started to suck on my pearl tongue just right, sliding his fingers in and outta me, reaching my G-spot. His tongue strokes went so deep into me I felt my peak harder than ever. "Oh shit." This was the best head job I had ever received.

After I came T-Hood pulled his pants down and his dick disappointed me; it was not all that big. He put on a condom and slid into me moaning like he was going crazy. T-Hood was stroking me so fast I wasn't enjoying it. "Slow down," I yelled.

"I can't. It's so good, oh shit, girl, *fucck,*" he screamed, and came quicker than a thirty-second TV commercial. "Shit, girl, that pussy right, oh wee," he moaned as his body shook.

I just sat there looking at him in disbelief. I didn't know what the hell he called that. He didn't even stroke me for five minutes. I was so disappointed I just got up and dressed myself. *At least I got paid,* I thought to myself as I left shaking my head.

# 10

## In Too Deep

Even though I told myself I wasn't going to fuck with T-Hood's little dick ass no more, he was a big spender. Andre fell off the face of the earth, and I hadn't heard from him in months. He hadn't answered any of my calls, come by to see me, or sent me any money. *Shit, I still need to live good.* Misty got me on as a top video girl in the industry, but she was cheap with her pay. I could barely afford my label fetish off what she was paying me. I also had to foot the bills because Andre left me without notice. I really didn't mind him being gone, though. I had more leg room to do what I wanted.

I fucked with a few other rappers here and there to trick up on some money, but most of them niggas were cheap. I kept a small list because I didn't want to create a name in the industry. I mainly fucked with niggas who had wives. It was much easier and no hassle. I kept Donald's broke ass and his crack dick around just in case Andre popped back up. Donald stayed blowing my back out so I didn't mind kicking it with him. I knew he cared for me more than I wanted him to. I didn't tell him to fall in love with me. Donald knew he couldn't afford me from the beginning. He knew my pussy was high priced. *He better be glad he getting it for free. He should just appreciate that,* I thought.

I let Donald stay over often unless I didn't feel like being bothered with him. I knew I was playing with fire. Andre would kill us both if he caught us. A part of me wanted him to catch me so I could make him hurt like he did me. But I wasn't crazy. I took some precautions. I never let Donald keep any clothes at my place. He brought his stuff in an overnight bag and I never let him hang around too late. It was no need for me to get boo'd up with him anyways. I mean, sometimes when he was hitting me with that crack, my thoughts got cloudy.

Donald called and told me he was on his way up. I walked to the door dressed in a teddy and these six-inch heels he loved to see me in. "Damn." He smiled. "You know I needed that, didn't you," he said as he entered my place and threw down his book bag.

"You know, I know how you like it." I took Donald's hand and walked him to my bathroom where I had his bathwater waiting. I undressed him and helped him in the tub. I took my loofah and scrubbed his body with his Axe Fresh. It smelled so good on his skin once he sprayed his King cologne on. Donald kept on smiling at me. I knew I probably spent way too much time with him. He was really cool but I just couldn't see myself with him. I mean, he would have made a great man for a woman who likes to live poor. *That shit ain't for me,* I thought to myself. I would never forget how sleeping on the streets felt.

I made Donald get out of the tub. He was looking mad sexy dripping wet. I dried his body off and oiled him up. I took his cologne and sprayed it on him and kissed him on his lips. "I want you tonight," I whispered in his ear softly.

Donald took me and placed me on top of him. "I want you forever," he said to me, pulling my breast out of my teddy. He licked my nipple softly, making my body moan. "I want to be with you," he repeated to me.

I hated it when he got emotional while we was having sex. I couldn't see why we couldn't just cut and keep it moving. I couldn't lie, he did touch and please me so much better when he got all mushy over me. "Bend over," he told me as I stood in front of the long mirror in my room. I bent over and grabbed ahold of my heels and arched my back.

"Like this, daddy," I moaned.

"Yeah," he agreed as he slid his long dick deep into my wetness as far as he could, making me lose my breath.

"I can take this dick," I screamed, throwing my ass back at his thrust.

Donald started stroking me right at my G-spot. He knew how to get me to say what he wanted. "Oh, be my girl," he said while his dick went deeper and deeper into my spot. "I will take care of you, I promise, I will get you anything that you want."

"Shit, daddy, what you want from me?" I slipped up and said to him. I couldn't help it, I was speechless.

"I want you," he scolded, pulling my hair back, working me even deeper and harder than before. I couldn't do nothing but take it. He had me pinned down and there was no space to break away. "You want me too?"

"Oh yeah, I want it." Donald was making my pussy cry out for him. I lost control of myself. "Oh, I want you, you need to keep doing me like this." I lost my focus. My body started going through motions. I felt my peak coming and I couldn't get back in control of the situation. I didn't know if I wanted to throw my ass back or run. The feeling was coming on too strong. "Oh, I can't take it," I screamed, trying to break away from him. Donald pulled me back and told me to take his dick like a big girl. I took in a deep breath and arched my back as high I could get it.

"This my pussy," Donald moaned as he fucked me harder, trying to get me to say it too. Once my body tensed up again tears started rolling down my face. Donald pushed my head down in the bed. "You finna take this dick," he ordered. I felt like I was about to black out. My eyes rolled in the back of my head and my body was shaking recklessly. Once my legs went numb my pussy juices streamed out of me. I grabbed ahold of my covers and took in another deep breath once Donald came. My body was so weak I couldn't move. I just sat there staring at him. I couldn't believe he had fucked me until I lost control.

I sat in silence trying to gather my thoughts and pull myself together. Donald was cool peoples but he was not on my level. He was a doorman and he lived in the ghetto. There was no need for me to even think about being with him. I wanted to marry a rich man so I could have security. This just wouldn't work. *Bitch, get your mind right,* I told myself. I couldn't let my throbbing pussy make stupid decisions for my life. "Look, Donald, we're just having fun, okay?" I had to bring things back to reality.

He looked at me. "I want to be with you. I never felt this way about a woman."

"Donald, why can't you just enjoy the ride? You already knew the deal."

"I can give you everything."

"Donald, please, you're broke, and ain't nobody checking for no doorman. Let's be real. You need to stop playing yourself. You can't afford a woman like me. Just stay in your lane."

"Stay in my lane! What the fuck that's supposed to mean?"

"Just like it sounds. Don't get mad at me because you chose the wrong career path. I would never date a broke nigga, okay."

"But you will suck my dick, lick my ass and balls though." Donald looked at me. He was salty, it was written all over his face.

"Well, not normally, but I like your dick, so I hook you up. Why can't you just be grateful for that?"

"Grateful, bitch, you got me fucked up." Donald looked like he wanted to punch me in my face. "You think what you're doing is funny, but I promise I will get the last laugh off your trick ass."

"Why you up in my place disrespecting me? You can get the fuck out."

Donald laughed at me. "We cool, shorty. If you want me to treat you like a ho I will."

"Whatever," I said as I rolled over. I knew Donald was talking crazy because he was salty at me. Niggas try to act hard but they catch feeling just like we do. He'd be alright.

I was tired. I pulled the covers over my head so I could catch a nap. I had some casting calls to go out on. Donald went into my bathroom and turned on the shower. I thought about getting in with him but my body was drained. I closed my eyes and dosed off to sleep.

Donald woke me up outta my sleep telling me he was leaving. I knew he was still mad at me from the way he spoke to me. "Listen, I hope we're still cool. I mean, you're a cool dude and all. I just want us to be friends."

He looked at me and gave me a devious smile. "I'm good now." He laughed. "Thank you for your stamp of approval. I know I'm a good man."

I nodded my head, saying yes. "You are a good dude."

"Good dude." He laughed again. "You whores cost too much to keep around. Anyways, little broke niggas like myself should stay in their lane with hood bitches."

I knew Donald was being sarcastic so I wanted to be sarcastic too. "Yeah, y'all really should. That what I was telling you."

Donald got even more pissed off at me. I just laughed at him. *Don't dish shit you can't take.*

"I'm not worried, Kandy. I just fucked you real good. Your ass will be calling me and needing me. I put that on everything you'll learn about playing with people's emotions."

Donald was talking like a pussy-whipped bitch. I just blew him off; he'd be alright in a day or two.

# 11

## *Payback's a Bitch*

*I* hit up SoHo to cop that crocodile bag I'd been wanting. My money was right so I figured I'd trick on myself. Donald still had an attitude with me. He came through once since we fell out and the sex wasn't even the same. *Oh well,* I thought. I was cool with us calling it quits. As long as he kept his promise I was good. I walked into the boutique and grabbed the croc bag in pink and black. I saw some YSL pumps that gonna kill the game with this bag. The sales clerk was taking all day to wrap up my bags. I still needed to go cop a few other things. Once she rang me up my bill came to a little over three thousand dollars. I took a couple of knots out of my stash before I left. I knew I needed to stop playing and get me a bank account so I didn't have to carry cash on me. I gave her thirty one-hundred dollar bills. She took her counterfeit marker and ran it across the money. "Excuse me, ma'am," she said, looking as if something was wrong.

"Is there something wrong?" I asked, concerned.

"Oh no, I have to let my supervisor approve anything over a thousand dollars," she claimed as she walked to the back with all the money in her hand. After ten minutes I became angry. *What's taking her so damn long? Something must be wrong,* I thought.

Once she and her manager merged to the front of the store, I yelled, "Is there a problem?"

"Ma'am, do you have another form of payment?"

"What's the matter with the money I gave you?"

They looked at each other. "Ma'am, this money is not real. It's counterfeit."

"What?" I yelled. "That's impossible." I took the money back and looked through it. The money looked real to me. "Are you trying to play me because I'm black?"

"Ma'am, I have been in business for over fifteen years now. I've seen your type come through here trying to get over on me. Now you can either pay for this with another form of payment or I can call the police on you."

"This is impossible. I just spent some of this same money last week and they marked it. This money has to be real."

"You see this," the lady said as she took out another hundred dollar bill and ran her marker across it. Then she ran a marker across mine and it showed up way darker.

"What if that bill is fake?"

"The marker shows up dark only on phony money."

I was in deep shock. Was Misty paying me with fake money? Did some nigga I tricked with hit me with some phony cheese? I had no other way to pay for the bags; I had never been so embarrassed in my entire life. "Listen, I do not know what's going on, I swear, I don't want to start any trouble. I just want to leave." I grabbed my Marc Jacobs bag and ran like hell; my face was red from embarrassment. I sat back and racked my brain. I had just paid my bills and shopped at the Gucci store two weeks ago. How could this money be fake all of a sudden? Misty had just paid me that day me and Donald got into it. Was Misty stiffing me? I didn't want to call her and accuse her of it before I got some proof.

I racked my brain for hours. The only thing that popped into my mind was Donald saying he fucked me real good. *Donald must'a switched my money while I was asleep.* I remembered the look he gave me that night, then all of sudden he asked me about spending money. He did this to me.

I wasn't going to call and ask him about it. That's what he wanted me to do. He thinks he fucked me. I needed to be sure Donald indeed called himself pimping me and Misty wasn't the person I needed to go to war with. I went back to my place and took out the marker I picked up on my way in. I threw all my money on my bed and started to mark it. All of it was fake. *Fuck,* I screamed, trying not to lose my head. This was all the money I had. I sat down and thought about what I needed to do about this. I wrapped the twenty thousand dollars up in rubber bands. I took five grand of it and rolled it in a knot and headed down to Donald.

"Hey, sweetie." I smiled at Donald.

"Yes, Ms. High Price."

"Baby, I thought we was over that. I need you to do me a favor."

"A favor? What do you need from me?"

I took out the knot of money and handed it to him. "I need you to deposit that in your bank for me."

"What?" he yelled.

"Yeah, I'm trying to get a loan and I need a deposit slip from a bank. You can't do that for me? I will pay you."

"Umm," he said. I knew right then he was the one.

"Come on now, sweetie. I'd help you if you needed me to."

"I can't get this done until next week 'cause I'm having car trouble and my bank is far. So if you need this right now you probably should ask somebody else."

*Car trouble? Nigga, please.* "You got change for hundred?"

"No."

I sat there looking at Donald, who had brand-new earrings and a diamond-face watch on. "Damn, I need some change," I said, looking around. When the elevator doors opened, Officer Michael came off. *Perfect timing.* "Officer Michael, can you come here," I said as I waved him over to me.

"Yes, baby girl?"

"You got change for a hundred?"

"Yes, I do."

"Donald, give Officer Michael one of them hundreds so I can get change." Donald sat there looking crazy. "Did you hear me, Donald?" I asked him once again.

Donald sat with the stupidest look on his face. "I ain't got it," Officer Michael said after he looked in his wallet. "I'm sorry, sweetie."

"Don't be, thanks." I didn't need anything else. I saw what I needed to see. "You know what, Donald, you're right. I need the loan now, so I'ma get somebody else to do it." I reached my hand out for my money. Once he gave it to me I smiled at him. "Thanks anyway, honey. I like your new watch and earrings. Nice."

Donald thought he played me, but he just joined my fucked list with Andre. *He can floss now but I will make his ass pay.* I reached over and gave him a hug and kissed him softly on his lips. I told him I wanted some of his dick later and if he felt like it he could come through. There was no need for me to get mad at him. I'd much rather get even with him in the worst way.

# 12

## *More than Friends*

*I* hailed a cab over to Park Avenue to Misty's place. She was living large and she'd told me there were several famous people in her building. She said she always bumps into Tommy Banks, the head honcho over at Columbia Records' Urban division. Misty's building was much more secure than mine. They checked your ID and took down all your information like the airport. After I got through that massive screening I made it to the twenty-eighth floor and Misty was waiting on me. "Hey, girl," she said as she greeted me with a kiss on the cheek.

"Hey, girl, you have to get checked harder here than at the airport," I said as I walked in and couldn't believe my eyes. Misty's place made my apartment look run-down. Her home was breathtaking. "Your home is beautiful."

"Thank you, girlie."

If being a talent scout paid this well then maybe I needed to switch my position within the industry. "Well, I see where the real money is at," I said to Misty jokingly.

"No, it's not; the money comes from the hard work, the building of a brand, me keeping my team together. This industry is tough and it's the survival of the fittest. It is not easy, trust me. It took me years to get where I'm at. You can't get it all over night."

*I never believed that shit, you can get it all overnight. Shit, life moves as slow as you do. There's always a way around things and a quicker way to get something done.* After talking to Misty for hours I knew what I finally wanted to do with my life. I wanted a company of my own. I wanted to make my own rules and get paid just like Misty, and I knew the quickest way in was through her. She already knew the game inside out. Who better to help me rise to the top than her? Misty had been trying to get me into her lair for months but I always passed on it. I felt like she was on some gay shit and I ain't with that.

"You want something to eat or drink?" Misty asked me, breaking my thoughts.

"Yes, please." I walked around Misty's house admiring the details she had throughout her place. Everything was so neat and perfect. The view from her balcony showed the New York City skyline perfectly. Misty was sitting on top of the world and that's right where I needed to be.

"So, Kandy, how's the shoots been going?"

"They've been going great, why do you ask?"

"Oh, nothing," she said, but the look on her face already told me what she was trying to hold back.

"I mean, we both grown. If you got something to say, say it."

She looked at me and then got up and went into her closet and pulled down a box of pictures. Misty handed me pictures of some random girls. I didn't know her purpose for showing me this.

"Why are you showing me this?"

"These are girls who used to work for me. Honey was my favorite but she would never listen to me." She pulled out a picture of this real pretty dark-skin girl who looked like Gabrielle Union. "Co Co was my number one girl; it's hard to push a dark-skin girl to the top in this industry. But Co Co did it." As she talked I started to remember the videos these girls did, but I was still clueless to her purpose.

"I still don't know your point."

"Kandy, my point is, these girls didn't last more than six months because they wanted to sleep their way to the top, thinking these rappers really had money. Once you get a name for yourself in this industry, you've washed away your chances to get ahead and have longevity. The only way to the top is working hard and keeping your legs closed. These rappers don't have any money and they don't make any decisions. They work for the record label that makes all the money and tells them what they want them to do. If you're out here groupie playing yourself you won't last, either, because as you can see, all these girls were pretty and they still didn't make it."

*Groupie playing myself,* this bitch had a lot of nerve to call me a groupie. "Misty, let me tell you something. I graduated high school at sixteen with a 4.0 GPA. I'm very smart.

I learned how to hustle from my father, Kane. I know the streets and the game very well."

"So you're Kane's daughter. I heard all about him, growing up. I'm sorry about your loss. I'm not calling you dumb, I'm just giving you the skinny about this industry. Once you sleep with one person he'll tell another, and before you know it you have a name for yourself. I just want you to be careful; I'm not sure what you're looking for. I just wanted to keep it real. Ninety-five percent of these rappers are broke and struggling to keep up their image. They really don't have any money to trick on you, so I wanted you to know that before you got that big idea *he's gonna save me.* He ain't. Shit, I'm caking more than them niggas, don't none of them sign my checks. They basically don't matter in my world."

I understood where Misty was coming from. Them niggas is broke as hell. "I hear you. So the bigwigs got the money. Like, umm, what's his name you said lived in this building?"

"Tommy, yeah, now he is caked up. I've been trying for months to get a contract from him. He's an asshole, so I don't bother with him much. I do fine with my other contracts and spot work."

"What do you mean by contract? I mean, I know what a contract is, I just wanted to know what that means to you."

"Well, that means security. I usually sign a six-month exclusive deal with the major labels to use my modeling company for their videos. That's why I'm always looking for new girls, so it won't be the same ole girls over and over again."

I knew I couldn't flood Misty with too many questions at

once. I had to calculate and plan my takeover precisely. I knew what Misty thought of me, but she had me all figured out wrong—*a groupie bitch, please*. I was taking over her spot. There's only room for one of us at the top. *I'ma bring the Kandy Girlz back and we'll be better than ever.*

Misty sat on her couch staring at me and it was making me uncomfortable. *Here she go again,* I thought. "So," I said, getting off the couch, trying to stop her from looking at me like she wanted to take a bite of me. "Where's your man at?"

Misty knocked back her drink and busted out laughing. I looked at her. "What's so funny?"

"Nothing," she said. "I don't have a man."

"Why is that?" Misty was gorgeous. What man wouldn't want a driven woman with so much going on for herself?

"I don't like them," she said as she looked me in the eyes. At that point I knew where the conversation was going. I went to grab my purse and get my things so I could leave.

"Well," I said, trying to get around her, "what videos do you have lined up? I have to get home before my boyfriend gets in."

Misty reached in the top drawer of her desk and handed me four leads. "You know, Kandy, I'm going to be real with you. I like you. I think you're beautiful. I would like to get to know you better if you would like to."

*What the fuck, I'm strictly dickly.* "Misty, I'm not a lover of women, so I guess I'm flawed, but that's not my thing."

"Fine, but if you change your mind you can get at me."

"Okay," I said as I ran out of there as fast as I could.

I jumped into the elevator as soon as the doors opened. I was confused and felt crazy. I just couldn't understand why such a pretty woman would want to be gay. I reached in and pressed the lobby key but it wouldn't light up.

"This is going up," an older gentleman advised me.

I turned around and looked at him. "Sorry, I wasn't paying attention." I blushed. "I guess I have to ride up and go back down." The button was lit for the thirty-eighth floor. I looked at him. He looked familiar to me. He was very handsome for an older man. His smooth caramel skin glowed. His voice was very deep and sexy, and he smelled great. "You smell great. What's that scent?" I asked.

"Marc Jacobs," he said quickly. "You smell great too," he complimented me back.

I smiled. "Thank you."

"You live in the building?" he asked.

"No, I was here visiting my friend. She lives on the twenty-eighth floor."

"My name is Tommy," he told me as he held out his hand for a shake. I knew he looked familiar to me.

"Kandy," I said back.

"Like that Cameo song."

"I'm sorry—Cameo—I'm not sure who that is."

He started laughing at me. "I guess you're too young." He smiled.

"I guess," I replied. The elevator doors opened and there was only one door on the entire floor.

"I have to let you back down," he said as he took out his key card and scanned it. "Here's my card. Call me sometime. Maybe I can catch you up on some good music."

I took out one of my old business cards I had made when I was in high school and handed it to him. "Sure, you can call me as well." It may have been outdated but I knew you should never pass by a chance to network, and my number was still the same.

"Kandy Girlz, what's that?"

"Oh, I own a modeling agency. Well, I'm starting it back up. That card is a little outdated. I'm working on updating my business."

"Okay," he said. "I will call you, Kandy."

When the doors shut I let out a loud laugh. I couldn't believe I bumped into the largest music executive by chance. Misty was right, there was no need wasting my time and pussy on these broke niggas. If I wanted to rise to the top, I needed to start at the top.

# 13

## Daddy's Home

I thought I was dreaming when I heard my doorknob turning. I was in a deep sleep, so I didn't bother checking. When I heard the front door slam I knew I wasn't dreaming anymore. I knew it was Andre. He was the only other person who had a key to my place. Andre had been missing for months now. I hadn't seen or heard a word from him. Now he wanted to show his ass up in the middle of the night? I was too pissed. The nerve of him—he left me with no money, no phone calls; he basically said fuck me and now he wanted to come back around my way. I heard him stomping through the house knocking shit over. I didn't even bother to get up. He wasn't worth my time. *Whatever,* I mumbled to myself.

"Wake up," he yelled, flashing on my lights.

I didn't move. I just pulled the covers over my head. *This Negro has a lot of damn balls to still think he running a show,* I mumbled. Andre pulled the covers back off my naked body. I had just finished fucking Donald four hours ago. "Get yo stanky ass up."

"Nigga, don't be coming up in my house with that shit."

"What did I tell you about playing with me?"

"Andre, don't come in here trying to regulate shit. I haven't seen or heard anything from you in months."

"Bitch, I was in jail. I didn't hear from you or see you. But guess who I see shaking her ass in some nigga's video."

*Jail*, I thought. "How was I supposed to know you were in jail, Andre?"

"You didn't bother to look for me, did you?"

"I'm not your wife. You didn't even try to get in contact with me, did you?"

"I did—you kept hanging up the fucking phone on me."

Damn, that was Andre calling here with them private calls. "I thought that was your wife calling here playing on the phone."

Andre looked stressed the hell out. He didn't even look the same anymore. "Man," he yelled as he paced the floor in my bedroom.

"What's the matter with you, why you so jumpy?"

"Man, shit fucked up."

I didn't understand him or why he acting like he was on drugs. "What did you go to jail for?"

"Man, I got set up."

"Set up—look, Andre, I don't know what the hell is going on, but you need to tell me something."

Andre looked at me. "Who you have up in here?" he

yelled, sticking his fingers in my pussy. I did my kegals daily so I wasn't worried about my pussy being loose.

"What," I yelled, trying to hold a straight face. "I didn't have nobody up in here. Don't come here with this shit, Andre. I can leave," I yelled as I got out the bed reaching for some clothes.

"Look," he said as he grabbed the back of my head and pulled me close to him. "I need you, Kandy," he cried. He broke out into tears like somebody made him their bitch in jail. I had never seen him get emotional; I didn't know what to say to him. I took my hands and rubbed his back and gave him a kiss on his forehead.

"It's going to be okay." My feelings for Andre were gone. I never really allowed myself to fall in love with him anyways. I knew he was married so I just enjoyed the ride, but I did feel sorry for him. I'd never seen him be weak and needy. "Tell me what happened," I said, making him sit down on the bed.

"It was June and my wife, they set me up and took everything. I don't have nothing, I'ma kill them when I find them. *I'ma kill 'em*," he yelled, balling his fist up.

Andre always meant business. He ran his ship with an iron fist so I didn't see how he let this happen. The only person he told everything to was June. I guess he trusted him and got fucked by him.

"So what do you need me to do?"

He looked at me and rubbed the side of my face so softly, I knew what he needed from me. I pulled his shirt off; I hadn't felt Andre's touch in a while. I missed it a little. I kissed him softly on his lips while I unbuckled his pants. I took his hand and he followed me into the bathroom while I turned on the shower. I pushed him against the sink and asked him again, "So what do you need from me?"

Andre picked me up and opened the shower door and we got in. The shower nozzle shot hot water all over our bodies at full force. Andre pulled me by my hair as he sucked my neck and licked me down to my rock-hard nipples. "I need you," he whispered in my ear as his free hand caressed my breast, driving me wild. He slid his manhood inside of me. He felt bigger than I remembered. My body cringed as he pushed himself so deep in me I felt him in my stomach. "Oh shit, I missed him," I moaned into Andre's ear.

"We missed you too," he said as he gave it to me like it was the first time he'd gotten pussy in his life. After Andre finished me I couldn't do nothing but look at him. I couldn't even front he tore my shit up.

"Damn, boy, you trying to kill me."

He looked at me and smiled. "No, man, I just been missing you. I been dreaming about the way you would feel. I'm sorry for yelling at you earlier. I just got so much shit on my mind and I feel like everything in my life is fucked up."

I really wasn't paying Andre any mind. I mean, it was fucked up and all what he was going through. But that shit wasn't my problem nor my business. When his wife was around, his ass played me to the left with the quickness. Then the nigga had the nerve to fuck my friend. Karma is a motherfucker. "I'm sorry about what happened to you." I knew how to play the game with Andre. I sat down in his lap and rubbed his head. "It's going to be okay, poppa, you know I got you."

"I hope so," he said as he looked into my eyes. "I need you, Kandy. Please tell me that you won't do me dirty."

"Andre, stop tripping. Is there something you're not telling me?" I didn't want to sit there and lie to his face, but I would if I needed to.

Andre held his head down. "I might be getting locked up."

"Locked up, you just got out. You've been gone over six months almost."

"Yeah, but I got to go to trial. I mean, my lawyer saying it's looking good for me to beat the case. But I'm fucked up. They took all my money. Even the money I had stashed away, they took that too."

I looked at him. *Broke.* I don't like that word one bit. "So how you're going to pay for your lawyer?"

"I got a little money stashed here, but that's all I got. I see you're working. How much money are you making?"

I looked at him. There was no need for him to be worried about my money. "Not much. I got a few dollars, maybe twenty-five hundred saved."

"Well, I don't agree with you being around them niggas but I'm fucked up right now, so I guess you can work and maintain the bills around here until I get back on my feet."

I just smiled at him and gave him a kiss. I was cutting him off the first chance I got. I didn't trick on no niggas.

# 14

## *Every Man for Himself*

*A*ndre had been the perfect boyfriend since he'd been home from jail. His court date was coming and he had me running around like a chicken with its head cut off. I had my own reasoning for wanting to help him. I didn't care how nice Andre was to me, it still didn't change the fact he hurt me. I didn't believe in forgiveness so I would never forgive him. Donald became a pain in my ass, he was blowing me hard. He had the nerve to be demanding shit like he didn't steal my fucking money. *Dirty niggas,* them fuckers had my nerves bad. I couldn't wait to rid them from my life.

I set my sights on doing big things. I wanted The Kandy Girlz to take over the game quickly. Getting my company started up was very easy for me, thanks to my new friend Mr. Bigg. Mr. Bigg had a lot of experience in the music industry and shared his knowledge with me. It was hard for me to see him because Andre's insecure ass was hawking me like he was the damn FBI. I liked hanging out with Mr. Bigg;

he put me in contact with one of his lawyer friends to help me out. Dave was an entertainment lawyer and he promised Mr. Bigg he would help since he owed him a favor. Dave did all my legal work and papers and found me office space in Manhattan.

My money started running short because I had to pay all the bills because Andre's broke ass refused to get a job. He kept his pipe dreams of getting back in the game and getting paid. I didn't see how he figured he was going to make any money sitting on his ass all day. I barely had enough money left to buy me a pair of panties out of Victoria's Secret. I didn't have time for that broke shit. I had to make moves and get rid of my dead weight.

I finally agreed to see Donald so he could stop blowing up my phone. It still amazed me how people felt they could hurt you and get away with it. I couldn't believe that dirty nigga switched my money with fake cash; he just didn't know I was dirty too and I don't play fair. I walked up to Donald's door and rang the doorbell and waited for him to answer.

"Who is it?" he yelled through the door.

"It's me, Kandy." Donald stayed in the heart of the hood. I'd never been to this side of town. I didn't know why he ever thought he had a chance with a girl like me, and I don't know why he ever tried to play a girl like me. I knew he cared for me deeply. It was written all over his face. But that was his fault falling in love with me. I told him from the get-go I was just fucking him.

"Hey," Donald said as he let me into his place. This was the first time I'd seen the inside of his apartment. It was fully loaded thanks to my money he stole. He had LCD TVs and two iMac computers. He was living it up. All his shit was top of the line, I wasn't even mad at little daddy hustle. I'm a working girl too.

"Nice place. Your job must pay you well," I said, trying to crack a joke.

"I do okay. I know it's not the good life like you want, Ms. Kandy, but I like it."

"I'm sorry if I offended you in any way," I said as I took a seat across from him and took off my shades.

"What happened to your face?" he asked me.

"It's nothing," I said, trying to put back on my glasses.

"Kandy, tell me what happened. Did that nigga hit you?"

"Just forget about it, Donald. I came to see you."

"I'ma kill him," Donald said as he got out his seat, pacing around his front room.

"Donald," I yelled as I got up and removed my coat, revealing my naked body. "Don't worry about it. I told him I was leaving him for you and he got mad. I'm fine with it. I just want to know if you still love me like you said you do." I sat back down on the couch as the tears poured from my eyes. "I'm sorry for hurting you. I didn't want anybody to get hurt. I love you. I need you. I just want to know if you still want me too."

Donald walked over to me and bent down on his knees. He pushed my face up and rubbed the side of my cheek gently. "I do love you, Kandy. I want to be with you. You can stay with me. I mean, I will get us a better place. I just need you to believe in me. I can give you what you need and I will never hurt you."

"You promise?" I asked him as my tears started to pour harder.

"I promise, I'll give my life before I let somebody hurt you again."

I kissed Donald on his lips, biting his bottom lip softly. "I want you inside of me. I want to feel him inside of me, all of him." I put Donald's finger in my mouth, sucking on it like an ice cube. I got on my knees and began to suck Donald's manhood like I never did before. I knew he loved it from the way he screamed my name out loud. He loved it just as much as I did. Once he climaxed into my mouth I slurped all his juices down until he pulled me roughly by the hair. "Give him to me hard, Donald," I demanded. Donald reached over into his top drawer and pulled out a condom. "No, I want to feel him, please. I want you to fuck me hard and bust inside of me."

I knew his dick was throbbing for me. He hadn't had any of this kush in a while. Donald grabbed me by the neck and slammed me against the wall. "Yes, choke me harder," I screamed. "I can take this dick, boy, show me who's the boss." Donald pushed his dick so hard in me I jumped for dear life. I didn't run; this was how I needed it. I wanted him to fuck me until I couldn't walk straight. "Yeah, big daddy, fuck me harder. I don't want to walk after this." Even though Donald was pushing himself into me as hard and deep as he could, it didn't hurt me. I loved pain.

"Oh girl, I finna come, shit, I finna come, Kandy."

"Oh poppa, explode in this pussy. It yours, you can do what you want to." After he humped me faster than a jackrabbit I felt all his and my juices running down my legs.

"I don't want you going back to that nigga."

"Okay, daddy, I just need to go back tonight to get my stuff. When you get off work I will leave with you."

"Okay," he said as he stroked my head gently.

"What if he acts crazy? Andre is crazy. I don't want you getting hurt."

"I'm crazy too. I got something for his bitch ass anyway, putting his hands on you."

I got up and put my clothes back on. My pussy felt like he had ripped it two to three inches. I could barely walk. I looked into the mirror. Donald had choked me so hard his fingerprints were showing around my neck. I wrapped my scarf around my neck and headed back home.

# 15

## It's a Dirty Game

It's a dirty game out here. When you play with fire sometimes you end up getting burned. You have to be careful how you treat people because it might turn around on you. I could barely make it down the hall to my place, my body was hurting so bad. I felt like passing out. When I stumbled through the door Andre was sitting on the sofa watching TV. I couldn't bear walking any longer so I fell to the floor. "Kandy, what happened?" Andre yelled as he picked me up off the floor.

"I got raped," I said as I felt my body become lifeless.

"What!" Andre yelled as he looked at my face and neck and saw the bruises I had all over me. "Who did this to you?" He demanded that I tell him but I refused.

"No, he said he is going to kill me and you too. I can't."

Andre became furious and started hollering and screaming at me. "Who the fuck did this to you?" Tears started forming in his eyes. "Tell me now," he demanded again as his voice cracked up.

"It was the doorman. He said you paid him to watch me. He is obsessed with me. He made me get into his car and he raped me." I cried like a baby. "It's all your fault. How could you, Andre? I thought you said you loved and trusted me."

"I'm finna kill him," Andre said. "He's a dead man."

"Andre, no, let's just call the police, baby. I don't want you going to jail. You know if you get into any trouble you are going to have to finish doing your time in jail."

"Fuck that," Andre yelled as he got up and grabbed his gun out of the top of the closet and cocked it back.

"Baby, wait," I yelled, trying to run behind him.

"Call the police," Andre advised. I knew the police would be there in a matter of minutes. The station was right around the corner. I followed Andre down to the lobby where Donald was seated at the front desk. Donald rose out of his seat and looked Andre in the eyes. "Wait, Andre," I said as I tried to get in front of him, but he pushed me out of his way, making me fall.

I was scared once the police swarmed the place. I started yelling, "He did this to me."

Andre and Donald both had loaded guns on them. They exchanged words back and forth like the police wasn't there.

"Drop your weapons," the police yelled as they tazered them both down.

"They raped me," I started screaming like a fool.

The police called for an ambulance for Donald because he was barely moving. "Ma'am, calm down and tell me what happened," the officer said.

"They raped me. I was visiting a friend and they made

me get into a car and raped me." I cried the police a river. A woman officer arrived on the scene and took me to the hospital. The doctor performed a rape analysis on me; he advised them that I had been raped and torn badly. The police told me that they found both Andre's and Donald's semen in me. I gave another statement to them and told them I was scared for my life and was moving out of town. The police told me the law protects me if I didn't want to physically testify against them. They said my statement was good enough to put both of them behind bars.

*Eye for an eye.* Andre and Donald fucked me, and I fucked them back up the ass. I bet them motherfuckers will think twice before they do somebody else dirty. I had to do what was best for me. I took Andre's money and bounced.

# 16

## The Takeover

In a matter of weeks Andre and Donald were doing hard time. I didn't attend the trial because the judge granted me immunity. They had all the evidence they needed to convict them. The prosecutor had it out for Andre, anyways. Oh well, easy come, easy go. Black men really don't have a chance in the legal system, especially when they're broke. I wrote them a letter explaining why they were sitting behind bars. I knew they wanted to kill me but I'd be long gone before they got out.

I didn't feel safe at my old place so Misty told me I could crash with her until I got me a place. I figured all I needed was a month or two and I'll be on and gone. My business was almost open. I knew Misty had a thang for me and I wanted to get closer to her so I could find out more about the business. I already had Mr. Bigg eating out the palm of my hands. He was so open, he contacted his lawyer about leaving his wife. I talked him out of it. I didn't want him to wife me up; he was old enough to be my dad. I enjoyed hanging out with

him, and the sex was good once he popped a Viagra, but I
didn't like him like that. I played my position with him because I needed him to give me a contract with Columbia.
Securing that contract would help me put The Kandy Girlz
on the map.

"Kandy, come and eat. I fixed dinner," Misty yelled as she
came in and disturbed my thoughts. Misty had fixed us New
York strip steak and a chopped salad. Once I sat down across
from her, she stared at me again. I knew I had to take it
there with Misty even though I didn't want to. Pussy rocks;
men and women love it. I was just using what I got to get
what I want.

"Thanks for the meal," I said to her.

"No problem. You're my guest, so I will take care of you."

*Take care of me.* I bet she would. "Okay." I smiled. "So,
Misty, if you don't mind me asking, how long have you been
running Envy Girls?"

"No, not at all. I been in business for the last three years.
I started with three girls and ended up with what I have
today."

"Oh, I want to start a business, maybe a clothing store
since I like to shop so much."

"Well, you should do that. You only live once."

*That's right, you do only live once.* That's why you shouldn't
care about nobody but yourself. Misty invited me into her
bedroom to watch a movie after dinner, so of course I took
her invitation. I knew I wasn't gay, I was just doing what was
needed to get Misty to open up and trust me. I had to do
what I had to do to make The Kandy Girlz happen.

Misty's room was huge. I liked that her red and black decor stood out against her modern pieces. *Misty is doing it big*, I thought to myself. *I see where all the money is going.* It was obvious Misty was clocking mad paper. *She pimping me*, I thought. *We do all the work and she keep all the profit to herself. That shit seems unfair to me.* Listening to Misty talk about how she got this from Paris and that from Spain made me want to rob her even more. I sat down at the foot of her bed waiting for her to put her moves on me. Misty came over and sat beside me, and her perfume smelled really good on her. "What are you wearing?" I asked her.

"Ed Hardy."

"It smells good."

"I'll buy you some," she responded.

I felt weird being in the same room with another woman. I climbed to the head of the bed and got underneath Misty's covers. "I'm cold," I told her as I buried my body underneath the luxury of her four-thousand-thread-count sheets. She got into the bed with me from the other side.

When she got closer to me I closed my eyes and reached in and kissed her on her lips softly. Misty ran her fingers through my hair and caressed my back gently; it actually didn't feel all that bad. She grabbed my breast and licked my nipple perfectly. I couldn't believe how much I was enjoying the way she touched me. She kissed me from my neck to my stomach, rubbing her hand up and down my pussy. Once she licked me on my lips I closed my eyes tight. My heart started racing. I felt so ashamed because I was enjoying what she was doing to me.

Misty took her tongue and licked me all over my coochie. She was in sync with my body and it was driving me crazy. She kept her tongue rolling in rhythm, which made me reach my peak quicker than I ever had before. "Fuck," I screamed as my body was doing things it had never done before.

After I came I sat there looking at her. *I can get with this,* I told myself. I let her do whatever she wanted to do to me! I filled her head with everything she wanted to hear, and when we were done I knew she was mine. I had her opened wide and I went to bed that night satisfied.

# 17

## Can't Knock the Hustle

*I* convinced Misty that it would be best if I was her assistant and she agreed. After that, it wasn't hard getting Misty to fall for me. I knew all the right things to say and do to get her gone in the head. Being Misty's assistant was a benefit to me—she showed me everything about her day-in and day-out functions. I was practically running the place after three weeks of training. I learned everything about the business; I booked all of Misty's appointments and meetings.

I established relationships with all of Misty's contacts, letting them know about The Kandy Girlz. I had everything I needed, but my model search wasn't going as well. I wanted to get some fresh faces in the industry, some girls who would set my company apart from everyone else's. Misty was holding a casting call for new girls and I was over it, so I figured I'd picked the good ones for my company and give her the leftovers.

Misty could be a little emotional and controlling at times,

which got on my damn nerves. I had to constantly remind her that she wasn't my man and I never told her I was exclusively hers. I knew things between us would end messy but I didn't care, I just wanted what I wanted from her. I was excited because I signed my first two major contracts. Mr. Bigg introduced me to Kenny Burns, who owned Urban TV. He put in a good word for me over there and I got an exclusive one-year contract to staff the extras for their television programs. I also got my exclusive one-year deal with Columbia Records. All I needed was the girls and I was ready to take over.

My personal life got crazy too. I liked kicking it with Mr. Bigg, but he was catching feelings too deep. I told him he was too old for me and to stay with his wife, but he seemed not to care about her anymore. He offered to put me up in a condo in his building on Park Avenue, but I passed on that. I'd learned my lesson from Andre. I purchased an estate in New Rochelle, away from the hustle of New York. I wanted to move someplace where I felt safe. I didn't tell Misty about my place. I didn't want her knowing where I stayed.

I planned on moving my things little by little, and once I stopped coming over, she would get the picture.

I had a lunch date scheduled at Mr. Chow's with Bigg and he was bringing me my advance check and some papers to sign.

I loved Mr. Chow's but I only ate there when somebody was treating me. When I arrived at the restaurant and told the waiter who I was, he took me in the back behind some long, black drape curtains. I didn't see Bigg anywhere, just a younger man who looked like a spitting image of him. "Hi, I'm looking for Tommy," I told him.

"Oh, my dad went to the washroom. He should be back soon. I'm DJ," he said as he reached his hand out to shake mine.

DJ looked familiar, like I'd seen him on TV or something. "I'm Kandy. You look familiar."

"I play for the Knicks." He smiled.

"Right. Wow, good luck on the season." Bigg had been holding out on me. DJ was *fine.* He was much taller than his dad, his dark skin was smooth and silky, and his body was right. DJ's swag was mean and his aura commanded the room. I was feeling him. Bigg came in and kissed me on the cheek.

"Son, this is Kandy. She is the owner of The Kandy Girlz Modeling Agency. We just signed an exclusive contract with her."

"Congrats, Kandy. Doing it big, I see," DJ said as he smiled hard at me.

I couldn't take my eyes off DJ throughout the dinner. I wanted to get with him. I'd never met a man that I was feeling this much. I wanted DJ.

We talked over drinks about basketball and sports. He had me laughing because he had a great sense of humor. Before we left, he asked me for my number and I gave it to him. Hell, Bigg already had a wife and he couldn't tell me who I could see. After I said my good-byes to DJ, Bigg told me he needed to speak with me. I could tell by the tone of his voice he was upset. I sat back down and waited for him to walk his son out.

"What's up? I have some runs to make," I advised him.

"What was that all about?" he scolded.

"What about? I don't know what you mean."

"Don't play dumb with me, Kandy. You giving my son your number."

"He asked for it, and I can give my number to whomever I want."

"Are you going to sleep with him too?" he yelled at me, pissing me off.

"If I want to," I said as I got out of my seat and brushed by him. "You don't own me. You have a wife, so worry about her."

"But I love you."

"Please, nobody told you to fall in love with another woman. You have a wife and I will not let you control my life."

"I'm going to tell him about us."

"So," I said, shrugging my shoulders. "How about I tell your wife about us, or show her those pictures you took. When she leaves you and takes half your money, you'll feel differently." I was far from a fool. I had covered my ass just in case something like this happened with him.

Bigg just stood there staring at me. I really had no more use for him. He could kick rocks. My contract with Columbia was solid and there was nothing he could do about it. My lawyer had finalized all my deals, so Mr. Bigg couldn't do nothing but man up and deal with it. "We don't have to see each other if you don't want to," I said to him, grabbing my bag so I could leave.

"I can't believe I let you play me for a fool." Bigg scratched his head, trying to figure out how he had let this happen. "I love you."

"I love me too, and I love money just as much. Cheer up, Daddy," I said as I kissed him on the cheek. "At least you enjoyed the ride while you were on it, but I think we both know it's best we end this thing now."

"But I don't want to," Bigg begged me. He stood there begging and looking so desperate, but I was done with him. As I shouldered my purse and walked away, I gave him some advice. "Maybe you should treat your wife right." Then I was on my way.

# 18

## Girls Girls Girls

$\mathcal{I}$ was running late for my casting call. I had a meeting over at Columbia about upcoming video shoots. On my way out, I bumped into Bigg and he started acting a fool. DJ and I had hooked up and we'd been going strong for six months now. Bigg wanted me to break it off, but he knew better. I was very much in love with his son. DJ loved me as well; I had met his mother and their entire family.

DJ's mother was great. She'd aged beautifully and didn't look a day over forty. His mother and I became close, and on some days I felt horrible when she would talk about how much she liked me. Bigg tried his best to come between me and DJ, but he knew I would fuck him up if I needed to.

I finally pulled up to my casting call and saw that the line was still around the corner. I scanned the line as I walked in. I was impressed at some talent in the crowd. I was looking forward to selecting my crew, just like I'd done in high school. My vision was to create a team of girls who looked very different from the girls that other companies had.

When I walked into the conference room, a sudden sadness came over me. I did feel somewhat bad for Misty, for taking over the game like I did. *Maybe I'll give her a job*, I said to myself.

"So this is what you wanted," I heard coming from a familiar voice. I turned around and Misty was leaned up against the wall, looking upset.

"I was just thinking about you," I said to her. I was pretty sure she'd gotten word that I was running The Kandy Girlz.

"You didn't have to sneak to start your company. I would have helped you."

"Sneak? Girl, please. I don't share my personal business."

"So you think you can sleep your way to the top and stay there?"

"Misty, I know it's probably pretty hard for you because you've lost so much business to me, but that's how the games go. Not my problem, sweetheart, but if you ever need a job, I can hook you up." Misty looked disgusted. *Hey, it's not my fault you got caught slipping.*

"You're really smart, Kandy, and a good manipulator, but every dog has its day. I give you three months, tops, and you're gone. Snakes only slither for so long before they get stomped on. Karma will get you."

"Oh, Misty," I said as I leaned in and kissed her on her lips. "I know what the problem is. You still want me, right?"

"Please!"

"Oh, I can see it all over your face. Too bad I have a man now." If I didn't love DJ so much, I would have dipped with her. I did feel a little bad; I'd heard she's practically broke now.

"I wouldn't want you if you were the last person on this earth. You're a lowlife and you use people, but I hope you can see when somebody is using you," Misty said as she walked off.

I knew Misty was speaking from an angry place, but the world was mine now. I ran this city, and The Kandy Girls would reign.

# 19

## The Reign of a Kandy Girl

*D*J's big hands caressed my thighs so tenderly, and the smell of his cologne filled the air, driving me insane. I'd never felt this way for a man; I didn't think I would ever be in love like this. DJ pulled my body closer to him as he licked my bottom lip with his moist tongue.

"I need you," I whispered gently into his ear as I positioned myself on top of him. "I love you," I said softly as I ran my fingers up and down the small of his back.

"I love you, too," he whispered, making my heart tremble.

I always tried to please him, no matter what he wanted me to do. I knew he cared about me, and it was a different kind of love, not like what Andre had shown me. I felt he wanted me and he showed me he did with his actions. After I rode him to ecstasy, I rolled over and lay next to him. I knew DJ was the one for me. I had it all—a good man and a career.

* * *

I needed to get away, so DJ and I decided to vacation out of the country. I really didn't want to leave before I picked the rest of my team. I still needed to get two bad white girls to complete my takeover. I gave orders to my assistant and let her know I would fire her ass if she let me down. DJ's dad owned a big home and yacht in Saint-Tropez, so we flew in and chilled for the weekend. It was my first time there and I didn't want to leave, but after three days I had to accept reality, and it was time to go back to work.

I was rejuvenated when I got back to my office. Def Jam gave me six casting calls to fill. My schedule with Columbia was packed; I had a few commercial spots to fill, and some extras to send over to Sony Pictures. The Kandy Girlz had officially arrived at the top like I knew I would.

"Kim, send in the girls," I directed my assistant. I wanted to meet the models she'd picked while I was away.

"Thank you," I heard come from a voice that annoyed me. Before the door swung open, I knew who it was.

"Vanilla!" I screamed.

"Kandy," she said, surprised to see me seated behind my oversized oak desk.

"What the fuck?" I screamed. There was no way this little tramp was going to be a part of my team. She was a little backstabbing bitch and I would never give her the time of day.

"Kim!" I yelled as I rose from my seat.

"Yes, Ms. Johnson," Kim asked as she rushed to my office.

"Who hired this bitch? She's fucking fired, so have security remove her now."

"There's no need. I'm out," Vanilla said as she walked away.

"Ms. Johnson, I don't know what that was about, but she was one of the best-looking girls we've had come out. Her body is dope, and the trend is something new for a white girl with a black-girl body. She has the it factor that we need. Besides, we have two jobs that need to be done today. There is no time to look for somebody else. We need her."

Kim was right, and I hated to bite my tongue and tell Vanilla I needed her. Vanilla did look good, much better than she did a couple of years ago. I knew I needed her to take me to the top spot. I had no choice but to swallow my pride, suck up our past, and work it out. I ran out into the hallway to catch her. "Vanilla, look. I do need you to work for me. That Andre shit was the past and I've moved on, so let's not sweat it, and get this money."

"Cool," she said as she turned around and followed me back into my agency. I gave her forms to fill out and sent that bitch to make me my money. What better way to get payback on a trick than to pimp her out for her paper. *Yeah, she my bitch now and I'ma make sure I get my money's worth off her ass before I dismiss her.*

## 20

### *Pimping Ain't Easy*

$\mathcal{M}$y decision to keep Vanilla on was the best one I ever made. Vanilla was in high demand; she was in every other video and commercial, and even got picked up for small roles in a couple of movies. I was laughing all the way to the bank. It's funny how the one person who hurt you can be the same one to make you rich. I kept tabs on Vanilla; she was an investment and I'd banked over five million dollars in the last four months off of her. I still wanted more and planned to ride her until she was washed up and dried out.

It seemed that the more my business picked up, the more I got pulled away from DJ. I started to get worried about him regretting being with me. At times I had to leave him for weeks and I felt like I was slipping. I took off the weekend as often as I could so I could focus on him and only him. DJ never made me feel like he was leaving or unhappy. He was right by my side whenever I needed him. He was supportive of my career and me making my own name. He told me that he admired having a woman who could take care of her home, have a booming career, and put the smack down in the bed. I never revealed my insecurities to him because I knew he loved me.

I cooked DJ one of his favorite meals, smothered pork chops, mac and cheese, and homemade biscuits. I made a sweet potato cake for dessert and prepared the evening for fun and passion. I set up my steam room and spa with hot oils and sweet scents. I sprinkled red and white rose petals on the floor from the front door all the way to the dinner table. I trailed the rose petals to the spa, then to the tub and ending in our bedroom. I had a surprise for DJ. He'd mentioned to me the other day that he had a dream about a threesome. I'd asked him if he'd ever had one, and he told me no. I still don't believe that shit—he's an NBA player, so I'm pretty sure he has had a few.

I figured that since I'd been working a lot and not able to please him like I should, I would give him a great time to make up for my slacking off. I wrote out little note cards and placed them around each destination point. I poured him a glass of Ace of Spade and had his dinner on the table waiting for him with a note card telling him to eat up his food and follow the rose petals to his next pleasure. I made sure I was looking real fly; my black lace La Perla nightie was hugging my curvy body. I oiled my long sexy legs just the way he liked me to and put on my red six-inch Gucci heels. My j'adore sank into my pores and filled the room—DJ loved the way it smelled on my body. I pulled out my red lipstick, which I only wore in the house because I felt like a hooker when it was on my lips. I wanted to feel like a big hooker, and I wanted DJ to feel like he had a girl who had it all, money, power, respect, and independence, but could still please him and take care of his needs and the home just fine.

I wanted DJ to marry me. I wanted us to last forever and I really didn't care what I needed to do to show him I was down for him. I heard DJ's footsteps come closer to me as the Isley Brothers sang "Let's Lay Together." When DJ entered the room, my pussy became moist; I'd never felt this way for a man. I pulled him close to me and ripped his clothes off while I stared into his eyes. "You did all this for me, babe?" he asked me in his deep Barry White voice.

"Yes, I'd do anything to please you and make you happy, Poppa."

"Yeah," he murmured as he shoved his sweet tongue deep down my throat. I was ready to take him but I knew I needed to back down.

"Baby, wait. We gone get to that, but first I need you to enjoy every moment. I'm doing this all for you, to show you I love you and I'm willing to do anything to make you happy."

"A'ight," DJ said as he lay down on the massage table. I took the hot oil I had warming up and poured it over his upper and lower back. I took my hands and massaged every inch of his body. I made sure he enjoyed every second of it. After I finished, I handed him a note card and walked off. I wanted to switch to my belly-dancing outfit. I'd put up my

Flirty Girl Fitness pole in the bathroom so I could strip for him. The note I'd handed DJ told him to go to the guest room. I popped in his favorite sex tape to give him an example of what was to come.

Once DJ came into the bathroom, I undressed him and pushed him into the tub. I turned on the music and started my routine. I danced for ten minutes before he demanded I get into the tub with him. I reached in and kissed him as I slowly slid down onto his rock-hard love muscle. After we played around in the Jacuzzi for an hour, we got out, dried off, and headed to my bedroom. DJ's eyes bucked wide when he saw Vanilla lying in the bed buck-ass naked.

"What's going on?" he asked me, ready to dive in.

"She's for you."

"Word, are you sure you want to do this?"

"Yeah, have fun and enjoy it. I'll do anything for you."

DJ took off his towel and climbed in between Vanilla and me. I'd never had a threesome before in my life, but I was open to it. I just wanted to make DJ happy, so if this would keep him loving me, then I wouldn't mind doing it from time to time. Vanilla wasted no time slurping DJ's dick in her mouth. I sat and watched her. She was not all that she bragged about. I pushed her off him and took DJ's dick into my hand. I had to show her how a real woman handled a big dick. I licked his shaft just the way he liked it, made my mouth water, and took him deep down into my warm throat. I sucked DJ better than I ever had, just because I wanted to show this bitch she was not better than me. She thought she was gonna snatch Andre from me and he stayed. Now she'd see that I throws the pussy like a free-throw line. I was such a beast I ripped into DJ's dick like he was my last meal, and he busted within five minutes of me doing my thing. I sucked all his nut out of his dick and held it in my mouth. I pulled Vanilla by the hair, made her open her mouth, and spit all of DJ's nut into her mouth.

Vanilla didn't mind. She swallowed it down like a G. I grabbed a condom and slid it down DJ's dick. I'd be damn if he ran into her ho ass raw. Vanilla bent over and DJ pushed himself into her; I got behind him so I could lick and kiss his back. Vanilla and me switched positions with him for hours, until he couldn't get it up any longer. I was drained. I climbed underneath my sheets and Vanilla thought she was staying as well. I had to get her mind right. "Beat it, bitch," I told her. I didn't need that tramp getting confused. This was a one-time thing. Once she left, DJ pulled me close to him, kissed me on my forehead, and told me he loved me.

"Did you like your gift?" I asked him.

"Yeah, it was cool. Thank you."

"No need to thank me. I just want to make you happy."

"Well, you make me happy regardless, and you didn't have to do that. But since you did, it's all good. I appreciate it."

I hugged him closer and went to sleep.

# 21

## *Betrayed*

*Five Months Later*

*V*anilla had been acting real brand new. She missed photo shoots and skipped showing up for music videos. I scouted two more white girls, Co Co and Dime Piece, to replace her, but I couldn't figure out what the deal was with her. She ignored me totally, but I couldn't spend too much time worrying about it. I was on my way to London and couldn't waste time worrying about a trick. DJ and I were still going strong, and I believed we were headed to the altar. Bigg finally let go of me and moved on to somebody else. I was just happy he'd stopped hating on me to DJ. I kissed DJ goodbye and ran out the door, heading to meet my contacts in London. I needed to secure contracts for some up-and-coming acts the label had over there.

The flight was long and tedious. Once we landed, I checked into my hotel and rested before I made my way to the label. I loved London—the shopping was great, the people were great, and it was such a beautiful place to visit. After my meetings, locking down deals, and a little shopping, I was more than ready to get back to my baby. I had been away for two weeks and DJ was getting ready to go away to basketball camp. I got myself prepared for the long flight back to New York as I boarded Virgin America. My flight took forever to get back into New York. I was so ready to lie down, I jumped into my Aston Martin and headed straight to my estate in New Rochelle.

And that's when I found Vanilla in bed with my man.

After I threw that bitch out my house, I knew things wouldn't be the same between me and DJ.

I was betrayed, and payback is a bitch. I looked at DJ. I couldn't believe this was the same man who'd said he loved me. Once I laid my head down, it dawned on me that I'd heard rumors that Vanilla was pregnant. I jumped up and turned the lights on and snatched DJ's pillow from under his head so he could wake up. "Nigga, did you get this bitch pregnant?" I demanded.

DJ sat up and looked at me. He didn't speak, so I knew he was thinking up a lie. The look he was giving me told me the truth. *Damn,* I thought as my stomach started to turn. "I can't believe you," I screamed. "Why did you do me like this?"

"Wait, let's talk about this, baby," DJ said as he tried to smooth things over, but I wasn't having it.

"Wait?" I yelled, jumping up and slapping him. "Why you get this trick knocked up? You wasn't gonna tell me." My head was spinning at Vanilla's payday. Having a baby by a rich man, she didn't need to work. It all made sense to me now, her not returning my phone calls, missing work. But DJ had me fooled. I thought he loved me. Man, this was all my fault. I should have never trusted her. *Fuck*.

"I was . . . I'm just trying to figure shit out."

"Get out," I screamed like I had just gotten robbed. "Get out of my house now."

"Come on, baby. Let's talk about this. We can work this out."

"We can *not* work this out. You got a tramp stank whore as your baby mother. You sleeping with her behind my back; you running up into her raw and sleeping with me. I was faithful to you. I did whatever you wanted me to. How could you do this to me, DJ?"

"Well, it was your fault. You the one who let me sleep with her in the first place. I told you in the beginning that I liked the pussy, but I ain't finna leave you, though. Your pussy good, too."

I looked at him. Was this the same man I was in love with yesterday sitting here talking to me like this? "And I'm sup-posed to be cool with that, DJ? Just let it be what it's gonna be and work it out and forgive you. Keep this shit pushing and help raise your baby because it was my fault for letting her in our bed?"

"Yeah, shit. A lesson learned. I still love you and I'm sorry, but the shit is done, so deal with it." DJ picked up his pillow, turned off the lights, and rolled over. My blood was boiling; I wanted to make him hurt like he'd hurt me; I wanted to tell him to deal with it. I couldn't hold it in any longer; I wanted to crush him in the worst way.

"Well, I'm not the only person who needs to deal with shit," I said as I looked at him. "I fucked your father for months before I met you, so you deal with *that*." Before I knew it, DJ had slapped me senseless. He jumped on the bed and choked me until I turned red, and then he let me go. I was scared and gasping for air. I couldn't believe he hit me. I had never been hit by a man in my entire life, not even my dad.

"Bitch, I knew that shit was true. You a dirty ass tramp. I should kill your ass."

I was too scared to pop shit back to him. I'd never seen him this mad before and I didn't know if he meant what he said about killing me. DJ got up, got dressed, and pushed me against the wall. "Bitch, we are through. I don't ever want to see your whore ass again."

"DJ, wait," I begged as I fell to my knees, trying to make him stay. "Let's work this out and talk this thing through. Please, don't leave me."

DJ turned and walked away and didn't look back at me. I had lost him trying to get payback. It didn't feel as good as I'd thought. I'd lost the love of my life and I didn't know how to fix this.

## 22

# *What Goes Up Must Come Down*

*I* tried to get DJ to forgive me for months, but he refused to answer any of my calls. I did everything I could do to show him how sorry I was, but he didn't want to forgive me. My life was useless without him; I didn't care about anything anymore, not even The Kandy Girlz. I rarely went to the office and skipped business meetings because nothing mattered to me but getting DJ back. This whole mess was all my fault. I should have never let that thirsty bucket into my bed, and now I was paying for it. I kept my cell phone glued to my side because I wanted to make sure I didn't miss DJ's call.

I had just turned on my Mary J Blige *My Life* CD when my doorbell rang, and I broke my neck running down the stairs to answer it. I prayed that it was DJ. I opened the door and it was Kim. "What do you want?" I asked, slamming the door behind her.

"Girl, what is your problem? Do you understand you are losing business sitting in here down and out?"

"Who cares?"

"Kandy, listen. Get your shit together. Fuck DJ and that trick. You need to fix your business. Do you know that Misty is trying to take over again? She just opened another agency called Re-Vamped."

"So? I don't even care anymore."

"Girl, are you serious?"

"Yeah."

Kim turned on the news and handed me a package. "Everything you worked hard for, you gonna let it go over a nigga?"

Kim didn't know the things I did to start The Kandy Girlz, all the schemes I pulled and the hurt I caused. I felt that same pain now; I was a heartbreaker, but I wasn't prepared to feel the same pain back. It hurt like a knife slicing my heart with no codeine. I knew I was dirty; I basically schemed out Misty, so I didn't deserve to have nothing. I never knew how depressing the news was until now. I saw the headline flashing across the bottom of *Prison Break*. The anchor was reading an emergency bulletin:

*"This is Connie with Channel Five News. Two inmates escaped from Rickers Prison late last night. Andre Walters and Donald Jones escaped in the wee hours of the night. Some say this was an inside job, but the NYPD have yet to respond to that allegation. A massive manhunt is on to find the two men who where convicted of raping a young girl, and they are considered armed and dangerous. More on this breaking story as we get information."*

Shit, once they flashed Andre's and Donald's pictures, my heart started racing. I'd known one day I would have to face them, but not this soon.

"What's the matter?" Kim asked me.

"Nothing. Listen, if anybody comes by the agency asking for me, tell them I sold it."

"What? Kandy, what's going on?"

I opened the package Kim had handed me, which didn't have a return address on it. When I took the contents out of the envelope, I saw that they were pictures of me going into my home. Pictures of me going into the agency and getting into my car. My heart started pounding. "When did this package come?" I screamed.

"Last week. I called you and you said hold your mail. Why, what's going on?"

My head started spinning and I felt like the walls were caving in on me.

"Kandy, are you okay?" Kim said, but I tuned her out. My doorbell rang again and my heart started beating like a drum.

Kim got up to go to the door. "No," I screamed.

"Kandy, please, you're acting like a fucking psycho." Kim opened the door and I could barely breathe. "It's FedEx, you nut," she said as she signed for another package. "What's the deal?" she said, handing me a letter. I shook it to make sure nothing was in there. I opened the letter and it read:

*YOU'RE A DEAD BITCH.*

*I see you're living real hood rich, baby girl. I guess you forgot what goes up must come down. It's time for you to receive some Kandy Coated Karma.*

*See you when I see you. Tick tock goes the clock.*

I looked at Kim. I knew I had to tell somebody I could trust. Somebody who wouldn't rat on me, somebody I could feel safe with. Kim wasn't close to me, and the less she knew, the better. There was only one person I could depend on, and I hoped she would forgive me and help me.

I met with Misty and told her everything I'd done and I told her how sorry I was. Despite being a bitch and putting her out of business, she agreed to help me. Of course, it meant me signing over some of my company to her. I was at her mercy, at this point, and I needed to leave town quickly. I didn't tell her where I was going or when I was coming back. I boarded a plane going as far away from New York as possible. The one thing I'd learned in life was you gotta treat people the way you want to be treated. Being a heartbreaker was all good until you got the broken heart. Then it didn't seem so great. I didn't know what my future held or if I would receive my Kandy Coated Karma. But I made my bed. I knew one day I would have to lie in it. It didn't matter, I was still a Kandy Girl, and Kandy Girls don't cry, we get even.